She was leaving.

"Let's not part this way," Marshall protested. "We should talk."

"About what?"

"You're supposed to be the expert."

"On pregnancy?" she asked.

"On relationships."

"Well, here's my opinion," Franca said. "We're not compatible, Marshall. I wish we were, and sometimes... No. I refuse to delude myself. Let's just leave it at that."

Her footsteps rapped across the tile floor toward the hall. Then he heard the door latch behind her with a loud click.

He sat at the counter, bewildered. How could she deny the intimacy they'd shared last night? Yet judging from her words, she regretted the whole night with a man she could never love. What had seemed a transformative experience to him had been entirely one-sided.

He and Franca had always been opposites. Why expect things to be different now?

Because, in a few weeks, they'd learn whether they were going to be parents...

Dear Reader,

Opposites may attract, but can they find common ground? That's the dilemma psychologist Franca Brightman faces as she reconnects with the man she secretly loved in college, but who chose her roommate over her. Then he dropped the woman with a vague explanation and moved away.

Now Dr. Marshall Davis is a prominent men's fertility surgeon at Safe Harbor Medical, where Franca has joined the staff. Struggling to cope with the loss of a beloved foster daughter she hoped to adopt, she finds in him an unexpected source of support. But the personality traits that separated them in college present fresh challenges. And when a stolen night of passion results in a pregnancy, their conflicts come to a head.

We previously met Marshall in *The Doctor's Accidental Family* as the estranged cousin of obstetrician Nick Davis. In a subplot, the book explored their complex relationship and a shocking discovery about their past. Even if you didn't read that book, you can easily pick up the thread as Marshall copes with the consequences.

This is the seventeenth book in the Safe Harbor Medical series. You'll find a complete list, plus recipes from earlier books, on my website, jacquelinediamond.com, where you can sign up for my free monthly newsletter. Welcome to Safe Harbor!

Best,

Jacqueline Diamond

THE WOULD-BE DADDY

JACQUELINE DIAMOND

———

HARLEQUIN® AMERICAN ROMANCE®

ISBN-13: 978-0-373-75607-0

The Would-Be Daddy

Copyright © 2016 by Jackie Hyman

The publisher acknowledges the copyright holder of the additional work:

My Funny Valentine
Copyright © 1991 by Debbie Macomber

Recycling programs for this product may not exist in your area.

This edition published by arrangement with Harlequin Books S.A.

For questions and comments about the quality of this book, please contact us at CustomerService@Harlequin.com.

Printed in U.S.A.

CONTENTS

Medical themes play a prominent role in many of **Jacqueline Diamond**'s one hundred published novels, including her Safe Harbor Medical miniseries for Harlequin American Romance. Her father was a small-town doctor before becoming a psychiatrist, and Jackie developed an interest in fertility issues after successfully undergoing treatment to have her two sons. A former Associated Press reporter and TV columnist, Jackie lives with her husband of thirty-seven years in Orange County, California, where she's active in Romance Writers of America. You can sign up for her free newsletter at jacquelinediamond.com and say hello to Jackie on her Facebook page, JacquelineDiamondAuthor. On Twitter, she's @jacquediamond.

Books by Jacqueline Diamond

Harlequin American Romance

Safe Harbor Medical

Officer Daddy
Falling for the Nanny
The Surgeon's Surprise Twins
The Detective's Accidental Baby
The Baby Dilemma
The M.D.'s Secret Daughter
The Baby Jackpot
His Baby Dream
The Surprise Holiday Dad
A Baby for the Doctor
The Surprise Triplets
The Baby Bonanza
The Doctor's Accidental Family

Visit the Author Profile page
at Harlequin.com for more titles.

THE WOULD-BE DADDY

Jacqueline Diamond

To Hunter and Brooke

Chapter One

It was unfair, dangerous and cruel. That poor little girl. If Franca Brightman didn't figure out a way to rescue four-year-old Jazz, she'd burst into a fireball that would bring down the Safe Harbor Medical Center parking structure on top of her.

She'd tried to work off her fury by staying late on a Friday night at her office. She'd spent hours reviewing the patient files that had come with her new job as staff psychologist. Plunging into the records and assessing patients' need for additional treatments should have blunted her pain and outrage.

Instead, the click of her medium-high heels on the concrete floor rang in a fierce staccato as she tore through the nearly empty lower level of the garage toward her aging white station wagon. At least at this hour she didn't have to feel embarrassed by her car, which was dented and old compared with the others, particularly the sleek silver sedan parked a short distance up the ramp.

Franca's last glimpse of Jazz had been riding off in a junkmobile far worse than this. The decrepit state of the car had intensified her fear about where and how the child would be living now that she'd gone back to her biological mother.

Where was Jazz right now? Had her mom bothered to fix dinner, or were they eating out of a can? Crammed into a rent-by-the-week motel unit, the four-year-old must miss her beautiful princess bedroom. Did she believe Franca had relinquished her by choice?

White-hot rage swirled inside Franca as she unlocked her station wagon and dropped into the driver's seat. It was a wonder that, despite the chilly March air, she hadn't already set the building ablaze.

Franca wished she could figure out a safe way to vent her anger, which had been simmering all day. With a PhD in psychology and years of counseling experience here in Southern California, she ought to be an expert on releasing emotions.

Instead, her mind returned to an image of the black-haired little girl, her blue eyes brimming with tears. Handing Jazz over to her unstable mother at the lawyer's office this morning had nearly torn Franca apart. How could she expect her foster daughter to understand why the planned adoption had fallen apart?

I shouldn't have come to work today. But being new at her job, Franca didn't want to ask for personal leave. After a lifetime of careful control, she'd assumed she could handle this.

She'd been wrong.

On the steering wheel, her hands trembled. She hated to drive in this condition, but she couldn't sit here indefinitely. Sucking in a breath, she switched on the ignition.

A rock song from the radio filled the car. The singer's voice rose in a ragged lament: "I can't take it anymore!"

There must have been half a dozen songs with similar lyrics, but right there, right then, this one seemed meant for her. Smacking the dashboard, Franca cranked up the volume and sang along in shared disgust, her voice ringing through the garage.

"I can't take it anymore! I can't take it anymore!" That felt good. Childish and self-indulgent, but good.

A drum solo followed, which Franca accompanied by thumping the steering wheel. When the chorus returned, she howled even louder: "I can't take it anymore!" The acoustics in this garage were odd, she noted as she paused for a breath. It sounded as if the music was echoing from up the ramp, underscored by...could that be a man's voice rasping out the same lyrics?

It might be her imagination, but to make sure, she muted the radio. The music continued in the distance, with a ragged masculine voice trumpeting, "I can't take it anymore!" over the recording. The words and melody were emanating from the silver sedan.

Although Franca had done her best to meet her fellow professionals at the hospital during the past few months, she couldn't identify them all. Maybe it was best if she *didn't* recognize her fellow sufferer. She hadn't meant to intrude on anyone's privacy.

Embarrassed by her outburst, Franca adjusted the radio so it played at a lower volume. The man, little more than a silhouette against a safety light, turned in her direction, as if he'd registered the change.

Had he heard her singing earlier? She hoped not.

Franca was about to pull out of her spot when the silver sedan shot in reverse. In a moment, the car would drive past her parked vehicle as it headed for the exit. The driver would be able to identify Franca by the reddish-blond hair floating around her shoulders.

How awkward for the staff counselor, who was supposed to be strong and supportive, to be caught screeching like a teenager. Should she try to beat him out of the garage and pray he hadn't already figured out who she was?

Too late. His car was closing in, and she might back into it by accident.

Hunkering down, Franca trained her gaze on the concrete pillar visible through her windshield. *Just zip on past, whoever you are.* He was probably as eager as she was to pretend this scene never happened.

But she couldn't resist sneaking a glance in the rear-view mirror…at precisely the wrong instant.

Brown eyes, surprisingly clear in the dim light, locked onto hers. That angular face had thinned since they'd first met fifteen years ago in college, but she experienced the same jolt of electricity, the same powerful sense of connection.

Why did this persist, this ridiculously misguided notion that they meant something to each other? She wished Dr. Marshall Davis hadn't come home to California. He'd spent more than a decade out east, completing his medical training and earning respect as a skilled men's fertility surgeon. Even though he had grown up around here, he should have stayed put.

Instead, Marshall had joined Safe Harbor's urology program last fall, she'd discovered when she was hired about a month later. Encountering him had been inevitable. At the cafeteria and staff meetings, they'd chatted pleasantly but impersonally.

Given her professional acquaintance with Marshall, there was no reason for her to react so strongly when their eyes met, yet electricity snapped through her. Did he feel it, too?

Apparently not. As cold as ever, Marshall whipped his gaze away and drove out of the parking structure. Gone in a flash of silver, he left her shivering.

So much for setting the building on fire.

Exiting the garage into the hospital's circular drive, Franca spotted his car skimming onto the street. Nothing else stirred. Only scattered lights glowed in the windows of the six-story main structure and the adjacent medical building.

She struggled to put the weird encounter out of her mind. She and Marshall had always had an inexplicable habit of stumbling into the same place at the same time, as with their hiring at Safe Harbor. It meant nothing except that they'd both been drawn to an exciting place to work.

The former community hospital had been remodeled to specialize in fertility treatments and maternity care, featuring the latest high-tech facilities and outstanding physicians hired from around the country. Across the drive, the recently acquired five-story dental building stood dark save for safety illumination. It was undergoing renovation to serve as a center for the expanding men's fertility program, in which Marshall played a key role.

There he was again, popping into her brain with his sharp, intelligent gaze and rare, brilliant smile.

Their first meeting at a student party near the UC Berkeley campus was as clear in Franca's mind as if it had been weeks instead of well over a decade ago. Tall and broodingly handsome, Marshall had stood out in the crowded room. She'd been a freshman and he, she later learned, a junior.

Franca's breath had caught when he'd started toward her. She'd been rooted to the spot, overwhelmed by the sense that something life-altering was about to shake her world. Until then, she'd never considered herself the romantic type. To her, boyfriends had been just that— boys who were friends.

As Marshall wove through the tangle of beer-drinking undergrads, the intensity of his gaze had made her acutely aware of her Little Orphan Annie red hair—now dyed a less strident shade—and her curvy figure beneath a tank top and jeans. She'd read his response in his parted lips and the warmth infusing his face.

As she started to greet him, however, a nerdy guy from her psych class darted up and tugged her hair. Startled, Franca spilled her plastic cup of soda and ice.

By the time she finished cleaning it up, Marshall was deep in conversation with her roommate, who'd been at her elbow. Tall and slim with ash-blond hair and tailored clothes, Belle radiated cool sophistication in contrast to Franca's scruffiness.

When Belle introduced them, Marshall had responded with a brief "hello" and a nod, nothing more. *Okay, so I'm not his type after all,* she'd thought. And had been reminded of that for the next two years as he and Belle dated.

Yet they kept running into each other at events that would have bored her roommate: a lecture on recent archaeological finds, an experimental theater performance, a poetry reading. Afterward, she and Marshall had shared fervent discussions over coffee, discussions that only revealed their different opinions on everything from politics to the value of therapy to attitudes toward family.

His views on child rearing were almost Victorian, while Franca had an affinity for hard-luck kids and a desire to become a foster parent. As with Jazz.

Steeling her nerve, Franca turned left onto Safe Harbor Boulevard. No sign of Marshall's car ahead, but then, she'd lingered for quite a while.

She remembered Belle's tear-streaked face when he'd broken it off with her after his graduation. Apparently Belle hadn't met his high standards because she was struggling academically. Never mind that her troubles had stemmed from her attempt to cram in extra classes and finish early so she could move to Boston to be near him.

Although the way he'd treated his devoted girlfriend had been cruel, it would be unfair to call him heartless, Franca reflected as she headed for the freeway and the half-hour drive to her apartment. Especially in view of his rumpled hair and distraught expression tonight.

What could have reduced him to screaming in a parking garage? Well, one thing was certain: he wouldn't be calling Franca Brightman, PhD, for a consultation.

IF LIFE WERE as precise, clean and well-structured as an operating room, Marshall would be a much happier man, he reflected the next morning as he performed microsurgery. Although he wasn't fond of working on Saturdays, the scheduling was necessary due to the shortage of ORs. That would change once the new building opened, thank goodness.

The patient, Art Lomax, a thirty-three-year-old ex-marine, suffered from a low sperm count and reduced sex drive. He longed to be a father and to satisfy his wife in bed. A man who'd fought for his country deserved a break, and Marshall was glad to be able to provide it.

Seated at the console of the microsurgical system, he trained his eyes on the 3-D high-definition image of the patient's body. Marshall enjoyed the way the controls translated his slightest hand movement to the in-

struments inserted into Lomax's body. The delicate
procedure, a varicocelectomy, would repair blood vessels attached to the patient's testes, which produced
both sperm and testosterone. Restoring them to normal
functioning would enhance Lomax's ability to father
children and improve his sex drive, along with muscle
strength and energy level.

Around him, the surgical team functioned with
smooth efficiency, from Dr. Reid Winfrey, the urolo-
gist assisting him, to the nurses who ensured that the
right tools were ready to be attached to the machine's
robotic arms. The OR was a technophile's dream. The
overhead lighting generated no heat, while suspended
cameras recorded the surgery for later review. An adjacent pathology lab allowed tissue to be tested during
surgery so the surgeon could review the results without
leaving the sterile field.

Early in Marshall's medical training, he'd felt uncomfortable in clinical settings because he lacked the
gift of relating easily to people. The discovery of his
talent for surgery had revolutionized his dreams.

Focusing on the screen, he took little notice of the
chatter among the surgical team. Then a name caught
his attention.

"Isn't it awful about Franca Brightman's little girl?"
a nurse, Erica, commented to the anesthesiologist.

"What about her?" The slender fellow, who sported
a trim gray beard, perked up at the prospect of fresh
gossip.

"She was adopting this adorable four-year-old girl
whose mom's a convicted drug dealer," the nurse said.
"Apparently the mother had agreed to the adoption,
but then she got sprung from prison due to an evidence

snafu at the lab. Just like that, *wham*, she took the lit-tle girl away."

"That's rotten." Reid, an African-American urolo-gist who shared Marshall's office suite, frowned at her. The man did volunteer work with underprivileged kids, and had more than once described the harsh impact of parental drug use on children. "Surely a court wouldn't hand a child over to a mother like that."

The petite blonde shrugged. "She isn't a convict any-more, and the adoption was voluntary."

"How long was the girl with Franca?" asked Mar-shall. Belatedly, he realized he should have used the title Dr. Brightman. But it was too late, anyway, to keep their acquaintance a secret. When he'd referred several staffers and patients to Franca for consults, he'd men-tioned they had a prior acquaintance.

More than an acquaintance. Her anguish last night had shaken him. But he had no clue how to comfort anyone, especially a parent deprived of a child.

He'd never fathomed why Franca planned to become a foster and adoptive mom to troubled kids when she could presumably bear children of her own. Sure, Mar-shall sympathized with the youngsters Reid counseled; he'd donated scholarship money to an organization his colleague recommended. But no matter how much he sympathized with their plight, wasn't it natural to yearn for a little boy or girl who was yours from birth?

"She's been with Franca for a couple of years, half the kid's life." Erica peered up at the high-definition screen that showed the same image of the patient's body Marshall was viewing on his terminal. Observing it helped the staff anticipate Marshall's needs, plus many nurses took an interest in anatomy and physiology. "Jazz was pretty wild when Franca became her foster mom,

I gather, but she was learning to trust that the world is a safe place. Until now."

"You seem to know a lot about it." Marshall registered that the anesthesiologist gave him a speculative look due to his uncharacteristic show of interest, but he was too curious to care.

"Jazz's been attending the hospital day care center these past few months," the nurse explained. "My son Jordan is friends with her."

Erica and her husband had a toddler, Marshall recalled. Recently, he'd become more aware of who had children.

Part of the reason stemmed from learning he had a young nephew, and part of it from turning thirty-five. Many doctors delayed marriage and parenthood during their long training, but he'd moved past that stage. As his medical practice showed, men as well as women experienced a powerful urge to procreate. That was an intellectual way of rationalizing his gut-level desire to be a dad.

But Marshall couldn't consider fatherhood until he sorted out the shock he'd received less than a week ago. He'd never imagined that everything he thought he knew about himself could disintegrate with a single stunning revelation.

That didn't excuse him for howling like a banshee in his car last night. Luckily, the only person who'd overheard had been Franca, and he respected her discretion.

With the last of the blood vessels repaired, Marshall yielded his position at the controls to Reid, who would close the tiny incisions. The surgery was only minimally invasive, so the patient should be able to go home later that day.

As for Marshall, he was heading home now, having completed three operations this morning. Much as he loved the two-story house he'd bought here in Safe Harbor, though, he was in no hurry to get there.

In the hallway, his footsteps dragged. Marshall needed someone to talk to, someone who could set him straight and provide perspective. Someone like Franca.

That would be a big mistake. In college, he'd recognized almost immediately that his attraction to her was wrong for them both. Instead, he'd tried in vain to fall in love with her roommate, who met all his requirements, or so he'd believed.

He'd survived for more than a decade without Franca to bounce ideas off. And he would continue to manage just fine.

At the elevators, Marshall punched the down button. A second later, the doors opened to reveal the *other* person he didn't care to face right now. A man almost the same height, build and coloring as Marshall himself.

Dark circles underscored Dr. Nick Davis's eyes from an overnight shift in Labor and Delivery that had obviously run long. He gave a start at the sight of Marshall, and for a moment, the air bristled between them.

Stiffly, Marshall stepped inside. "Hey."

"Hey back at you," said the cousin he'd disliked and resented all his life. And whom he'd just learned was his biological brother.

As the elevator descended, Marshall searched for a polite way to break the silence. "Rough night, Nicholas?"

"Buckets of babies." Nick cleared his throat. "Say, I have a question."

Marshall braced for whatever barb might come next. "Shoot."

"Will you be the best man at my wedding?"

Chapter Two

After meeting with a family at her private office in Garden Grove, fifteen miles north of Safe Harbor, Franca drove to her nearby home Saturday morning with her mind in turmoil. She'd insisted on retaining her old practice when she'd joined the hospital staff, partly in case the new job didn't work out and partly because she refused to drop loyal clients.

She wasn't sure how much good she'd done today, though; it had been an effort to concentrate on the conflict between an adolescent girl and her parents. However, they'd shown progress in their ability to set reasonable boundaries while respecting the teenager's right to privacy.

At her apartment complex, Franca followed the walkway between calla lilies and red, purple and yellow pansies. In the spring, Jazz had been unable to keep herself from plucking the flowers until Franca explained that the blooms were for all the residents to enjoy. After that, the child had taken care to avoid picking or trampling them.

What a change from when she'd entered foster care. Jazz had lacked self-control, even for a two-year-old. Having a regular bedtime, eating three meals a day at a table and following rules about storing toys after use—

everything was a fight. But beneath the stubbornness, Franca had sensed the child's anger over having her world torn apart and her hurt at feeling abandoned. Distraught about facing trial, her mother, Bridget Oberly, had been a frequent no-show at arranged visits.

As a foster parent, it was Franca's job to prepare the child to return to her mother's care. The more self-sufficient Jazz became in terms of potty training and dressing, and the more she was able to obey rules, the better she'd handle her mother's unpredictable lifestyle. Since her father had died in a gang shooting, her mom was parenting solo.

Gradually, she'd bonded with Franca, running to her for hugs and curling in her lap for story time. When Bridget agreed to an adoption, Franca had been deeply grateful.

She'd never imagined that her world could shatter so utterly.

Now she stepped inside her second-floor unit with a sense of entering paradise lost. She'd tried to enliven her simple apartment with personal touches: a multi-colored comforter crocheted by her mother was draped over the couch, while on the walls, she'd hung framed photographs shot by her brother, Glenn, of the wildflowers and summer meadows near his Montana home.

At the doorway to Jazz's bedroom, tears blurred Franca's vision. The fairy-tale bedspread and curtains that she'd sewn herself, the shelf of books and the sparkly dolls remained unchanged, yet their princess was gone. Bridget had told Jazz she could take only a single suitcase because of their cramped unit. Franca wished she could drop by to check on the preschooler's well-being and reassure her.

The ringing of the phone drew Franca back to the

present. The caller was Ada Humphreys, owner of the Bear and Doll Boutique, where Franca had often taken Jazz to pick out toys and books.

"I just got a new catalog of doll-clothes patterns," Ada said after they exchanged greetings. "That little girl of yours will adore them."

Franca kept running into people who hadn't heard the bad news. Despite a catch in her throat, she forced out the words, "Jazz is…gone."

"Gone?" Ada repeated.

Franca summarized what had happened. "She trusted me to take care of her and I let her down."

"I don't mean to be nosy, but with her mother's history of drug use, couldn't you sue for custody?" Ada asked.

"My lawyer advised against it. He said there was no guarantee I'd win, and it might be counterproductive."

"In what way?"

"Jazz's mom may face retrial on the same drug charges," Franca explained. "If that happens, it's better for me to stay on good terms."

"So if she's convicted, she might relinquish Jazz to you again," Ada said.

"Exactly." Franca couldn't keep the quaver from her voice. "Otherwise, my little girl could end up in the foster care system and I'd have no claim on her."

"How awful," Ada said. "But it's fortunate Jazz had you during such an important part of her childhood. You've prepared her to succeed in school and life." The mother of a second-grade teacher, Ada understood a lot about learning and child development.

"That's a positive attitude." Franca wandered into her own bedroom. On a side table, her sewing machine sat idle, threaded with pink from the Valentine's Day dress she'd stitched for Jazz.

"I can understand you might not be making doll clothes for a while," Ada said. "It's too bad. Sewing is such a relaxing hobby."

"I do enjoy it." A puffy blue concoction on a hanger caught Franca's eye—the bridesmaid's dress from Belle's wedding. Considering Belle's usual good taste, why had she chosen such ugly gowns for her attendants?

Last month, Belle had pulled out all the stops in her wedding to a likable CPA. Franca had been glad to serve as a bridesmaid, despite the strain on her budget to pay for this awful creation, its bows and lacy trim more suitable for a Pollyanna costume than for a woman in her thirties. She wondered what the rest of the half dozen attendants would do with their froufrou getups. Donate them to charity? Use them in community theater productions? Clean the garage with them?

"Well, don't be a stranger," Ada said. "You never can tell when you might need a gift, or be in the mood to sew for fun."

On a shelf, a couple of dolls that doubled as bookends caught Franca's eye. How shabby they'd become, as had the dolls in her office. They underwent plenty of wear and tear in play therapy, where she used them along with stuffed animals, coloring materials and building blocks.

Franca hadn't planned to drive to Safe Harbor today, but she refused to sit here and stew in her unhappiness. A visit to the Bear and Doll Boutique was exactly what she needed.

"You're an inspiration," she said to Ada. "My dolls deserve a new wardrobe, and I have a perfectly hideous bridesmaid dress to cut up."

"Some of these new patterns are darling." A bell

tinkled in the background, signaling the arrival of a customer. "I'll see you soon."

After clicking off, Franca changed from her skirt and jacket into jeans and an old sweater. Since her hair was frizzing out of its bun, she shook it loose and ran a brush through it, which did little to tame the bushiness. But Ada wouldn't care about Franca's appearance, and she doubted she'd run into anyone else she knew.

Out Franca went, her mood lifting.

"Best man at your wedding?" Marshall repeated. He wasn't ready to answer, nor to ask the question uppermost in his mind until he had a better grasp of the situation. "Have you set a date?"

"Yep, three weeks from now." When the elevator arrived at the ground floor, Nick let him exit first. "There's nothing like an April wedding, Zady says. Lucky for us, the Seaside Wedding Chapel had a cancellation."

"Not so lucky for the couple who canceled, I presume," Marshall said.

"Maybe they decided to elope instead." How typical of Nick to look on the bright side.

As they passed a couple of nurses' aides in the hall, Marshall heard the murmur that often greeted their rare appearance side-by-side: "Are they twins?"

He'd been irked in school by the striking resemblance between him and his cousin, who was a year younger. Wasn't it obvious that Nick's brown hair was a shade lighter, and that at six feet tall he lacked an inch of Marshall's height?

Nevertheless, people considered them look-alikes. And since they were also close in age and shared a surname, teachers at their magnet science high school had often compared them academically. How unfair that Marshall had studied until his head hurt to earn top grades, while Nick, with his quick grasp of essentials and his unusually good memory, sailed from A to A.

After attending different colleges and medical schools, they'd accidentally landed at Safe Harbor Medical at almost the same time, which had created confusion among their colleagues. Good thing they specialized in different fields, Nick in obstetrics and Marshall in urology, or their patients might wind up in the wrong examining rooms. Or worse, the wrong ORs.

Nick must have heard the muttering, too. Rather than stiffening, he draped an arm over Marshall's shoulders. "If they want to yammer about us, bro, let's show 'em what pals we are. Okay if I mess up your hair?"

"No." Marshall eased away from his brother.

Nick removed his arm. "Loosen up, man."

"I'd rather not." However, Marshall had no desire to renew the friction that had flared between them over the years. His perfectionist, high-achieving parents had encouraged him to scorn his freewheeling cousin and Nick's irresponsible parents. They'd hidden a dark secret, though: unable to have children, Upton and Mildred Davis had adopted Marshall, their nephew, as a toddler. In exchange for their silence, Mildred and Upton promised to help pay the younger Davises' household expenses.

That silence had lasted for nearly thirty-five years, until last Monday. Out of the blue, Uncle Quentin had confronted Nick and Marshall with the truth, explaining that he wanted to repair past wrongs. Instead, he'd simply dumped his burden on his sons, then taken off for his home a hundred and fifty miles away in Bakersfield.

Everything Marshall believed he knew about himself and his parents had been thrown into turmoil. Why had they been ashamed of his origins? Had they been so strict because they feared he'd turn out a mess like his birth parents?

As they exited the hospital via a side door, Nick asked, "Is that a no? I assure you, I have the bride's approval."

"Considering that Zady's my office nurse, I should hope so." Marshall didn't wish to offend either his brother or the future Mrs. Davis, whom he liked and respected. Besides, being invited to serve as best man was an honor. "Of course I'll stand up with you."

On the path toward the parking structure, their strides synchronized. "Maybe we should rent different color tuxes," Nick said cheerfully. "I'd hate for the bride to get confused and marry the wrong guy."

Leave it to Nick to find humor in their embarrassing resemblance. "What exactly does a best man do?" Marshall asked. "Aside from making sure the groom shows up and doesn't lose the ring."

Halting in his tracks, Nick whipped out his phone. "Let's see."

"I didn't mean for you to research it now."

"We've only got a few weeks." He tapped the screen.

Marshall gazed across the curved drive to the newly acquired building, where construction equipment buzzed. The Portia and Vincent Adams Memorial Medical Building—popularly referred to as the Porvamm—would provide much-needed operating suites, laboratories and other facilities for the men's fertility program.

A little over a week earlier, two groups of doctors had nearly come to blows over how to allot the two floors of office space. Marshall and Nick had taken opposite sides, with Marshall in favor of keeping the entire Porvamm for the men's program, while Nick and his comrades protested that they deserved a break from their cramped quarters.

Before open warfare could break out with scalpels flashing in the corridors, they'd reached a compromise. Encouraged by Zady, Marshall had proposed a concession, and last Monday the administration had agreed to assign a quarter of the offices to obstetricians and pediatricians.

"Duties of a best man," Nick read aloud from the phone. "Serve as the groom's adviser on clothing and etiquette. I think we can skip that part."

"I know nothing about weddings, so I concur," Marshall said.

"Organize the bachelor party," his brother continued.

"Okay to video games and pizza," Marshall said. "I draw the line at strippers."

Nick laughed. "I'd love to see you plan a party with strippers, just to watch your face get redder than a blood specimen, but you're off the hook. Because of the tight time frame, Zady's skipping the bachelorette party, too."

What other land mines lay in wait? Co-opting the phone, Marshall scanned the list. "I can make a toast at the reception, and I'll be glad to dance with the bride and the maid of honor. Should I be squiring around the other bridesmaids, too?"

"There aren't any." Reclaiming the device, Nick resumed their walk toward the garage. "Just Zora as matron of honor." The bride's twin sister was an ultrasound technician. "You might have to ride herd on my future mother-in-law, though. She's reputed to be a dragon."

"You haven't met her?" Marshall had presumed that introductions to the bride's parents would be a priority.

"Zady doesn't plan to invite her until a few days before the ceremony. That's enough notice for her to fly down from Oregon but short enough to minimize the damage." Nick shrugged. "I've heard many stories about the woman's drinking and trouble-making. Zady's plan seems sensible."

Marshall hadn't given any thought to what kind of wedding he'd have. If he'd ever spared a moment's reflection on the subject, however, it wouldn't include misbehaving in-laws. That brought up a delicate subject. "Will my mother be invited?"

"I put Aunt Mildred on the guest list." Inside the parking structure, Nick halted beside his battered blue sedan. "Unless that's a problem for you."

"I doubt she'll accept," Marshall blurted. In response to his brother's quizzical expression, he explained, "I tried to talk to her after Uncle Quentin dropped his bomb, and got nowhere."

He still couldn't refer to Nick's father as "Dad." That title belonged to Quentin's older brother, who, to be fair, had been as hard on himself as he'd been on his adoptive son. A brilliant inventor of medical devices and a savvy businessman, Upton Davis had amassed a fortune. After his death five years ago of an aneurysm, he'd left half his estate to Marshall, along with a request to take care of his mother.

Marshall had done his best. How sad that his mother no longer wanted his help.

"You told her that you now know you're adopted?" Nick leaned against his car.

"Uncle Quentin beat me to it."

"How did she react?"

"Badly." When Marshall had called Thursday night to confirm their usual dinner date on Sunday, she'd dismissed him coldly. "She said now that I've learned I'm not really her son, not to bother. Then she hung up."

"That's harsh, even for Aunt Mildred," Nick said.

"I've called but all I get is her voice mail." How could his mother reject him for something that wasn't his fault? She was the one who should be apologizing, yet Marshall hadn't asked for that.

To him, Mildred would always be Mom. His birth mother, Adina Davis, had died of lung cancer two years ago. Thanks to the family's secrets, Marshall had never had a chance to know the woman who'd given birth to him except as a charming but volatile aunt.

"Give her a chance to recover," Nick said. "She's never been the warm, cuddly type."

"There's an understatement." Might as well raise the other issue on Marshall's mind. "I suppose your father is on the guest list."

"Yes. Zady requested it. She's more generous than I am after he let us down." In addition to hiding the truth about Marshall, Uncle Quentin had abandoned his wife and son when Nick was ten. "I may tolerate his presence, but that doesn't mean I forgive him."

For once, the two of them agreed on something, Marshall thought. And for all that he'd lost by his parents' deception, at least they'd been there for him.

Mercifully, neither he nor his brother showed signs of their parents' mental instability. Although about 50 percent of the children of bipolar patients suffered from a psychiatric disorder, sometimes the odds worked in your favor.

"The important thing is that you and Zady enjoy your wedding." Curiosity propelled Marshall to ask, "How's Caleb reacting?"

Although his nephew's conception four years ago had

been an accident, he'd proved a blessing to Nick. Named after their grandfather, the boy had come to live with his dad after his mother's death in a boating accident.

"He's excited about being the ring bearer." Nick grinned. "That's another duty of the best man—supervising my son. Hope that's okay."

"It's fine. More than fine." Marshall had felt an immediate attachment to his nephew when they'd met a few months ago. If he had a kid, he'd relish every minute of the boy's—or girl's—childhood.

"I'll email you with whatever we decide about tuxedos. I'd prefer a dark suit, but I doubt Zady will go for that," Nick said.

"I'm sure she'll keep me informed." Noting the exhaustion on his brother's face, Marshall remembered that the man had been on duty all night. "Go home."

"Gladly." Lifting a hand in farewell, Nick ducked into his car.

Marshall surveyed the scattering of vehicles for a familiar white station wagon. Its absence brought a pang of disappointment. What had he expected, a repeat of last night's impromptu karaoke duet?

Recalling what the surgical nurse had said about Franca's foster child brought a wave of sympathy. She must be grieving.

While Marshall respected her decision to take in a troubled child, he had to be honest. If he and his future wife were unable to have kids, he'd be happy to adopt, but only if they nurtured the child from infancy. He'd never invite trouble by taking in a foster kid. The discovery that his own parents had been so ashamed of adopting him that they'd kept him at arm's length reinforced his reservations.

His footsteps slowed as he neared the silver sedan,

his earlier reluctance to go home closing over him. He could call Franca to offer his support, he mused. He had her cell number, which she'd provided to the staff.

Then he got another, better idea. Since his best-man duties involved Caleb, why not buy the boy a gift? A teddy bear dressed in a tux, perhaps.

Marshall recalled passing a shop on Safe Harbor Boulevard...the Bear and Doll Boutique, that was the name.

And since Franca was no doubt clearing away reminders of her foster daughter rather than acquiring more toys, he didn't have to worry about an awkward encounter, or the possibility of a heart-to-heart conversation. As he'd learned from his father, it was his responsibility to deal with his own problems, and he intended to do just that.

Chapter Three

The rainbow colors of the toy store brightened Franca's mood. What a joyful array of bears, dolls, accessories and children's books, plus there was a large craft table that Ada used for classes. Although the store appeared small from the front, its depth encompassed several rooms, which was part of its charm: you never knew what delightful surprise lay around the corner.

Near the front counter, stuffed animals in fairy-tale outfits filled a shelf. A pink-gowned Cinderella pig beamed at her porcine prince. A polar bear Snow White shepherded an assembly of penguins, while a Little Red Riding Hood sheep held out her basket to a wolf in fleecy clothing.

"They're darling!" Franca told the owner.

At the compliment, Ada tipped her head of champagne-colored hair. "I ran across them last week in the storage room. I try to rotate my stock."

"They're too precious to hide." Wary of soiling the merchandise, Franca avoided picking up the wolf, despite her curiosity about how its fleecy costume had been constructed.

"I'll fetch that new catalog," Ada said. "Hang on." She ducked behind the counter.

From within the store appeared a familiar dark-haired woman. As the hospital's public relations director, Jennifer Serra Martin had interviewed Franca for the employee newsletter a few months ago. Discovering that they had a lot in common, they'd started meeting for lunch and scheduling play dates for their little girls.

"I heard about your daughter," Jennifer said. "Franca, I'm so sorry. I can't imagine what I'd have done if Rosalie's birth mother had changed her mind."

The five-year-old, a cutie with blond ringlets, trotted after her mother, clutching a panda. "Where's Jazz?"

"I told you, Rosalie, she's gone to live with her birth mommy," Jennifer reminded her. "Honey, can you read a story to your new bear for a minute? I'm busy with Dr. Brightman."

"You're just talking!"

"Remember what I said about that?"

Rosalie screwed up her face as she searched for the answer. "Talking is how grown-ups play."

"That's right. And you hate when I interrupt *your* play," Jennifer said.

"Okay, Mommy." Rosalie perched on a chair and, panda in lap, picked up a picture book.

With her daughter settled, the PR director turned to Franca. "Have you thought any more about what we discussed?"

Franca's memory yielded no clues as to what the woman was talking about. Suppressing an instinct to screw up her face like Rosalie, she asked, "What was that?"

"Ideas for new counseling groups," Jennifer reminded her.

"Oh, yes. I've been reviewing possibilities." The previous psychologist had established programs for infertile couples, for surrogate moms and for several other categories of patients. However, the hospital was expanding into many areas, and Jennifer had volunteered to brainstorm new groups with her.

"I had an idea I meant to share. Now, what was it?" Jennifer sighed. "Too bad I forgot to write it down."

"It'll come back to you," Franca assured her.

"Probably at a totally inappropriate moment." The dark-haired woman smiled. "When it does, I'll text you immediately."

Ada joined them with a pattern catalog. "I can order these at my discount—I'll split the difference with you."

"I'll pay full price," Franca told her. "I want you to stay in business."

"Every little bit helps," the older woman admitted.

Jennifer peered at the catalog. "What adorable little dresses!"

"Here's the fabric I plan to use." On her phone, Franca clicked to a photo of Belle resplendent in white, flanked by a half dozen attendants bedecked in frothy blue. "I'll never wear my bridesmaid dress again."

"Oh, dear," Jennifer said. "Those are fascinatingly hideous."

Ada took an amused peek. "Some insecure brides try to enhance their image by making their attendants as ugly as possible."

Franca shook her head. "I doubt Belle did it intentionally."

She halted as the shop's glass door opened to admit a tall and much-too-handsome man with a shadowed expression. Even though Marshall instantly assumed a polite smile, her heart twisted. What was troubling him?

Still, his rumpled appearance from last night had yielded to smooth hair, pressed slacks and a navy polo shirt—a marked contrast to Franca's scruffy state. She wished she hadn't worn her oldest jeans and stained sweater. As for the condition of her hair, the less she thought about that, the better.

Distractedly, she said hello, and after Marshall exchanged greetings with Jennifer, Franca introduced him to Ada. She'd forgotten the phone in her hand until the picture caught his gaze.

"Belle got married?" His voice rang hollow.

"Last month." Was this the cause of his distress? But that didn't make sense after all these years.

Franca supposed she ought to mind her own business about whatever was troubling Marshall. But it wasn't in her nature to ignore friends' distress…even if they hadn't consciously sought her input.

How ironic, Marshall mused as his pulse quickened. He'd been naive to believe himself safe from running into Franca here. Not that he was sorry.

In college, they'd frequently bumped into each other, as if drawn to the same locations. In truth, it hadn't always been a coincidence. If he learned Franca was attending an event that interested him, he'd make a point of going, too. But there'd also been a synchronicity at work, he believed.

Now here they were. And Belle was still between them. Speaking of Belle, she appeared happy in the picture. No doubt she'd long ago forgotten her disappointment in him.

"She's beautiful." That was true of all brides, but especially of Belle, with her blond radiance. Yet her image failed to eclipse one particular bridesmaid. "As are you."

Peripherally, he observed the PR director taking her little girl to the counter to pay for their purchases. He was glad not to have to include them in the conversation.

"No one could look beautiful in that dress." Franca chuckled. "I plan to cut it into doll clothes. I'm here to pick out patterns."

Marshall decided to explain why he'd stopped in, as well. "I figured my nephew, Caleb, might like a bear in a tux."

"You have a nephew?" A pucker formed between her eyebrows. "But you're an only child."

They'd had a conversation once about the advantages and disadvantages of their situations, him as a single-ton and her as the middle of three kids. How odd that the normally hyperactive hospital grapevine hadn't yet broadcast the news to her.

"Nick and I were raised as cousins. We just learned that was a lie." To his embarrassment, he had to clear his throat. *Pull yourself together.* "The short version is, we're brothers and I was adopted by my aunt and uncle. Anyway, Nick asked me to be best man at his wedding next month, and Caleb's the ring bearer. He's engaged to my nurse, Zady. Nick is, not Caleb. But you got that." He rarely stumbled over words. How embarrassing.

"Zady told me she was engaged," Franca said. "I was honored that she asked me to save the date."

"I see." Up close, her cloud of reddish-blond hair made her amber eyes appear extra large, but Marshall noted there was something different. "Why did you change your hair color?"

Franca shrugged. "I was tired of feeling like Rag-gedy Ann."

"I liked it."

"You liked that I resembled a rag doll with red yarn for hair?"

"It was...you."

"Exactly," she said. "A mess. And I'm not fishing for compliments."

"May I offer a word of advice?" Marshall plunged ahead before she could respond. "I realize you're the expert on psychology, but you shouldn't put yourself down."

"Where's this coming from?" Franca asked.

"From…" He broke off. In college, he'd been aware that Franca felt eclipsed by her stunning roommate. But he'd been in no position to explain that whenever he was around her, Belle faded. Nor did he wish to bring it up now.

Fundamentally, nothing had changed. Marshall had recognized from the start that his attraction to Franca was destructive. They were opposites who disagreed on many important topics, and whenever they were together for long, their arguments brought out the worst in each other.

"Never mind," he said. "I shouldn't have spoken."

"Actually, you're right," she responded. "I was indulging in either self-pity or false modesty."

"Nothing about you is false." That skated too close to flattery for Marshall's taste. He decided on a quick exit. "Good luck with your patterns."

"Happy bear hunting."

"Thanks."

Before he could escape, Jennifer Martin turned from the counter and cried, "I remember!"

"Remember what?" Franca asked.

"I'll leave you two to chat." Marshall started to retreat.

"Wait, Dr. Davis!" Jennifer protested. "This concerns you."

"Excuse me?"

"I have an idea for a new therapy group," Jennifer burst out. "For men undergoing fertility treatments. How perfect if the pair of you ran it as a team!"

Teaming up with Franca to plumb patients' emotions? The concept struck him as anything but perfect. "I'm not a counselor," Marshall said. "Dr. Brightman is well qualified to lead such a group."

"Men might hesitate to talk freely with a woman," Jennifer said. "Also, while she's a counselor, you have medical expertise. You'd be a great team."

"She has a point," Franca conceded.

"Any male urologist would do." That was the best argument that came to mind. "Preferably one who has better people skills than mine."

"Such as who?" Jennifer demanded.

Marshall's mind skimmed over the urology staff. The head of the department, Dr. Cole Rattigan, had no spare time, since he and his wife were juggling fifteen-month-old triplets. Marshall's suitemates were even newer to the hospital than he was and still honing their surgical skills under his supervision. It seemed wrong to pressure them into the job.

So how did he get out of this?

FRANCA SYMPATHIZED WITH Marshall's deer-in-the-headlights reaction. However, she couldn't dispute Jennifer's reasoning.

"It's worth considering," she said. "Dr. Davis and I will discuss it."

"Great!" Jennifer said. "Okay if I mention it to Mark?" Dr. Mark Rayburn was the hospital administrator. "Oh, and Cole, too?"

"What's the rush?" Marshall asked irritably.

"Things are slow after the holidays. There's not a lot

happening in March. I'd love to publicize a new therapy group in the newsletter," Jennifer explained.

"Give us a chance to consider how we might organize it and whether it fits into Dr. Davis's schedule," Franca said firmly. "Nice to see you and Rosalie."

"Nice to see you, too." To the obvious relief of her daughter, who was hopping up and down, the PR director departed.

"She doesn't take no for an answer, does she?" Marshall growled.

"She's not usually pushy," Franca assured him. "But if we don't want this foisted on us willy-nilly, we'd better present a united front."

His jaw twitched as if he were about to dismiss the notion entirely. But Ada was observing them from the counter, and other voices were approaching from outside. "Let's finish shopping and meet elsewhere to resolve this."

"Good idea." Not at her apartment, and Franca wasn't about to suggest his place. "How about the Sea Star Café down by the harbor? I haven't had lunch."

"Is that still there?" Like Franca, Marshall had grown up in inland Orange County, but must have visited the harbor town over the years. "Yes, I'm hungry, too."

Into the shop surged a couple of women shepherding children.

"See you there," she said.

"Done." He drew himself up to his full, rather impressive height. "Let's get this squared away before it blows up in our faces."

Would it be so terrible for them to coordinate a weekly group? she wondered, watching him move deeper into the store. Surely they could maintain a professional distance, despite her awareness of him as a man. And despite his disappointment in her new hair color. The picky comment reminded Franca of how exacting Marshall could be.

Franca flipped through the catalog and selected half a dozen patterns with adjustable fastenings, easy to remove for washing. After writing the pattern numbers on a notepad, she handed it to Ada.

The shopkeeper promised to order them that day. "I'll text you when they come in."

"Great."

In an angled wall mirror, Franca spotted Marshall in the next room, lifting a formally dressed bear for inspection. Yearning transformed his face as he fingered the soft fur.

With a start, she recognized that look. She'd seen it on the face of her older sister, Gail, when one of their cousins had brought her baby to a family gathering. Gail had been devastated by repeated miscarriages.

Was Marshall eager to be a father? Perhaps Belle's wedding photo had reminded him of how much he'd thrown away. But whatever promptings he experienced toward parenthood, Franca doubted he'd understand her torment over losing Jazz.

Marshall had made it clear long ago that he saw no reason to "invite trouble," as he put it, from a foster child. For him, fatherhood meant a traditional home with two or three genetic children.

To Franca, motherhood meant loving children regardless of their origins. Despite growing up in a happy household with a psychologist father and a devoted mother, she'd had an immediate bond with the neglected and abused youngsters she'd met as a teen volunteer, along with a sense of destiny. In her twenties, she'd gone through the process to qualify as a foster mom. After caring for several youngsters, she'd given her heart to Jazz.

She had no desire to return to her lonely apartment. In contrast, eating lunch with Marshall didn't seem so bad.

Reminded of their plans, Franca said goodbye to Ada and went out.

Chapter Four

Marshall inhaled the crisp sea air as he swiped his credit card in the parking meter. On a Saturday afternoon, he'd been lucky to find a space.

Seagulls mewed overhead as he descended the steps to the quay. Surf and souvenir shops lined the inland side of the wooden wharf, while small piers thrust outward into the harbor, tethered boats bobbing beside them in the water. In the breezy March sunshine, white sails filled the harbor.

To his right, past a tumble of rocks, stretched a beach dotted with a few brave sunbathers. During his teens, the beach had been popular with Marshall's classmates, but he'd been too busy with Advanced Placement and International Baccalaureate classes to hang out at such places. However, he'd enjoyed the sounds and smells of the ocean on rare jaunts with family friends who'd owned a powerboat.

Ahead, at the Sea Star Café, outdoor diners basked in the comfort of warming devices shaped like metal umbrellas. No sign of Franca.

Inside the café, the scents of coffee and spices greeted him. Families and couples had claimed all the tables, and he was wondering if they should have chosen a less popular locale when he spotted a tumble of red-gold hair at a booth.

Hands cupped around a mug, Franca gazed out the window to her left toward the open ocean. In profile, she had a straight nose, a determined chin and long lashes. When she swung toward him, her mouth curved in welcome. She waved at almost the same moment that the loudspeaker squawked her name.

"I went ahead and ordered," she explained when he reached her. "Hope you like pita sandwiches. You can have either the falafel and hummus or the Swiss and turkey."

"Take whichever you prefer." Marshall usually picked items that could be trimmed, such as sandwiches on bread. Still, he refused to become one of those fussy eaters who drove everyone around them crazy. He had even recently discovered the pleasures of pizza. "I'll pick up the order."

"I'll hold down the table," she said. "Either sandwich is fine with me."

Marshall claimed their tray and on his return, handed her the falafel and hummus pita—definitely messier. He slid several bills across the table to cover his check. "No arguing."

"Wasn't going to," she said.

He removed the plates, utensils and glasses of water from the tray, then carried it to a disposal station. "You're always so neat," Franca remarked.

"As opposed to?" He raised an eyebrow.

"Me." She indicated a glop of hummus she'd spilled on the table.

"A little mess doesn't bother me as long as it's not mine." Marshall had the sense he was being perpetually judged, thanks to his parents' habitual criticism. He tried, not always successfully, to cut others more slack.

After a few bites of pita, he brought up the proposed counseling group. "Any suggestion for how to get out of this?"

"Are you sure we should?" Responding to his frown, Franca said, "This would benefit many patients. It also could reinforce Dr. Rattigan's view of you as a key player in the department's expansion."

Marshall mulled the idea as he ate. Adding such a group did seem logical. "What exactly happens in a counseling group? If that isn't a bonehead question."

"It's more a reflection on what medical schools teach doctors, or fail to teach them," she said.

"I took courses in psychopathology and clinical psychiatry," Marshall countered. "As well as serving a rotation in psychiatry." Psychopathology was the study of the genetic, biological and other causes of mental disorders, along with their symptoms and treatments.

"Dealing with psychotics and how to medicate them?" Franca summarized.

"Basically, yes."

"I figured." Her nose wrinkled. "We won't be dealing with psychotics. We'll be helping ordinary people whose infertility creates problems for them." Having finished her pita, she wiped her hands on her paper napkin.

Marshall reached across with his own napkin to dab the corner of her mouth. "Missed a spot."

Startled, Franca lifted her chin, and her cheek brushed his hand. An electric tingle ran along his arm. "I could use an aide to follow me around and clean me up," she said.

"Why bother, when I'm here?" he teased.

She smiled. "Promise you won't do that in front of patients."

"Promise you won't eat a pita in front of patients."

"It's a deal."

He returned to their topic. "I don't mean to be dismissive, but why not refer troubled patients to Resolve?" The national organization assisted people coping with infertility.

"It's a terrific group, but it's a complement to therapy," Franca said. "It doesn't replace it. But I never answered your question."

"About what happens in counseling?"

She nodded. "Infertility is a stressful experience. People often feel out of control and that they've failed. There's loss and grief as well as financial concerns." Fertility treatments could cost tens of thousands of dollars and were rarely covered by insurance. "Sharing your pain with others who are in the same boat can be a relief."

"But why have a separate group for men?"

Franca took a sip from her mug. "Most infertility counseling focuses on the woman or on the couple's relationship. But when the man is the source of the infertility, that can affect his feelings of masculinity and self-worth. And men in general have a harder time expressing their emotions."

"That's true of me," Marshall conceded. Although he wasn't entirely convinced, he'd run out of arguments. Moreover, an earlier comment of hers was rattling inside his head.

He'd assumed that by adopting, his parents had put to rest the issues associated with their infertility. Perhaps he'd been wrong. "Could those concerns persist after the couple adopts?"

"Certainly." Sunlight through the window brought out the sprinkling of freckles across Franca's cheeks. "A lot depends on the patients' self-esteem and how they view adoption."

"And therapy can help?" Too bad his parents hadn't availed themselves of it. But that wouldn't have suited their superior, stiff-upper-lip attitude.

"It isn't a cure-all, but yes," Franca said. "For example, adoptive parents worry whether there'll be a temperamental mismatch and whether the child will bond with them as strongly as with a birth parent."

"Or whether they'll bond with the child?" Marshall asked.

"That, too."

"You raise interesting points," he said. "To me, therapy has always seemed unscientific, perhaps even..." He paused as a couple moved past them to claim an empty table.

"A weakness?"

"Yes." He regarded her steadily. "I realize patients find it helpful. I've just never understood why."

"I wish doctors underwent therapy the way psychologists do," Franca said. "It's part of our training."

"Was it helpful to you?"

"Very."

"In what way?"

"I learned to stop assuming I'm responsible for my mother's happiness." She tilted her head as she reflected. "Ten years ago, after my father died, my brother went his own way. My sister was already married and living out of state. So Mom focused her energies on me, insisting we talk for an hour every night. Sometimes she'd phone at lunch, too. It was intrusive, but I couldn't bear to disappoint her. She'd always been more invested emotionally in her children than in my dad, despite their good relationship."

"Why was that?" It had never occurred to him that children could be more important to a parent than the husband-wife bond.

"My mother had been married once before and had several miscarriages." Franca hesitated, as if reluctant to confide too much. Odd, considering how readily she invited *his* confidences. Then she continued, "Her first husband couldn't handle the disappointment and left. Mom never entirely recovered from that betrayal. So as you can see, I know about the fallout from fertility problems in my own family."

"Surely things changed after she married your father, right?" He'd liked the elder Dr. Brightman when they'd met once at a campus event, although the man hadn't spoken much. He'd puffed on an aromatic pipe and listened attentively to the conversation involving his wife, Franca and Belle.

"Yes," Franca said. "Fortunately, there were no more miscarriages. But in a sense, I think she felt his loyalty had never truly been tested."

An interesting insight—but not really relevant to today's topic. "How did counseling help with your mom?"

"I had a frank talk with her about respecting boundaries," Franca said. "I also suggested activities for her."

"How'd she take it?"

"It upset her, and that upset me." She sighed. "After a few rough weeks, she reluctantly joined a senior center. A couple of months later, she met a widower, and married him."

"Is she happy?"

"Extremely." Franca folded her hands on the table. "They moved to Reno, where his children live. She's surrounded by grandkids, and except for the holidays, I've become barely more than a Facebook friend. A victim of my own success."

That wasn't the worst thing in the world. "If I were on Facebook, my mother would unfriend me," Marshall muttered.

"Because of you and Nick being brothers? I don't really understand how that happened." Franca broke off as a server offered them each a chocolate chip cookie, courtesy of the café. "Thanks." She set one on her napkin. Marshall accepted his and enjoyed the chocolate melting in his mouth while weighing how much to reveal.

He might as well spill it. The details would soon be all over the hospital anyway. "Nick's parents allowed my parents to adopt me as a toddler. Upton Davis was much more successful financially, while my birth parents were nearly homeless. I gather they hadn't planned on having two kids a year apart."

Quentin Davis had stumbled from job to job, drinking heavily and refusing treatment for his bipolar disorder. Aunt Adina had held a series of low-paying positions, spending money whenever she had it and expecting it to fall out of the sky when she didn't.

"How unusual that they chose to adopt the toddler rather than the baby," Franca said.

"I presume Nick was still breastfeeding. Also, with a toddler, they had a better idea of how well the child was developing."

"Aren't you being a bit severe?" she asked.

"I know my parents." Rather than elaborate, Marshall moved on. "My folks paid Adina and Quentin for an apartment and other living expenses, and insisted on secrecy in return. Until last week, I had no idea I was adopted."

Franca rested her chin on her palm. "How'd you discover it?"

"Uncle Quentin had a crisis of conscience and decided to get it off his chest. He corralled Nick and me and dumped it on us." Marshall pictured the graying, slightly stooped man as he'd sat at a conference table in the medical building just last Monday.

"Your mom must have been upset."

"She implied I'm not her son anymore and refuses to have dinner with me or even talk to me." When Marshall inhaled, his lungs hurt.

"It might be a knee-jerk reaction," Franca said. "I can't believe she means it."

"She didn't leave much room for doubt."

"What about your birth mother? Do you have a relationship with her?"

"Aunt Adina died a couple of years ago. I never especially connected with her," Marshall said. "But at thirty-five, I don't suppose I need a mother."

"Everyone needs a mother." Reaching across the table, Franca cupped her hand over his fist. Instinctively, he relaxed beneath her touch. "Give your mom time. She's hurting, and she lashed out at the person most closely associated with her secret—you."

"If she refuses to see me, what am I supposed to do?" he asked bitterly.

"Write her a letter," Franca advised. "Tell her you love her and that you're here for her. She's a mother, and once her initial shock eases, she'll view things differently. Don't let pride keep you apart."

Pride. Marshall had plenty of that. "I suppose that's good advice."

Her smile froze on her face. Following her gaze, he spotted a little girl with black hair clinging to a woman's hand as they entered.

Anguish transformed Franca's expression, stabbing into Marshall as if the pain were his own. He'd never experienced another person's emotions this keenly.

He didn't have to ask what had hurt her. This must be her foster daughter.

EVERYTHING AROUND FRANCA VANISHED. All the light in the world haloed the little girl she loved.

Hard-won self-control barely held her in place. Then Jazz spotted her and the girl pelted across the restaurant screaming, "Mommy Franca!"

In an instant, the child was climbing onto her lap, hugging her. And Franca hugged back, tears flowing.

Bridget stalked toward them. Despite her jeans and cartoon-printed T-shirt, she looked older than her twenty-three years, thanks to her drug use. "What do you think you're doing?"

"I'm sorry." Franca struggled to catch her breath.

"Jazz, get down right now!" Bridget's command whiplashed through the air.

"No!" The child burrowed into Franca.

Marshall sat quietly, observing. Franca felt both his sympathy and his reserve.

Around them, the café fell silent. Everyone was watching.

"Honey, you have to do what your mommy says." Gently, Franca pried the little fingers from around her neck. "Don't worry. I'm keeping your dolls safe and they'll join you as soon as you have room."

"I'm s'posed to stay with you. You promised!" The heartbreak in Jazz's voice tore at Franca.

When she'd joyfully informed the child about the adoption, she'd never imagined that it might fall through. How could a child understand that grown-ups didn't always have the power to keep their word?

"You live with your mother now." Her chest tight, Franca eased Jazz to the floor. "How lucky you are. You have two mommies who love you."

Bridget's steely eyes lit with rage. "No, she doesn't. She has one mother—me!"

Franca forced out the words, "That's right."

"Damn straight it is." Until the man spoke, she hadn't noticed him looming behind Bridget, his muscles bulging beneath a sleeveless T-shirt. Shaved head, coarse features and a scorpion tattoo on his neck. When had Bridget hooked up with this guy?

The notion of him having access to Jazz chilled Franca. But there were no bruises on the girl's face or arms. She wasn't sure whether to be grateful or dismayed that she had no grounds to call the police.

"Come on." Bridget reached for her daughter's hand.

The girl snatched it away. "No."

"You heard your mother!" As if he'd been waiting for a chance to throw his weight around, the man grabbed the child's arm. "Not another word out of you." The man gave Jazz's arm a yank.

"Axel," Bridget warned.

Marshall uncoiled from his seat. He stood several inches taller, but lacked the other man's heft. "You're hurting the child."

The man's lip curled in a sneer. Then, as if becoming aware of the observers around them, he released Jazz. "Yeah, well, do what your mother tells you, kid."

Jazz stood motionless, her tearstained cheeks a match

for Franca's. Clasping her daughter's hand, Bridget led her along the aisle to the other side of the café.

Franca couldn't remain there another instant. "I have to go."

"Understood." Marshall followed protectively as she headed for the door.

Franca supposed she ought to thank him for standing up to Axel, but she could hardly think for the noise in her head. Outside, she said a quick goodbye to him and rushed along the quay, pushing through the midday crowd.

But no sea breeze could dissipate her grief and guilt. She'd failed Jazz, regardless of where the fault lay. It burned like fire.

She lost track of Marshall until he started up the steps to the closest parking area. He paused, his forehead creased with worry. Kind of him, but this wasn't his problem.

On Franca stumbled, toward the more distant lot where she'd left her car. She tried in vain to outrun the realization that swept over her, obliterating the destiny she'd pictured so clearly.

Franca could endure almost anything for a child in her care, but when she'd imagined relinquishment, it had been to a home where the little one could be happy and safe. Not this wrenching sense that she'd betrayed the girl's trust.

She couldn't go through this again, couldn't risk letting down another child and having her heart shredded. But if she didn't foster troubled children, what did that leave? She still wanted to be a mother.

Despite counseling fertility patients, Franca had never considered whether or under what circumstances she might give birth, because she didn't plan to. Nor had she worried about finding the right man to be a father.

Her desire to foster children had struck a chord with her own mom. Franca was a middle child who had often gotten lost in the shuffle at home. It had been exciting and validating to see her mother's excitement. Partly as a result, instead of dreaming about finding Mr. Right as her sister had, Franca had embraced an identity focused on motherhood.

Leaning against her station wagon, she felt confused and lost. At thirty-three, she'd believed she had a firm grasp on the future. Instead, a burning question darkened her horizon:

Now what?

Chapter Five

Franca's heartbroken expression haunted Marshall over the next few days. She didn't contact him about starting the new counseling program, and he let the matter ride.

She must have been too upset about her foster daughter, and he wasn't eager to pursue the matter. Despite her example of how therapy had changed her attitude toward her mother, Marshall doubted enough of his patients would sign up to make the effort worthwhile.

Recalling Franca's advice about writing to his mother, he tried to compose a letter. But after he penned the words *Dear Mom* on crisp gray stationery, nothing else came to mind. Writing, aside from the occasional prescription, had never been Marshall's forte. Perhaps they could gradually resume a normal relationship after the wedding. And if she still didn't return his phone calls, what more could he do? He couldn't force her to care about him.

On Sunday, Marshall accompanied Nick and Caleb to rent matching tuxedos, which Zady had decreed they should wear. While Caleb was being fitted, Marshall asked where the couple planned to go on their honeymoon. "Unless it's a secret." He'd read that some couples hid their destination, presumably to prevent crashers.

"We'd love a week or two in Italy," Nick said. "Gondola rides, Michelangelo and Roman ruins."

"Sounds like fun." As a high school graduation present, Marshall's parents had taken him on a tour of Europe.

"That's a joke," Nick said. "We're planning a three-day weekend in Las Vegas." That was a five-hour drive from Safe Harbor.

"Hard to get away for longer," Marshall sympathized.

"Yeah. Hard when you max out the credit cards, too."

As they left the shop, Marshall presented Caleb with his new bear. "Wow!" Dark eyes shining, the three-year-old inspected the furry animal in its tux.

Nick grinned his approval. "It's a cutie pie, like my son. Thanks, Marsh."

"My pleasure."

Gazing at his brother and nephew, with their dark hair and lopsided smiles, Marshall felt his throat tighten. *If only I had a son.* Before that was possible, though, he had to find the right woman, and not get distracted by one whose approach to life was incompatible with his.

After his breakup with Belle, Marshall had had a few casual relationships during medical school and his residency in Boston. As a fellow in reconstructive surgery at the Cleveland Clinic, he'd tried an online dating site. Of the half dozen women he'd met for coffee, one had lied about her profession, one had asked him to prescribe painkillers for her, and another had talked about how she'd always dreamed of marrying a doctor. The others had been pleasant but uninspiring. No one had generated the kind of connection he'd felt with Franca.

Why did his thoughts keep homing in on her?

As Marshall said goodbye to Nick and Caleb, he recalled the previous day's scene in the café, especially her distress over her foster daughter. It was exactly the kind of trouble that he suspected went hand-in-hand with fostering older children. How frustrating that she insisted on getting involved in such situations.

That fellow Axel could be dangerous, and in Marshall's opinion, to put her daughter at his mercy showed Bridget to be an unfit mother. And there was nothing Franca could do.

The next child she took in might come with an equally risky situation. But no matter how much Marshall wished to protect her, Franca had a right to live as she chose.

How lucky Nick and Zady were, to be well-suited and in love. Over the next few days, Marshall's nurse hummed as she went about her duties.

"What's that you're humming?" he asked on Thursday afternoon as he reviewed the face sheet for his next patient.

Zady's blushed to the roots of her short reddish-brown hair. "Uh…darn. I can't get it out of my mind. It's 'The Teddy Bears' Picnic.'"

"Not a bridal march?" he teased.

"It's Caleb's favorite." She leaned against the counter of the nurses' station. "We were dancing to it with the tuxedo bear you gave him."

"I'm glad he likes the toy." Marshall smiled at the notion of her and his nephew dancing the stuffed animal around.

Kids were resilient, as Caleb demonstrated. The little boy had lost his mother in a boating accident last year, then adjusted to moving from his maternal grandparents' large home to Nick's one-story rental.

Marshall had been surprised when his nurse, who had hardly known his cousin, agreed to move in and babysit during Nick's overnight shifts in exchange for room and board.

She'd explained that it was a great way to save money. Also, she'd been caring for her toddler god-daughter, Linda, for an extended period while the parents traveled on business. Zady had believed the little girl would enjoy having Caleb as a live-in playmate. Marshall, who'd stopped by with an occasional gift, had grown fond of both children.

One example where an untraditional model of parenting had worked out. Although with Zady and Nick getting married and Linda back with her parents, both children were now in more traditional situations. So what did that prove?

Marshall had no chance to dwell on it; his next patient was waiting. On the face sheet, the reason for the visit was listed as follow-up. Marshall had performed a vasectomy reversal on the patient eight months ago, and his sperm counts had risen and remained high since then.

"Why does Hank Driver need follow-up?" he asked Zady.

"He requested it," she said. "He declined to state a reason."

"Guess I'll find out." Marshall knocked on the examining room door, waited for a "Come in!" and entered.

A stocky man in slacks and a sport shirt swiveled toward him. "Hey, Doc." The other man thrust his hand out and Marshall shook it firmly. He already knew the patient's age was thirty-seven and his occupation was police detective, but he'd forgotten Hank's disconcerting gaze, as he had one blue eye and one brown.

"Nice to see you," Marshall said. "What seems to be the problem?"

Hank perched on the edge of the examining table. His light brown hair had begun to thin, but he was in good shape, without the potbelly that often signaled the approach of middle age for men.

"Are you sure everything's okay with my sperm, Doc?"

At the computer terminal, Marshall brought up Hank's records. "At your six-month checkup, your sperm count, motility and morphology were normal. Motility, you'll recall, is the sperm's ability to move effectively, and morphology refers to the shape. I can order a retest, but in my opinion, it's too soon. Is there something specific that's troubling you?"

Just because the surgery had succeeded didn't rule out some other medical problem. Any symptom might be meaningful.

"My wife's still not pregnant." Hank blew out a breath. Twice divorced, the other man had obtained a vasectomy in the belief that marriage and fatherhood had passed him by. Then he'd fallen in love with a police dispatcher and remarried. He'd promised his new wife to do his best to reverse the procedure.

"The average period from surgery to conception is about a year," Marshall advised him.

"Maybe so, but she's thirty-five and she's upset that it's taking so long."

Marshall read over the records again. "You told me previously that she had a full workup and no problems surfaced."

Hank began pacing. "Sex with my wife is starting to feel like a race against time. She denies blaming me, but we can hardly talk without fighting."

Marshall remembered the support group. Might as well see how Hank reacted. "Have you considered counseling? The hospital is considering starting a therapy group for male infertility patients."

"Stop right there." Hank scowled. "I'm not seeing some shrink."

"There would be a team running the sessions, including our staff psychologist and me," Marshall said. "I'd address medical questions that might arise."

Hank's expression softened. "Everybody in there would be guys?"

"Yes, except for the psychologist, Dr. Brightman."

"And you recommend this?"

Marshall had to be honest. "I'll admit I resisted when the idea was first raised." He recalled Franca's statements about the benefits of therapy. "However, I understand that infertility is stressful, and stress can have a medical impact."

"Worrying can add to the problem?"

"Yes," Marshall said. "Counseling can help you develop tools for dealing with the pressure. However, if you'd rather, you could both participate in a couple's group."

"Nah." Hank folded his arms. "I like the idea of it being all guys. Less touchy-feely stuff. When did you say this program starts?"

"We haven't set a date," Marshall said.

"Keep me in the loop, will you?" the patient replied.

"I will." Marshall jotted a note in the computer. After further discussion revealed no other concerns, they shook hands and Hank went out.

Marshall hadn't formally committed to co-leading the group. Still, the other man's interest indicated his patients might be more receptive than he had assumed.

Lost in thought, Marshall wandered down the hall. A throat-clearing sound drew his attention to Reid Winfrey, who tilted his head toward a commanding russet-haired figure standing near the nurses' station. "Here to see you," the other urologist murmured.

Fertility program director Owen Tartikoff seemed affable enough as he chatted with Reid's nurse, yet the usually relaxed, wisecracking Jeanine had gone rigid. Surely she didn't find the surgeon *that* intimidating. On the other hand, Owen had once fired a nurse who'd argued with him, Marshall recalled.

"Owen." As he stepped forward, hand outstretched, Jeanine seized the chance to vanish into the break room.

"Marshall." Tartikoff shook his hand firmly. "I heard from Jennifer Martin that you and Brightman might be starting a men's group. Excellent plan."

The director didn't beat around the bush. "I'm surprised Jennifer mentioned it."

"Her office is down the hall from mine. I stop in to keep current on hospital news," Owen said.

His thoroughness was impressive. Also inconvenient, from Marshall's perspective. "I assure you, the talks have been quite informal."

"Let's make them formal." A steely command underlay Owen's words. "It's important for Safe Harbor to stay ahead of the curve."

Talk about tipping points—the project had just flipped from potential to inevitable. "I'll get on it."

"Good man." Clapping him on the shoulder, the surgeon nodded to Reid, who'd remained on the sidelines, and strode out.

"Wow, the big man himself," Reid murmured. "I'll be curious about how this group pans out."

"Me, too." En route to his office, Marshall rejected the impulse to request a meeting with Franca over the weekend. This was business, not a personal matter, and should be conducted during regular hours. After checking his schedule, he wrote her a quick email mentioning Owen's interest and suggesting they confer Monday morning.

Marshall didn't usually schedule surgeries on Mondays so he could be available to patients who'd developed severe problems over the weekend. Although urology involved fewer emergencies than many specialties, they did occur, and he also sometimes received urgent referrals from other urologists due to his advanced training in microsurgery.

He sent the email and received an immediate response. Eleven a.m. Monday, my office, okay?

Marshall sent a confirmation, and squelched an impulse to inquire if she'd heard anything more about her foster daughter. Or to ask her opinion about the toast he'd begun composing for the bride and groom.

He had no reason to involve her in anything not work-related. No reason at all.

SEWING DOLL CLOTHES cleared Franca's mind. The simple tasks of laying out fabric on her cutting board, pinning the tiny pattern pieces, and cutting and then stitching them soothed her.

She jumped whenever her phone rang, though, in case it was news about Jazz. But it was always just the usual telemarketers. She struggled to be polite with them, since she'd read that many worked from home because they were disabled.

This past week, she hadn't been able to start on the doll clothes without breaking into tears. But over the weekend, the turmoil of the previous Saturday's encounter had yielded at last to a resolution.

If your dreams change, change with them. Instead of agonizing, she'd sorted through her options.

At thirty-three, Franca had a good chance of conceiving, but that would decrease with every year that passed while she searched for Mr. Right. Her best choice, she decided, would be to conceive via artificial insemination. She was fortunate to work at a hospital that offered a full range of services associated with AI.

Franca had no illusions about the challenge of raising a child on her own, and she believed fathers had an important role to play in children's lives. Too bad her younger brother, Glenn, lived in Montana and was too far away to serve as a father figure, she reflected as the sewing machine flew along a tiny seam. She planned to research the psychological implications for her baby, but other moms managed.

As her plan formed, her sense of helplessness, of having lost her goal in life, was fading. What a relief.

On Monday morning, however, her cheerful mood faltered when she entered the hospital by the staff door and heard the chatter of parents and children arriving at the day care center. Jazz ought to be skipping ahead of Franca, eager to join her friends.

No other child could replace the one Franca loved. Eyes stinging, she hurried to the elevator, and was grateful not to run into anyone with whom she'd have to converse.

Slowly, Franca regained her calm. Someday in the not-too-distant future, she would deliver a baby no one could take from her.

Her spirits rising, she exited the elevator on the fifth floor and followed the corridor past the administrative offices to her suite. Franca relished working in such a varied and challenging environment. The regular pay-check and benefits didn't hurt, either.

Her executive assistant, Maggie Majors, hadn't ar-rived yet. Since Franca was early and Maggie had to drop off her seven-year-old daughter at school, she didn't mind.

In the counseling room, Franca dressed the dolls in their new blue finery. How precious they looked! If only Jazz were here to play with them.

Stop torturing yourself. She hurried next door to her office.

The morning flew by. After administering psycho-logical tests to three potential egg donors, Franca met with a family about their newborn baby's heart defect. While surgery should eventually correct the problem, few people were emotionally prepared for such a fright-ening diagnosis. Franca offered both emotional support and information about the journey ahead.

She finished the consultation with fifteen minutes to prepare for Marshall's eleven o'clock visit. In her com-puter, she opened a file of ground rules she'd compiled for therapy groups.

Scanning them, she wondered what minefields lay ahead in co-leading a therapy group with Marshall. Not only did he lack experience, but he'd seemed cool to the idea. His cryptic message requesting today's confer-ence had puzzled her until Jennifer mentioned that Dr. Tartikoff had leaped on the proposal. Still, if Marshall opposed participating, he wasn't the sort of person to let a bigwig push him into it.

Her phone rang. *If he's canceling, I'll call him a cow-ard to his face...or ear.*

But the familiar male voice didn't belong to Mar-shall. "Hey, sis."

"Glenn!" He rarely called; he and his wife, Kerry, kept busy running a hardware store in a small Montana town. "What's up?"

"Can't I just call to say I miss you?" She pictured a teasing gleam animating his tanned face.

"Absolutely." She wished she'd had a chance to talk more with Glenn and Kerry at the holiday gathering in Reno. There'd been little opportunity, though, since the group at their mother's home had also included their sister, Gail, and her husband, plus their stepfather, his five children and their families. "But you have another reason, too, right?"

"Okay, so you're psychic. I mean, a psychologist," he said. "I'm calling with news. Kerry's pregnant."

"How wonderful!" she said. "I'm thrilled for you both." And at the confirmation that he was truly putting down roots.

Her brother had had a restless youth, moving from job to job and from state to state. In Montana, he'd fallen in love with Kerry and settled down, eventually winning both her hand and her parents' approval.

"I was afraid this might be painful, because of what happened with Jazz." He'd met her little girl at Christmas.

"Not at all." It occurred to Franca that he might have another reason for caution. "How did Gail react?"

He sighed. "She congratulated us—used all the right words, but her voice was really strained."

"I hope she hasn't had another miscarriage." That would make four.

"She didn't say," Glenn replied. "But she'd hardly bring it up, would she? Now, don't go calling her! She'll assume I put you up to it."

"I won't." Despite all her training, Franca wasn't equipped to comfort her sister's grief.

"I wish the doctors would figure out whether it's genetic," Glenn said. "If it is, maybe she could move on."

Genetic. The word hit Franca like a slap.

Their mother had lost two pregnancies during her first marriage, then gone on to bear three children. One of her aunts, after repeated miscarriages, had remained childless. Because Franca hadn't planned to bear children, she'd never connected the family history to herself. When she'd decided to pursue insemination, she'd assumed that she had a normal chance of carrying a child to term. What if she didn't?

Moreover, miscarriages could be not only heart-wrenching but dangerous for the mother. During Gail's last miscarriage, she'd suffered heavy blood loss and passed out. If her husband hadn't arrived home in time to summon paramedics, she might have died.

Franca struggled to avoid going overboard with her fears. A glance at her watch showed she had only a few minutes before her appointment, and Marshall was frighteningly punctual. "I'm sure Gail's as delighted for you and Kerry as I am. Thanks for calling and not just emailing."

"I love you," Glenn said.

"I love you, too, bro."

As she clicked off, a tall figure filled her door frame. Oh, damn. Despite an urge to run to the privacy of her car, where she could scream and cry and beat on her steering wheel again, she had to pull herself together fast.

"Good morning," she told Marshall, and assumed the most professional smile she could manage.

Chapter Six

Marshall respected Franca's cool manner—that was the right touch in this work setting. Yet he missed her usual warmth. At their meeting, she sat behind her desk, scarcely meeting his gaze. Was she angry at him for some reason?

Briskly, she began outlining protocols for the men's group. The first protocol was to state the group's goal: addressing issues that arose from male infertility and treatment.

"I agree." A mission statement would position the operation on a businesslike basis, which in his experience should appeal to men.

"Good." She'd tucked her hair into what Marshall believed was called a chignon. The style enhanced the heart shape of her face, while escaping twists of reddish-blond hair added an appealing touch. He just wished she'd chosen one of the comfortable chairs beside him rather than keeping a barrier between them.

Clearing her throat, Franca proceeded to item B on their list of protocols, designating the sessions as a safe zone where each participant could speak without interruption, without criticism and without receiving visual negativity such as eye rolling.

The subject of their meeting seemed straightforward,

yet there was an edge to her voice that hinted at tension. Marshall wished she'd explain why. But he'd resolved to avoid personal discussions, hadn't he?

"I'm on board with declaring a safe zone."

As item C, Franca proposed a guarantee of privacy for anything that was disclosed in a group session. "No sharing case histories or anecdotes, even with their spouses."

"Absolutely." While that might be difficult for the patients, they'd appreciate not having *their* personal details bandied about.

He also accepted her suggestions that they restrict participation to six to eight members, allow an hour and a half for each session, and schedule meetings on a weekday evening or on Saturdays. "Wednesday or Thursday nights are fine for me," Marshall said. "I reserve Saturdays for overflow surgeries."

Franca nodded. "I have a standing appointment at my private office on Wednesdays. Thursdays it is."

He entered the information in his calendar. "Anything else?"

"We should encourage a minimum of three sessions." Franca steepled her fingers. That, coupled with the fact that she'd worn glasses today rather than contacts, added to her remote air.

"Okay."

She closed the file in her computer. "May I ask you a question?"

Maybe they'd finally discuss something other than rules and schedules. "Shoot."

"What persuaded you to go ahead with this?" Her amber gaze skimmed his face. "Was it Dr. Tartikoff?"

While he'd hoped to learn what was bugging her, Marshall responded gamely. "A patient requested a surgical follow-up, not for medical reasons but because of personal concerns. When I mentioned this group, he expressed interest." To be candid, he clarified, "Guarded interest."

Franca smiled for the first time that morning. "How precise you are."

"And you, today." Marshall decided to press on. "Is everything all right?"

"What do you mean?"

Her defensive tone signaled him to back off. Instead, he said, "You were understandably upset when we ran into your..." How should he refer to a child who was no longer in her care? "Into Jazz. Is she okay?"

Franca's hands formed fists on the desk. "I'm not privy to that information."

A surge of protectiveness spurred Marshall to continue. "I'm glad you don't have to deal with that lout, the boyfriend. Although I suppose dealing with unsavory characters goes with the territory."

"Which territory?"

"Getting involved with dysfunctional families."

"I suppose it does."

Marshall had never seen her this frosty, nor experienced such a strong desire to push past another person's boundaries. "Surely there are experienced foster parents in a better position to deal with people like that. And group homes, although I don't suppose those are appropriate for such a young child."

"Marshall." Franca's eyes narrowed. "I'm well aware that you never approved of my plans to be a foster mom. There's no need to beat a dead horse."

"That's not my intent." He hated being misunderstood, especially by her. "I'm trying to..." Marshall stopped. He'd been about to say, "protect you."

What right did he have to do that? Judging by her current anger, he gathered her answer would be "none."

"To do what?" Franca prompted.

"Never mind." He rose, towering over her. "I can't expect to get through to you."

She leaped up to her full height, which was eight or nine inches shorter than his. "You're the most infuriating, arrogant man I ever met."

"Seriously?' he retorted. "As bad as all that?"

"Worse."

They glared at each other for about five seconds.

Marshall wasn't sure which of them crumbled first, but suddenly they were laughing. He had no idea what struck him as so funny, except that this was a ridiculous argument between two people who'd always known they were opposites.

"Well," Franca said when she regained control of herself. "That cleared the air."

"Are you sure you can work with such an infuriating man?" Marshall quirked an eyebrow.

"Guess I'll have to."

"Suits me. Oh, I'd appreciate if you'd email me a rough draft of our proposal," he said.

"Will do." Franca's mouth twisted ruefully. "I've heard that once Dr. T gets a bee in his bonnet, he expects results pronto."

The notion of Owen Tartikoff wearing a bonnet brought another chuckle. "Let's not provoke the great man any more than necessary." Marshall reached across the desk, and they shook hands. It felt strange, as he wanted to give her a hug. Perhaps it was fortunate she'd kept a barrier between them.

On his way out, Marshall caught a speculative glance

from Franca's assistant in the outer office, who must have heard their loud voices.

An unusual-looking woman with black hair and dramatic bone structure, she was named Maggie Mejia Majors, according to her nameplate. "How alliterative," he said.

"I beg your pardon?"

"Your names all start with the same letter." What was wrong with him? He never joked with strangers. "Have a nice day."

"You, too, Doctor."

If he weren't careful, Marshall reflected, he might soften his edges and become less arrogant. Then what would he and Franca quarrel about?

SHARING A LAUGH with Marshall might have eased their friction, but Franca remained wary of him. In any area other than their professions, they were impossibly far apart.

As if she weren't upset enough already, her attorney stopped by a few days later to report that he'd received a disturbing call from Bridget.

"She claims you influenced Jazz against her." Edmond Everhart's shirt was neatly pressed beneath his tailored suit, and his tie was smoothly knotted, as usual. A family attorney, he consulted at the medical center twice a week, advising patients and staff in areas outside the expertise of the regular hospital attorney. She'd also hired him as her private counsel to deal with the adoption.

"I did no such thing." Franca bristled at the accusation. "After she consented to the adoption, I naturally began treating Jazz as my own child, but I never spoke ill of her mother."

"I believe you." Normally, Franca found Edmond's calm manner reassuring. Today, she wasn't sure anything would have eased her temper. "The issue seems to be her boyfriend. She contends that Jazz is rude to him."

"Rude? He was yanking her around!" At the attorney's startled expression, Franca explained about running into them at the café. "I wouldn't be surprised if he's an ex-con or a gang member. Or both."

"You're probably right." Edmond studied her sympathetically. The father of four-month-old triplets, he also had custody of his eight-year-old niece, Dawn, while his sister served a prison sentence for robbery. His expertise with children of prisoners had been extremely valuable. "If Bridget were on parole, fraternizing with a felon would be a violation. But since her conviction was thrown out, she can associate with anyone she chooses."

"I'm not trying to send Bridget to prison, anyway," Franca said. "What specifically did she say?"

"That Jazz throws tantrums and refuses to call him Daddy," Edmond replied. "I have the impression she's torn between protecting her daughter and pleasing her boyfriend."

"What did you tell her?" Franca asked.

"That it's normal for a child to act up when she's removed from her usual care provider. She cooled down when she heard that. Mostly, she probably just wanted to vent." When his cell jingled, Edmond checked the readout. "I have to take this. But I wanted to inform you that I'd heard from her."

"Thanks for keeping me posted."

During the next few weeks, there was no further word about Jazz. That didn't relieve Franca's anxiety, but she struggled to steer her mind to other subjects so she didn't drive herself crazy.

With Marshall's input, she polished the therapy group proposal. The administrator and the directors of the fertility and men's programs approved it with minor changes. After Jennifer put out the word in the newsletter, referrals began arriving. The start date was set for late April.

Concerned about her older sister, Franca called Gail. Her sister commiserated about Jazz, inquired about Franca's new job and chatted about her husband, an electrician, whom Gail assisted in his business. She didn't bring up any medical issues, and Franca was too tactful to ask. Best to let Gail choose what and when she was willing to share.

Mid-April arrived, and with it the day of Zady and Nick's wedding, scheduled for 4:00 p.m. on a Saturday. It dawned cloudy with a chance of sprinkles, but the weather cleared by the afternoon.

Franca chose a pink dress with a matching print jacket. As she finished applying her makeup, her gaze fell on the last remnant of the blue bridesmaid's gown draped over the sewing machine table. Funny, she'd felt through Belle's entire wedding that Marshall was an unseen presence on the sidelines.

He'd be part of his brother's ceremony today, of course, but his best-man duties ought to keep him busy. There'd be little risk of personal interaction.

Just consider him a casual acquaintance. He wasn't involved in Franca's struggle to figure out whether she dared risk a pregnancy. Although the possibility of remaining childless haunted her, common sense warned her to be realistic. Then there was just plain fear. She'd gone so far as to scan Safe Harbor's computerized material on sperm donors, but whenever Franca started to schedule a consultation, her mind tortured her with scenarios of collapsing in agony, alone in her apartment.

For heaven's sake, she was about to attend a celebration. *Relax and have fun.*

The Seaside Wedding Chapel was perched on the bluffs above the harbor. Inside, a smiling woman handed Franca a printed program. The hum of voices and the tinkling of piano music greeted her as she stepped into the chapel.

Zady had kept the floral arrangements modest, preferring for guests to bask in the glorious view from the arched windows. The sight of colorful sailboats and, beyond the harbor, the blue sweep of the Pacific Ocean refreshed Franca's spirit.

While she was debating where to sit, two women gestured to her. She recognized them as nurses in Marshall's office who worked with Zady. The tall, thin one was Jeanine, Franca recalled, and the short, round woman was Ines.

She slid into a chair beside them, happy to join their banter. They volunteered that they'd leaped at the chance to leave their spouses home with the kids.

"My husband finds weddings boring," Ines said.

"Mine, too," Jeanine added. "Even our wedding, I suspect. Not the honeymoon, though."

"Speaking of honeymoons, any idea where Nick and Zady are going?" Franca asked.

"Las Vegas," Ines piped up.

"For a long weekend," Jeanine said.

A movement near the altar caught Franca's attention. The groom and his brother had emerged, a pair of strikingly handsome men in tuxedos with a mini lookalike trailing solemnly in their wake as the ring bearer.

A murmur ran through the crowd. "Isn't that boy cute?" Ines said.

"He's a doll," her fellow nurse agreed.

"Here we left our kids at home and we're drooling over someone else's child," Ines observed.

"Yes, but my sons don't wear tuxedos and resemble little movie stars," Jeanine said.

"I'll bet you a box of doughnuts he'll spill something on that tux at dinner."

"You're on. Any excuse for doughnuts."

Their banter barely penetrated Franca's awareness. It wasn't Caleb, darling as he was, who transfixed her.

Despite the resemblance between the brothers, Marshall stood out, with his erect stance and chiseled features. Everything about him evoked memories of his tenderness, his annoyance, his humor and his vulnerability.

She'd missed him these past weeks, more than she'd been willing to admit. Since he'd reappeared in her life, he'd become increasingly important to her. And her feelings had only grown stronger because of the recent distance.

Franca realized with a start that she was perilously close to crossing a dangerous line. She had to keep in mind, especially with a man as stiff-necked as Marshall, that however close you might become, ultimately you could only depend on yourself.

Chapter Seven

Marshall envied Nick's easy manner as they stood in front of the assembly. Any public appearance was uncomfortable for him, even accepting an honor. He couldn't escape the notion that he had a stain on his jacket or was about to blurt something idiotic.

You're here to support the groom, not obsess about your appearance.

Staring toward the far wall, he reviewed his ideas for the obligatory toast later this evening. He hadn't decided whether to bring up the fact that they'd recently discovered they were brothers, which would upset his mother. Yet he could hardly refer to Nick as his cousin.

When Marshall's gaze shifted toward his mother, Mildred Davis averted her face. It hurt that she refused to acknowledge him, for her sake as well as his. At seventy-two, she had few friends or relatives. It wasn't healthy to be so isolated.

Abruptly, he became aware of Franca. Wedged between two nurses from his office, she appeared to be listening intently to their conversation. Just knowing she was among the guests helped him to relax.

Marshall wasn't sure why she'd rigorously kept her distance over the past few weeks while they finalized plans for their group, communicating only by email and text. The loss of her daughter was obviously painful, and he supposed his tactless comment about foster parenting still rankled. But she'd always handled their differences with composure in the past.

The pianist finished her rendition of "We've Only Just Begun" and segued to the traditional wedding march. At the entrance appeared a little girl of about three, wearing a rose-colored dress tied with a gold sash and carrying a basket. Marshall smiled at the bride's goddaughter, Linda, whom he'd become fond of during the weeks she'd stayed with Zady.

Linda trotted forward, tossing handfuls of rose petals at the crowd, until she reached the halfway point. There she stopped, panic spreading over her features as if she'd suddenly noticed all the people staring at her.

Where was Zora, the matron of honor? She should have been right behind Linda, prepared to take her hand if needed.

The groom frowned toward the empty doorway as if willing Zady or her sister to appear. Naturally, he didn't want to risk spoiling the bride's big moment by intervening, but someone ought to act.

In the middle of a row, Linda's parents leaned forward uncertainly, also reluctant to intercede. Marshall whispered a request to Caleb, since the child was a natural choice to fetch his fellow Lilliputian, but the boy shook his head.

Might as well make a fool of himself for a good cause, Marshall mused. Up the aisle he strode and bent to take Linda's hand.

"Uncle Marsh!" With a cry, she flung herself into his arms and buried her face in his shoulder. Amid sympathetic chuckles from the crowd, he carried her to the altar.

As he lowered her to the ground, Marshall glimpsed Franca staring longingly at the child. Tears glittered on her cheeks.

She must be thinking of Jazz. It hadn't occurred to him what emotions the sight of a little girl might evoke. Then Franca gave him a shaky, approving smile that warmed him right down to his uncomfortably stiff shoes.

At the end of the aisle, the matron of honor entered belatedly in a swirl of dark pink. Judging by Zora's limp, the cause of the delay must be a hurt foot or ankle.

When she reached the altar, Linda scooted to join her. The music shifted to a familiar bridal melody and an excited rustle ran through the chapel.

The bride floated into view, radiant in a cream-colored gown and a hat trimmed with roses. She held the arm of her brother-in-law, Zora's husband, Lucky Mendez, who was grinning from ear to ear.

The lone sour note was the bride's pinch-faced mother, seated in the front row. At last night's rehearsal, she'd complained loudly about her last-minute invitation, while her husband glowered at everyone. Zady had explained earlier that her manipulative mother had lied to them for years, pitting her and Zora against each other so she could hold center stage. Today, Marshall hoped her grimace at the bridal party went unnoticed by the other guests.

When Lucky relinquished the bride to Nick, Marshall slipped the ring to Caleb. The three-year-old promptly handed it to his father.

"I helped pick it out for my new mom," he announced loudly. Appreciative chuckles rippled through the chapel.

"It was the sparkliest one we could find," Nick said.

"Yeah." His son beamed.

As the ceremony flew by, Marshall's chest squeezed. *My kid brother's getting married.* Too bad he hadn't known they were brothers while they were growing up. Their rivalry might have been less abrasive.

He still wasn't sure how to frame his toast. Well, if all else failed, he'd simply wish the bride and groom a long and happy life together. Boring, but safe.

After the exchange of vows, the minister introduced them as the new Dr. and Mrs. Davis, to the crowd's applause. With the children right behind, Zora and Nick strolled up the aisle, followed by Marshall with a limping Zady on his arm.

"Twist your ankle?" he asked.

"Damn shoes," she muttered. "The men who design high heels must be sadists."

"What about the women who buy them?"

"They're airheads," she responded cheerily. "Like me."

When they passed Franca, Marshall shot her a concerned glance. Her sadness had vanished, however, and she met his gaze with a friendly nod.

After the ceremony, the guests didn't have far to go: there was a ballroom connected to the wedding chapel. Decorated in rose and gold, the room was set up with round tables, a dance floor and long tables at the side for the food. Covered catering dishes indicated that dinner would soon be served.

The photographer had taken family and bridal party shots the previous evening, since Zady didn't wish to keep her guests waiting. She'd also ruled out a receiving line, thus avoiding the thorny problem of whether to include her mother and stepfather in it, as well as the groom's father. Uncle Quentin had attended, but kept a low profile befitting a man who'd abandoned Nick in childhood.

The waitstaff began to circulate with trays of hors d'oeuvres and wine, and Marshall helped himself. He still felt uncomfortable, and keeping his hands full eased his awkwardness. Rather than risk driving after drinking even a small amount, he'd walked to the chapel from his house, less than a mile from here along the bluffside road, and planned to either walk home or call a cab.

Around him, the guests mingled. Many said hello to him, but no one stopped to talk. As for Franca, she stuck close to the nurses.

How fortunate she was, to form attachments easily. Marshall hadn't left any close pals behind when he moved back to California from Ohio, nor had he reconnected with friends from high school or college. His mother was far from the only Davis who lived in isolation, he realized.

Speaking of isolation, Marshall spotted Uncle Quentin lingering uncertainly on the fringes of the gathering. Tall and bony, he'd had his graying brown hair trimmed and held a water glass rather than wine.

It was still hard to think of the man as his father. Upton Davis might have been a workaholic, with rigid expectations for his son, but he'd stuck by his family and provided for them, in contrast to his younger brother. However, Quentin deserved credit for finally seeking treatment for his bipolar disorder and for joining Alcoholics Anonymous.

Marshall sought out his designated spot at the wedding party's table. Zady had agonized over the seating chart, finally putting her mother and stepfather with Ca-

leb's grandparents and Linda's parents. She'd taken care
to position Marshall's mother far away from Quentin.

"I just hope my mom doesn't get drunk and act
rowdy," she'd said during a break at the office.

"Maybe you should hire an armed guard," Marshall
had joked.

"Too expensive," she'd said. "I'll keep a hypodermic
handy in case she requires sedating."

"Want a prescription?"

She'd laughed.

Smiling at the memory, Marshall slid into a chair
alongside his brother.

Having the ring bearer and flower girl with them
added to the wedding party's high spirits. Once dinner was served, Zady and Zora helped the children fill
their plates and tuck in their napkins.

Linda ate daintily, while Caleb stayed neat until, for
no discernible reason, he poured orange juice down his
front. At Franca's table, Marshall saw Ines and Jeanine
high-five each other, then enter into a joking dispute
featuring the word "doughnuts." Apparently there'd
been a bet but neither could recall who won.

Franca settled it with a word and a grin. She seemed
to have loosened up since her earlier distress, and she
soon joined her companions' giggling. Marshall wished
he'd invited her as his plus-one; if she'd accepted, she'd
be sitting beside him.

Nick leaned closer. "Do I detect an interest in a certain person?"

"We're old friends," Marshall responded.

"I'm surrounded by old friends. I somehow manage
to tear my eyes off them," the groom responded.

Marshall searched in vain for a clever retort. In truth,

he wasn't sure why every man in the room, aside from Nick, wasn't staring at Franca, whose soft pink outfit enhanced her natural glow.

"No smart reply? Wow. You *are* besotted," said his brother.

"Merely appreciative."

"Smooth answer," Nick said. "I wish I had your— what's the word—suaveness?"

"Or savoir faire," Marshall said.

"No normal person uses words like that."

Marshall regarded his brother in surprise. "With your exceptional memory, I'd assume your vocabulary would outstrip mine." His brother had indicated at family gatherings that he almost never had to study. In high school, Nick's easy cruise to academic honors had made Marshall question his own abilities, considering how hard he struggled with some subjects.

Nick ducked his head. "I have a confession."

"I'm all ears."

His brother shrugged. "My memory's pretty good, but I studied like a dog."

"Seriously?" In retrospect, Marshall supposed Nick's bragging had produced the desired effect—stemming his aunt and uncle's criticisms of his sloppy grooming and goof-off reputation. "I don't blame you for exaggerating, the way my parents put you down."

"They were hard on you, too," the groom said. "Damn hard."

"Yes, they were." Marshall had never been successful enough for them. Even though he'd become a National Merit Finalist, that had meant nothing when Nick had been named a scholarship winner. As for Marshall's grades, they'd all been As except for Bs in calculus and Spanish. When his father learned that Nick had earned straight As, he'd tossed Marshall's report card back without comment. His flared nostrils had spoken louder than words.

Did he wish they'd adopted the younger boy? It hurt like hell to think neither Upton nor Mildred had truly loved him because he wasn't perfect.

But why keep fighting a battle he could never win? His tension dissipated.

And, on the plus side, he'd just figured out what to say in his toast.

WHEN FRANCA ACCEPTED the wedding invitation, her focus had been on supporting Zady on her happy day and sharing the event with her colleagues. The sight of the adorable flower girl paralyzed in the middle of the aisle, however, had struck her with a rush of pain.

Where was Jazz right this minute? Was she suffering the same panic and fear, with far more reason than little Linda? Who would help her, when Franca was barred from intervening?

Marshall's actions had stirred her admiration. Not only because he made a handsome knight, riding to the little girl's rescue, but because he'd told Franca long ago of his anxiety at public events.

What a great father he'd be. For his ideal child, of course.

She snapped back to the present as a waiter handed her champagne for a toast. The tinkle of a spoon against a water glass drew everyone's attention to the head table, where Marshall got to his feet. "Someone mentioned that the best man is supposed to say something," he deadpanned.

Smiles greeted his comment. Not from Mildred

Davis at the next table, however. Franca had met Marshall's mother at campus events, and had found her cold. Tonight, the woman was subzero.

"Isn't Dr. Davis handsome in a tux?" Jeanine said.

"If I weren't married, I'd grab him," Ines agreed.

Franca stared straight ahead, wishing the crowd and her companions would settle down so Marshall could get this over with. Yet he didn't appear nervous, she was pleased to note.

"Not everyone here is aware that Nicholas and I were raised as cousins." Marshall spoke steadily. "We were rivals in high school, and frankly, we didn't much care for each other."

Somewhere, a piece of cutlery fell to the floor with a clink. In the silence, it sounded loud as a gunshot.

"Recently, we learned that we are actually brothers," Marshall continued. From the corner of her eye, Franca saw Mildred Davis's mouth open in a gasp.

"It's been said that you can pick your office nurse but you can't pick your relatives," Marshall joked. "Well, I picked Zady as my nurse and I'd do it again in a heartbeat." The bride beamed at him. "As for Nicholas, I'm glad he's my brother, and he's now my friend, too. I wish I'd learned the truth sooner. Here's to Zady and Nicholas and their future as a family."

He raised his glass to cries of "Hear, hear!" Amid the stir as everyone drank, Mildred hurried from the room.

Although most guests probably assumed Mrs. Davis was obeying an urgent call of nature, Marshall's jaw clenched. He stood, glass in hand, for a long moment.

The matron of honor started to rise for her toast, but Marshall signaled Zora with a "wait" gesture. "One more thing," he said.

Everyone quieted.

"It's come to my attention that the couple's ideal honeymoon trip would involve traveling to...what was it?" Marshall pretended to search his memory. "Death Valley? Antarctica? Chernobyl?"

Judging by the confusion on Nick's and Zady's faces, they had no idea what came next. Neither did Franca.

"Oh, yes, Italy." Marshall regarded his brother and sister-in-law. "I realize you have something planned for the next few days, but my gift to you guys is a trip to Italy whenever you have time to enjoy it at your leisure."

"You already gave us a houseful of towels," Zady blurted.

"That was to throw you off the scent," Marshall replied.

"Incredible," Nick said. "That's fantastic, bro."

"Double for me," Zady said. "Thank you!"

Zora sprang to her feet. "Lucky and I can't afford to send you to Italy, but we'll take care of our wonderful new nephew while you're gone. Here's to Nick, Zady and Caleb!"

She raised her glass, and everyone sipped. The bubbly tasted so delicious that Franca accepted a refill.

Her companions did the same. "Our husbands are picking us up," Jeanine announced. "Keep the champagne flowing."

"What's that Dorothy Parker quote?" Ines giggled. "'Three drinks and I'm under the table. Four drinks and I'm under the host.'"

"Someone ought to be under Dr. Davis," Jeanine said. "Not the married Dr. Davis. *Our* Dr. Davis."

"Considering how he keeps peeking at someone at our table, I know who it should be," Ines murmured.

Franca's cheeks felt hot. "I'm not sure why. He had

his chance years ago, but he bypassed me to date my college roommate."

Jeanine seized on the comment. "Who dumped who?"

"He dumped her," Franca said.

"Why?"

"Not brilliant enough to meet his high standards. She struggled with her grades and had to drop a class." Belle had never claimed to be the best student around, especially with the intense academic competition at UC Berkeley, and her goal of graduating early had been for *his* benefit.

"That was it? She couldn't match his level of genius?"

Franca tried to recall exactly what Belle had told her. "He was leaving for medical school at Harvard and she'd planned to graduate early so they wouldn't be separated too long. When she couldn't keep up, he broke it off."

"Maybe he had her best interests at heart."

"That wasn't her impression," Franca said. "And speaking of hearts, it shattered hers. They were practically engaged."

Mercifully, Ines changed the subject. "That was quite a gift he gave Zady and Nick."

"I heard his father left him a bundle," Jeanine said.

"It was still very generous."

"Excuse me. I need to walk around." Her friends were growing tipsy and their remarks becoming more and more personal.

Franca rose too quickly, and had to wait for her champagne-infused body to steady itself. If she stopped drinking now, she hoped to be sober enough to drive in a few hours.

Since there hadn't been a receiving line, this seemed

the right moment to offer her best wishes to the bride and groom before they started dancing.

A lanky man with thinning gray-brown hair reached them first. "Sorry about Mildred," he said. "I'd have pinned her to her seat, but I doubt she'd have appreciated it. Especially from me."

"It's okay, Dad." Nick clapped the man's arm.

So this was Marshall's birth father. Despite a similarity of height and bone structure, he was strikingly different from his older brother, Marshall's adoptive father, whom Franca had met in college. Upton Sinclair had held himself with pride, his shoulders straight, his thick hair a distinguished shade of silver.

"I feel responsible for the disruption." The newcomer addressed his sons. "Can you forgive me for shooting my mouth off?"

The mixed emotions on Marshall's face resolved into a smile. "If not for you, Uncle Quentin, I wouldn't know Zora was my sister-in-law and Caleb was my nephew. I wouldn't be best man at Nicholas's wedding, either."

"You can stop calling me Nicholas," his brother put in. "It sounds too formal."

"Okay, Nicky."

"On second thought, Nicholas is fine."

"Done."

She registered the exact moment when Marshall spotted her. The light in the room brightened, and warmth flowed over her skin.

"Quentin, there's someone I'd like you to meet." Moving to her, Marshall slipped his arm around her waist. "This is Dr. Brightman, our staff psychologist and an old friend of mine. Franca, this my birth father."

"My pleasure." The glint in Quentin's eyes as they

shook hands indicated he guessed there was more to this relationship. But then, the arm encircling her waist told everyone the same.

Franca wondered at Marshall's show of intimacy. Was this a couple of glasses of champagne speaking, or something more? And did she want it to be?

The pounding in her chest might mean almost anything. *Oh, stop kidding yourself.* No matter where this led, for tonight she and Marshall belonged in each other's company.

Beside the dance floor, the DJ took the microphone. "Dr. and Mrs. Nick Davis, how about you lead off the dancing?"

Zady gave a happy little hop. "This is my Cinderella moment! I've been dreaming about this."

Her new husband sketched a bow. "Milady, may I have the honor?"

"Let's go, my prince." Taking his elbow, she tugged him forward.

People gathered to watch the couple swooping around the floor to a romantic waltz. At a gesture from Zady, her sister and Lucky joined them.

Marshall removed his arm from Franca's waist. "May I have this dance?"

Her breath caught. She responded with a low, "I'd be delighted."

Taking her hand, he escorted her into the thickening crowd of dancers. It might be simply a waltz, but there was nothing ordinary about her reaction as Marshall held her close. They'd never had this much physical contact. Their bodies touched, their hands clasped, and an electric current coursed between them as they moved in sync.

Judging by his cheek brushing her hair and his grip tightening around her, Marshall shared her reaction. If this was a mistake, Franca longed to keep right on making it.

And tonight, she suspected she would.

Chapter Eight

Even though Marshall was aware he'd provoked his mother, her fury as she'd stalked from the room troubled him. But it also freed him to be generous with his inherited money in a manner she'd have resented.

What a pleasure to bring joy to Nick and Zady. As for his reservations about Quentin, they'd vanished. Without his birth father's revelation, as Marshall had stated earlier, he'd have missed being best man at this event.

His newfound sense of liberation extended to dancing with Franca, who seemed to have overcome whatever had been keeping her at bay, too. As he held her in his arms, the fresh scent of her hair filled him, and the music wrapped them in a private world. They melted together, and an unfamiliar happiness swelled within Marshall.

Their basic differences hadn't changed. Yet he prized this rare chance to have fun with the only person he could truly be himself with.

The music shifted to a Latin beat. He flowed with its seductive rhythm, and Franca moved with him as if they'd practiced it.

"I had no idea you were such a skillful dancer," she murmured. "Belle said you had two left feet."

Poor Belle! He'd always been tense with her, striving to match her perfection. "I was clumsy because I was trying too hard."

"And with me, you don't have to?"

"With you I'm…" He nearly said "home." Instead, he finished with "…comfortable."

"I'm glad." Quickly, she added, "I'm not sure my feet could take the punishment."

Their swift movements cut off further conversation. Soon, as the rhythm increased, they were both fast-stepping and breathing hard. Others paused to watch them, a development Marshall could have done without.

The music segued into a slower song. He and Franca were adjusting to the pace when people began staring off to the right and sneaking pictures with their phones. Peering over them, Marshall saw Caleb and Linda dancing in a classic waltz position. Both preschoolers wore earnest expressions as Caleb counted aloud: "*One* two three, *one* two three."

Franca stood on tiptoe to watch. "Oh! How cute."

"Priceless." *I wish they were our children.* Or rather, he meant, *my* children. Didn't he?

After a minute, Marshall tugged her into his embrace again. Time faded from awareness as they followed the changing patterns of the music. When other men cut in, Marshall squelched a flare of annoyance. But as the best man, he had other duties. He danced with the bride, the matron of honor and the bride's mother. Red-faced and with a tendency to giggle, Zady's mom, Delilah, brought uncoordinated energy to her dancing. Marshall was glad to relinquish her to her husband.

Another musical transition led to a rock song with the screaming lyrics, "I can't take it anymore!" Startled, Marshall caught Franca's gaze across the floor.

He'd been distraught that night in the parking garage,

wrenched by his mother's rejection. Catching Franca similarly howling had struck him as oddly reassuring. Now they made their way toward each other.

"They're playing our song." Franca draped her arms over his shoulders.

"Feeling better?" He encircled her waist.

"Better than what?"

"That night."

"No comparison." She swayed against him. Although everyone else was gyrating wildly, it was obvious to him that this was a love song.

"I'm six inches off the floor," Franca said. "I drank too much champagne."

"Weddings are magical." Marshall spoke close to her ear. "We could dance all the way home."

"Not me. I have a half-hour drive."

The music stopped. Into his mic, the DJ said, "I'm informed that the bride and groom are about to cut the cake. Don't miss getting your slice!"

People pushed by. Why were they in such a rush? The towering cake took up an entire side table. Did they believe it would run out?

The surging crowd made the room stuffy. Through the large side windows, the night appeared cool and inviting.

"Do you want dessert?" he asked. "Or would you rather take a walk?"

"A walk sounds lovely. Maybe it will clear my head."

After detouring for Franca to collect her purse, Marshall guided her outside. The only person who appeared to notice their departure was Nick, facing them at the cake table with the guests pressing around it. He winked.

Marshall supposed he might be criticized for aban-

doning his best-man duties, but he'd completed most of
them. Besides, if the groom didn't care, why should he?

Marshall wasn't usually one to flout the rules. Now
he was ready to crash through a thicket of them.

FROM THE BLUFFS, palm trees screened Franca's view of
the sparkling harbor. A fresh breeze filled her lungs,
although rather than sobering her, its invigorating effect
added to her sense of unreality. She could almost fly,
not that she was foolish enough to attempt it.

The scene dissolved her hurt and uncertainty. For tonight, she didn't care that Marshall was too judgmental
to rely on as she navigated through an uncertain future.
His tender side was exactly what she needed at the moment, so why not enjoy herself?

Marshall's arm anchored her as they strolled along
the walkway. When they stopped at an overlook facing
the ocean, the music resumed from the wedding chapel, muted but loud enough to serve as a melodic un-
dercurrent. Below, light twinkled from a yacht cruising
toward its mooring.

"Some evenings I can hear the music from the wedding chapel on my balcony." Leaning on the rail, Marshall's lean body shielded her from a gust of wind.

"You live that close?"

"Right there." He gestured across the street toward
a two-story home atop a rise. With its columns and the
lacy trim beneath the eaves, the architecture brought
to mind New Orleans.

"On the ocean? That must have cost a fortune!"
Franca felt her face growing hot despite the breeze.
"I'm sorry. That's the champagne talking."

"It cost a totally unreasonable amount," Marshall
said. "But my father left me enough to invest and still

buy my dream home. Now all I need is…" The words trailed off.

…a family to fill it. She understood. "I've never imagined my dream home."

His low chuckle rumbled through her. "How can you not imagine it, if it's your dream?"

"I'm too befuddled to untangle that sentence."

"Let me simplify," Marshall said. "What kind of house appeals to you?"

"A comfortable one. Warm colors, and a large kitchen." She'd grown up in a modest house with gingerbread-style trim and furniture that, while solid, was so worn that her mother had eventually thrown it out because the thrift shops wouldn't take it. But what had mattered were the gleeful interchanges around the dinner table, and the abundant laughter. "I never fantasized about Prince Charming or the perfect wedding, either."

"How did you and Belle become roommates?" His teeth gleamed in the darkness. "You're totally different."

"The college housing office paired us." They must have seemed similar on paper. Both had been nonsmokers who went to bed early, and they'd been focused on earning their degrees, hers in psychology, Belle's in business administration. "We had a lot in common."

"You could have fooled me." Marshall shook his head. "When she described in detail her plans for her wedding, right down to the cake decorations, I thought I'd strayed into the twilight zone. We hadn't even discussed marriage."

"Is that why you…" Realizing she had no right to pry into his reasons for the breakup, Franca switched to, "Did they include bridesmaid's dresses big enough to eat Chicago?"

He chuckled. "Accurate description." He'd viewed the photo on her phone, she recalled. "It's cold. May I entice you to enjoy the view from my house, madam? Perhaps with a glass of wine?"

"I'm already giddy," she protested, but weakly. It *did* sound like fun.

"You can sleep it off in my guest bedroom," Marshall offered.

Her answer ought to be a resounding no. Instead, Franca replied, "You're just showing off."

"How so?"

"Bachelors don't have guest bedrooms, they have couches," she said.

"There's a couch in my study." Against the moonlight, Marshall formed a muscular silhouette. "But you'd be more comfortable in one of the spare bedrooms."

Franca slapped his arm. "Spare bedrooms, plural? Now I *know* you're bragging."

"In the morning, I'll cook you breakfast in my catering-size kitchen," Marshall continued.

"Why not have your chef do it?"

"The upstairs maid could serve you breakfast in bed." He frowned. "Or would that be the butler's job?"

"Tell me you're kidding!"

"The cleaning crew mucks the house out twice a month," Marshall assured her. "That's the sum total of my staff."

"Don't you rattle around in your mansion?" Franca's curiosity was growing.

"I only bought it a few months ago," Marshall protested. "I've hardly had time to rattle. Or throw parties and create happy memories."

How different he sounded from the guy she remem-

bered from their university years. "You have a senti-
mental side."

"That surprises you?"

"It makes you dangerous." Had she actually said that
aloud?

"You *have* to explain that comment." Taking her arm,
Marshall continued their walk, heading away from the
wedding chapel. When she stumbled on a rough patch
of concrete, he caught her by the waist.

"I can't explain it," Franca said. "I'm not sure what
I meant."

That was a lie. The truth was that a tenderhearted
Marshall threatened her determination to keep him at
bay. Which she hadn't done very well this evening,
had she?

"I'd better head home," she concluded.

"You may not be sober enough to drive," he pointed
out.

"This from the man who just offered me a glass of
wine?"

"And the use of his guest room."

Franca yearned to tour his mansion and to watch this
very masculine man cook breakfast for her. Even though
she was almost certain it was the champagne addling
her brain, she said, "I am a little curious."

"I promise you, the sheets are clean." Marshall halted
at a crosswalk.

"You have guests often?" Franca asked as they
waited.

"Only one so far. Reid—Dr. Winfrey—stayed with
me for a few nights after he arrived from New York,"
Marshall said. "Since he didn't own a car, it was con-
venient for him to ride with me until he got situated."

"That was kind of you."

He shrugged. "Professional courtesy."

The signal changed and they crossed. Nearing the house, Franca saw that what she'd glimpsed so far was actually the back of the house. A concrete staircase led up a rise and around to the front.

There, she discovered, the mansion faced a cul-de-sac. It served a handful of similarly large homes, each with a unique design.

"My first sight of this place gave me pause." Marshall escorted her up the front steps to a broad porch. "I'd been living in hole-in-the-wall apartments, and I'd planned on buying something simpler. But I figured it would be a good investment."

"That's it?" Franca waited as he unlocked the door and deactivated the alarm. "It didn't grab your heart and refuse to let go?"

"That, too." He flicked a switch in the entrance hall. Overhead, a stained-glass chandelier cast amber and green light over the slate-tile floor.

The interior unrolled one delight after another: the spacious living room decorated in shades of aqua and peach, a dining room with a parquet oak table, a study that doubled as a workout room, the family room with big-screen TV—they were better than a showroom because Marshall's spirit infused them.

Nothing prepared her for the kitchen, though. From the oversize cooktop to the double ovens, the built-in refrigerator and walk-in pantry, it would make any caterer catch her breath. Every surface, every window treatment, every lighting fixture contributed to an aura of welcome. Meals would taste better just by being fixed here.

Franca was almost embarrassed by her reaction.

She'd never coveted wealth. But she could scarcely bear to live anywhere else after touring this place.

She searched for a neutral comment. "It's stunning. I'd pictured you in someplace more formal."

"Straight-backed chairs, dark woods and dim sconces?" Leaning against the center island, Marshall quirked an eyebrow. "That describes my parents' house."

A question occurred to her that might ease her sense of being caught up inside his personal realm. "Did you buy it already decorated?"

"The bones were here, but it was far too gloomy," he said. "I worked closely with a designer."

She sighed. "In spite of what I said, it suits you."

"Does it suit *you*?"

Caught off guard, Franca blurted, "I love every inch of it."

Marshall grinned. At ease in his palace, the rangy, rather stiff young man of their younger years had come into his own.

Franca had never experienced such longing around a man, despite the fact that they were spectacularly wrong for each other. Could she truly blame the champagne?

"I should go to bed." She nearly added *alone*, except that might reveal how tempted she was to do otherwise.

"Let's head upstairs."

As they returned to the hall with its curving staircase, Franca sensed that this was her last chance to assert a measure of common sense and beat a safe retreat. Sleeping here, even in a separate room, posed a huge risk. But she'd never felt more protected and sheltered than in Marshall's care.

Her feet barely touched the surface as she made her way up the stairs.

WHEN THE REAL estate agent had lured Marshall inside this house, there'd been a phantom along on the tour. Not that the house was haunted; rather, he'd sensed a woman's reactions.

His future wife, he'd assumed. Didn't everyone carry on conversations with "air people," folks who weren't actually there but who commented or argued in one's head? His usual air people were his parents, constantly criticizing and correcting his actions. But the person in his head when he'd viewed the house, he finally conceded, had been Franca.

Tonight, she more than matched her phantom alter ego, greeting each room with an exclamation. Marshall was proud of the smallest touches: the crown molding, the custom cabinetry, the embellished towels accenting the upstairs hall bathroom, and the low bookshelves and window seat in the room he'd mentally designated as a future playroom. Each cry of admiration was like a caress.

In the doorway to the master suite, Franca stopped ahead of him and inhaled deeply.

"Is anything wrong?" Marshall asked.

"It smells like you," she murmured.

Not the response he'd hoped for. "I assure you, I shower frequently."

"It's a good smell. But it's late, I should head to my own room." She turned abruptly and ran into his chest.

Marshall's arms closed around her. He could feel her heart racing.

She pulled away, and reluctantly, he released her. "Care to see the dressing room? It's equipped with a TV and a great sound system."

"I'd better not. I mean, no thanks." Her amber eyes blinked. "I'm afraid I'm not myself tonight."

She was entirely herself, in Marshall's opinion, the same intriguing person who'd drawn him magnetically fifteen years ago. He'd believed she was wrong for him, but tonight, she sparked magic in his bloodstream.

"Who else would you be?" he teased.

"I'll tell you after I've slept off the champagne." Franca scooted past him into the hall.

Despite his disappointment, Marshall respected her withdrawal. "Let's get you settled in the guest room."

"I'm not sure where it is."

He placed his palm on the small of her back to guide her. "You'll need towels. The linen closet is here, next to the bathroom."

Opening the closet door, he tugged on a china pull to turn on the light and reveal the neatly stacked sheets and towels. He selected a bath sheet along with smaller linens. "Okay?"

Franca smiled dreamily. "Just fine."

He couldn't resist pulling her against him, despite the armful of linens that formed a soft barrier. Their foreheads touched, and as they leaned toward each other, it seemed to Marshall that they completed an electrical circuit.

Or she might be falling asleep.

"The bedroom's just along here." After unloading the towels in the bathroom, he steered her into a peach-colored room with golden-yellow curtains and an oak bedstead. "I hope you'll feel at home. The bathroom's stocked with guest toiletries, but if there's anything lacking, just let me know."

Franca stared at him as if reaching a sudden conclusion. "Marshall."

"Yes?"

She caught him by his tuxedo lapels. "Do you have to be such a frustratingly perfect gentleman?"

"Is that what I am?" If only he had a clue about women. Especially her.

"Damn straight," she said, and tugged him toward the bed.

Chapter Nine

As she toured the house, Franca had become aware of an emotion unworthy of her: envy. Not of Marshall for owning this home, but of the woman who would some-day share it with him.

Why her, whoever she would be? Why had Belle been the lucky one in college, even if that hadn't ended happily? No matter how irrational it was, Franca ached to be selfish, just once. To take what *she* wanted instead of trying to recognize other people's wishes and help them come true.

Tonight, she wanted to act on impulse. To grab Marshall and watch his surprise turn to excitement. To feel his mouth claim hers. So she did.

She stood on tiptoe, her breasts rubbing his chest and her palms stroking his neck while her tongue played along his lips. A deep shudder ran through him, as if a dam had burst. His tux joined her print jacket on the floor and he swept her onto the bed.

Lifting himself on an elbow, Marshall probed her with his dark gaze. "Are you sure?" he asked.

"Aren't you?"

"More than I've ever been sure of anything."

"Then stop talking."

He kissed her again, gentleness shading into ferocity.

Franca treasured the whisper of Marshall's mouth trailing down her throat, the confidence of his hands as he released her dress, the joy of sharing her body with him.

She'd experienced nothing like this with the boyfriends who'd appeared briefly in her past. Why had she imagined Marshall was cold and distant? His passionate response thrilled her. And when he finally thrust deep inside her, Franca yielded to sensation.

Marshall withheld nothing, and neither did she. They became one wild creature, one glorious entity, one soul.

Everything else fell away.

MARSHALL HAD BOTH hoped for and feared the moment when he yielded to his desire for Franca and unleashed his long-suppressed recklessness. He'd always believed at some level that if he completely let go, he'd lose his direction, his purpose, and fail those he cared about. How absurd that struck him now.

The marvel was that Franca sought it as eagerly as he did. Her hands reached for him, her movements encouraged him, and her body invited him into a private dance.

The scent of her perfume intoxicated him; the touch of her skin thrilled him. Soaring together, they crested a giant wave and roared into free fall. Exultation obliterated the last limits of the familiar world.

For too long, Marshall had been caged, mistrusting every vulnerability. Now, a fresh vista unfolded, with Franca at its center.

Marshall held her close as they drifted to a far shore. He barely recovered enough awareness to pull the covers over them before sinking into blissful sleep.

FRANCA AWOKE IN the morning with the sense that she'd forgotten something important. But also that she'd done something wonderful and free.

Beside her under silky sheets lay the man she'd craved for years. Marshall's long body curved toward her, his tousled dark hair tickling her shoulder. In sleep, he had the openness of a young man. Had intimacy changed him, or was it her perceptions that had altered?

An ache at her temples reminded Franca that she'd had more to drink than usual last night. However, she couldn't blame her actions on the champagne. She'd chosen to sleep with Marshall, whatever the consequences.

He stirred. "Good morning." The brightness of his smile rivaled the sunshine glinting between the curtains.

"Hi." Now what? She shouldn't feel awkward, considering how well they knew each other. But in this context, they might as well be strangers.

"I promised to cook breakfast," Marshall murmured.

"That would be lovely." Franca still couldn't shake the notion that she'd been negligent somehow. Was it because she'd left her car at the wedding chapel? That didn't pose a problem; she could walk over to collect it. "Coffee first, please."

"You got it," he said. "I'll be downstairs in a minute." After planting a kiss on her nose, he arose, collected his tuxedo and departed. She missed him as soon as he was gone.

Rising, Franca reflected ruefully on an obvious omission: a change of clothes. She always carried a spare outfit in her car—a habit she'd started after a child client had thrown up on her. No point racing down the block for the clothes, though.

She took a shower and used a toothbrush and toothpaste from the basket of guest toiletries. Then she put on the same dress.

Franca was heading for the stairs when she passed a large, nearly empty room whose mint-green walls brought to mind a nursery. Perhaps that was what Marshall planned for it.

Then it hit her, what she'd forgotten.

Contraception. True, she'd been sleeping alone for the last few years, but how could she have been so careless?

"Oh, hell," Franca said.

She had to go downstairs and drop this on Marshall. That he, too, had been negligent didn't make it any easier. Nor was it his fault that she had a troubled family history when it came to pregnancies.

A remark came to her that she'd almost completely forgotten. After meeting Marshall at college, her mother had commented privately on how handsome he was—and how much he resembled her first husband. "A killer smile and gorgeous eyes," she'd murmured. "But Belle had better watch out. When he turns cold toward her, he'll be pure ice."

Don't get ahead of yourself. She'd better focus on one issue at a time, for her peace of mind as well as his.

MORNINGS-AFTER COULD be tricky, Marshall reflected as he switched on the coffeemaker and began fixing cheese omelets and toast. With other women over the years, there'd been the question of whether they'd see each other again, how often and on what basis. He'd never gone for one-night stands, but a few women preferred them.

Surely not Franca. They belonged to each other now. However fast or slowly their relationship progressed, they were in this together.

With rising anticipation, he heard the brush of footsteps on the stairs. Swiveling from the stovetop, he stared as slim legs and a swirl of pink skirt appeared. Against the soft colors surrounding her, Franca shone like a beacon. Marshall could scarcely breathe.

The sizzle from the stove top broke his reverie. "Breakfast's almost ready," he said.

"I'm not hungry." She scowled.

Uh-oh. "What's wrong?"

Franca crossed to kitchen. "We forgot to use contraception."

Oh, hell. Despite the packet of condoms in Marshall's bedside table, it simply hadn't occurred to him. Thoughts collided, but logic took command. "Is it the right time of the month for you to conceive?"

She glared at him. That must have been the wrong response.

She's a psychologist. Try to think the way she would. "How do you feel about it?" Marshall asked.

"I can't believe neither of us remembered." Striding to the coffeemaker, Franca poured a cup. "We work at a fertility hospital."

All was not necessarily lost. "You could take a morning-after pill."

Coffee sloshed onto the counter. "Easy answer for a guy," she snapped. "Besides, no matter how hard a pregnancy might be, I'd always regret it if I did that."

Her anger puzzled him, since Marshall would love to have a child. Still, he resolved to proceed with caution. "I understand why you're upset," he ventured. "Pregnancy is a huge undertaking for a woman."

"And for a man who'll get stuck with child support for the next twenty years." Before he could reply, Franca raised a hand. "Sorry. That was out of line. My head's throbbing, not that that's any excuse."

Afraid the omelets were getting overcooked, Marshall flipped them onto plates. He served them with a dish of sour cream and chives. "Whatever happens, we'll both be part of the decision making."

Franca splashed milk in and around her cup, adding to the mess on the counter. "I'm sorry, Marshall, but when it comes to my pregnancy, I'm the one who makes the decisions."

The baby that might be forming would be his son or daughter, too. "Legally, that's true, but morally, we're both involved. Please don't treat me like a bystander."

Franca plopped onto a stool at the island. "That doesn't give you the right to run my life."

"Don't exaggerate." This conversation was spiraling out of control. Marshall searched for a way to lower the tension. "It's not that common for a couple to conceive immediately. We might be worrying over nothing."

"Nothing?" Franca poked a fork at her eggs. "For the next few weeks, my entire future is up in the air."

This wasn't how he'd imagined conversing with her this morning. "Why are you picking a fight?" Usually, she was the most reasonable person around. "Let's not ruin a beautiful night together."

Jumping up, Franca carried her plate and cup to the counter. "Thanks for breakfast. I'm just not in the mood for—for whatever." She grabbed her purse.

She was leaving? "Let's not part this way," Marshall protested. "We should talk."

"About what?"

"You're supposed to be the expert."

"On pregnancy?" she asked.

"On relationships."

"Well, here's my opinion," Franca said. "We both know we're not compatible, Marshall. I wish we were and sometimes…no, I refuse to delude myself. Let's just leave it at that."

She barreled out of the kitchen and he heard her footsteps rap across the tile floor toward the door. He didn't deserve her anger, Marshall thought irritably, but he still cared about her. "Wait! I'll drive you to your car."

"I'll feel better if I burn off some energy." The door closed behind her with a loud *click*.

He sat at the counter, bewildered. How could she deny the intimacy they'd shared last night? Yet judging from her words, she didn't just regret the forgotten contraception; she regretted the champagne, the sex and the night with a man she could never love. What had seemed to him a transformative experience had been entirely one-sided.

A knot formed in Marshall's chest. *Well, so what if she rejected you?* He could almost hear his father's voice demanding he shape up and take it like a man.

True, he and Franca had always been opposites. He'd recognized that fifteen years ago. Why expect things to be different now?

This pain in his heart would ease. It had to. Meanwhile, in a few weeks, they'd learn whether they were going to be parents.

And if they were, Marshall had no intention of stepping meekly aside.

As a counselor, Franca often advised clients to take things one day at a time. So that was what she tried to do during the next week.

All the same, her calendar became her foe, announcing that her period was due on the following Friday. It didn't arrive. Not on Saturday or Sunday, either.

She'd been late before. Anxiety could cause that,

Franca cautioned herself, and redoubled her efforts to focus on her job.

It had been unfair to unload on Marshall, yet she couldn't bring herself to apologize. He'd been his usual high-handed self—all right, she conceded, he'd *tried* to understand her, but every word had rubbed salt into her wounds. She'd lost her daughter and then realized she might not be physically able to carry a child to term—and now she faced the prospect of an unplanned pregnancy. For once in her life, she had no compassion to spare.

Mercifully, no one appeared to notice her turmoil. Jeanine and Ines, who'd accepted the explanation that she'd left the reception early because of a headache, filled her in on the mother of the bride's shenanigans. After Franca had left, the woman had tossed a glass of champagne in the face of a waiter who'd accidentally trod on her foot. Lucky and Nick had politely but firmly escorted the miscreant and her complaining husband to a cab.

Attention in the cafeteria soon switched from the wedding to what was termed the Return of the Twins: Zady from her Las Vegas honeymoon and Zora from maternity leave. At lunch, people gathered to admire Zady's ring and coo over pictures of Zora's twins.

Thank goodness they had missed the juiciest piece of gossip stemming from the wedding. Franca shuddered. What a mess it would be if anyone found out what she and the best man had done.

Certainly no one would hear it from Marshall, who'd become cold and formal with her. Through the glass doors that separated the cafeteria from the patio where the doctors preferred to eat, she observed his rigid posture and stern expression.

She missed the warmth he'd shown her, the brilliance of his smile, the ease of his movements. Her anger had driven him into his shell, which she regretted, but she hadn't been wrong. Their differences were too profound to overcome for more than one night of drinking and dancing.

So why did she keep wishing he'd seek her out? Her hormones must be running riot. That was probably what had delayed her period, too. No, wait. If her hormones were surging, that might indicate pregnancy.

A week and a half later, she was still in turmoil. She sat at her desk and buried her face in her hands. Quickly recalling where she was, she straightened her shoulders. No weeping and wailing for a professional, especially since tonight marked the start of the men's counseling group. She had to project confidence and control.

In the therapy room, she cleared away the toys and drawing materials and arranged chairs in a circle for the half dozen men scheduled to participate. After communicating solely via email and text, she and Marshall would again be in the same room, side by side. Normally, Franca enjoyed meeting clients and beginning a journey with them. Now she simply hoped she could weather the session without a meltdown.

Someone tapped on the door. "Am I intruding?" Edmond adjusted the squarish glasses on his nose.

"Not at all." Franca gestured for the attorney to enter. "What did you find out?" She'd asked him to check on Jazz.

He came into the room but remained standing. "Bridget's moved into a two-bedroom apartment."

"Good." That meant Jazz had a room of her own. There'd be a kitchen, too, and a chance for healthier meals. "Does she want me to bring over Jazz's stuff?" Most of her clothes and toys remained at Franca's.

Edmond gave a regretful head shake. "They're sharing the apartment with her boyfriend. Axel doesn't want a bunch of toys littering the place, according to Bridget."

They were living with that awful man? "I'm sorry to hear that."

"There's more."

"More?" Her throat went dry.

"The district attorney has declined to refile the charges."

Franca's heartbeat thundered in her ears. Despite Edmond's cautions, she'd drawn comfort from the idea that she could bring her daughter home if Bridget was sent to prison. This development shattered that hope.

"There's nothing you can do?" As she stared at the attorney in his impeccable suit, an unreasoning anger tempted her to lash out at his smugness. But he was on her side.

"I'm afraid not. I'm sorry, Franca. You and Jazz deserve better."

She forced herself to politely acknowledge Edmond's sympathy. It was a relief when he left.

Despite a prickling behind her eyelids, no tears flowed. This cut too deep.

After a while, her breathing slowed. It was nearly five o'clock, which left an hour to grab a bite before the six o'clock session. Oddly, Franca discovered she had a ravenous appetite.

Typical of a mother-to-be.

In view of this fresh blow, she'd forgotten her other concern. Although it was early for results, she decided to pick up a test kit at the hospital pharmacy. She'd wait until after the counseling session to use it, in case the result was positive. Her emotions were tumultuous enough already.

Sucking in a deep breath, Franca headed for the elevator.

Chapter Ten

The past ten days since he and Franca made love, Marshall had instinctively watched for her everywhere. He'd listened for her voice, while mentally replaying their last scene, trying to figure out how it could have ended differently.

But he never managed to find the right responses for her. In many ways, she seemed contradictory, fearing a pregnancy yet refusing to consider a morning-after pill. Did that spring from her deep love of children? He wished he understood her.

Distracted at lunch that day, he'd struggled to join the laughter as Nick related funny incidents from his Las Vegas honeymoon, and been reduced to nodding vaguely because he scarcely heard what his brother said. It was as if Marshall had landed in a foreign country where he more or less understood the language but couldn't grasp its nuances.

Had Franca's period started? Surely she'd inform him. Until then, in view of how touchy she'd become, he decided to wait.

Meanwhile, he'd had no luck reconnecting with his mother. A few days after the wedding, Marshall had called to invite her to dinner again, but she'd declined curtly, citing prior plans. Much as he hated to abandon his efforts, he didn't see what else he could do.

His work had been his refuge. In the examining room, Marshall knew how to evaluate symptoms to reach a diagnosis, while for each operation, he had a carefully mapped-out strategy. At tonight's therapy group, however, the circle of men left him at a loss. Judging by the uneasy shifting in chairs and folding of arms, the clients were equally uncomfortable.

Keenly aware of Franca beside him, he scanned her out of his peripheral vision. She'd tucked her reddish-blond hair into a bun and put on dark-rimmed glasses. In spite of the buttoned-down impression, no one could miss the ripe curves beneath her suit or the softness of her lips.

Especially not me.

"Let's get started," she said. Around the room, the men slouched lower in their seats. Hank Driver, the detective whose vasectomy Marshall had reversed, was checking his phone. "Please mute your electronics."

"Sorry." He tapped the screen. Marshall was glad he'd remembered to put his own phone on vibrate.

"Let's set a few ground rules." Franca outlined the protocols. Everyone agreed about keeping the discussions private and listening without interrupting. "Do you have anything to add, Dr. Davis?"

He did. "Like most men, I was brought up to hold my emotions inside. I admire everyone for participating."

"Good point." Her gaze returned to the clients. "Let's introduce ourselves—first names only—and then you're welcome to raise any issues related to infertility or treatment."

What if no one spoke? However, after the introductions, a man named Cory broke the ice. "How do we tell our in-laws to butt out? That's our biggest problem. I mean, besides not having a baby." There were nods of recognition.

"Would you mind sharing your story?" Franca asked.

His mother-in-law called daily, advising her daughter to relax and let nature take its course. "After my wife hangs up, she bursts into tears," Cory said. "She's been through in vitro twice. Implying that she just ought to relax is cruel."

"Has she explained to her mother how hurtful these comments are?"

"She's tried," Cory said. "But her mother insists she's trying to make sure her daughter is happy. Well, that's my job, not hers."

Since Marshall's parents had been the opposite of over-involved, he had no idea what to recommend. Franca asked if anyone else had similar problems.

"We had to cut off contact with my sister-in-law," said a fellow named Burt. "She had the nerve to suggest my wife hang out with her to absorb her hormones, because she's pregnant with her third child."

Beside him, Marshall registered a wince from Franca. At the sister-in-law's insensitivity, or at the prospect of being pregnant?

"Can a woman really absorb someone else's hormones, Doc?" Hank asked.

Marshall wished Nick were here, with his experience in obstetrics. However, he was fairly certain of the answer. "There aren't any pregnancy pheromones that increase other women's fertility. If there were, I'm sure we'd be providing them to our patients."

Several men chuckled. Franca didn't crack a smile.

"Well, family interference appears to be a sore point

for many of you," she said. "Let's consider how infertility affects your family members."

"It's none of their business," Cory declared.

"That may be," she said. "But imagine how it would affect you if a person you love, especially your child, was suffering and hurting."

"I never considered it that way." He frowned. "I suppose I'd want to fix things for them."

"I wish our relatives didn't act as if this is our fault," another man said.

"Even if my sister-in-law has good intentions, that's no excuse for flaunting her pregnancy," Burt put in.

"Families are far from perfect," Franca said. "Any crisis, and infertility *is* a crisis, can highlight problem areas."

"My cousin went through infertility treatments and described it in detail on her Facebook page," one man said. "When she started urging us to do the same, my wife nearly strangled her."

"Each couple has a right to choose their own level of privacy," Franca said. "Let's discuss ways to set boundaries."

She recommended that, after making sure the partners were in agreement, they talk to each offending relative, stating explicitly what had to change. "Be polite but firm, and stay calm," she said. "Don't let people manipulate you by claiming you've hurt their feelings. And don't forget to reinforce their positive behavior."

"How do we do that?" Cory asked. "Give them treats, like my dog?"

Laughter rippled through the room.

"One reward might be spending more time together," Franca said. "Also, show an interest in what's happening with *them*."

Marshall admired her perceptiveness. He wished he had more to contribute, but aside from emphasizing a point here and there, he simply observed.

Toward the end, Hank Driver shot him a curve ball. "Do you have children, Dr. Davis?"

"No," he admitted. "I wish I did."

Franca's forehead furrowed.

"Just curious," Hank said.

After surveying the room in case anyone else wanted to speak, Franca said, "We've gone past our scheduled hour and a half. If you guys want to talk informally afterward, the cafeteria is open 24 hours."

"Thanks, but I had a long day," Hank replied. The rest of the men echoed his sentiment.

Finally the session ended. Chairs scraped as the men rose. Several shook hands with Marshall and Franca.

"I'm glad you're here, Doc," the detective told him. "No offense to Dr. Brightman, but having a medical expert gives it a stamp of authenticity. And it helps to hear a man's perspective."

"That's why we're both here," Franca said.

Once they were alone, Marshall gestured to the chairs. "I can put these away for you."

"The cleaning crew will straighten up tomorrow." She fidgeted with the strap of her purse. "Don't you have to be up early for surgery?"

"I'm in no rush."

"I'm tired, and the powers that be have requested I write up my observations on tonight's session for the morning." She peered at her notes. "Whatever you'd like to include, please email me ASAP."

"I'll do that." He recognized she was giving him his cue to depart. But she sounded shaky, and he couldn't leave her.

After she locked the office, Marshall accompanied her along the hallway. Near the elevators, she said, "Don't bother to wait," and vanished into the ladies' room.

Although it was only 8:00 p.m. and security patrolled the hospital, a woman alone could be vulnerable. Taking out his phone, he leaned against the wall and checked his email.

PINK. FRANCA STARED at the stick. According to the directions, that meant a 99 percent chance she was pregnant.

Most of her clients would be delirious with joy at such a result, but pregnancy posed a major risk to her health. All the same, it was miraculous, Franca thought as she rested a hand on her abdomen. A life had started that depended utterly on her—on a woman who hadn't planned for it and whose womb might not be able to nurture it to term.

Take it one day at a time. Oh, dear. That advice had been hard enough to follow during the past ten days. Now it frustrated her, because, ready or not, Franca had to prepare for the future.

She wished her stomach weren't churning, from hormones or anxiety or both. The awareness that she'd brought this about by practically dragging Marshall into bed did nothing to ease her discomfort.

Marshall. Oddly, she longed for his presence—until she recalled that he'd suggested a morning-after pill. Despite her fears, she had to give any child its chance. Didn't he? The man certainly sent mixed signals about wanting to be a father.

Franca had to pull herself together. It would be unprofessional to lurch downstairs, visibly upset. There might not be many patients wandering about at this hour, but staff members would see her.

She splashed water on her face, too upset to be careful where it splattered. As she stretched for the towel dispenser, she felt her foot slip on the wet floor.

She grabbed the edge of the counter, but its smooth surface defied her. She couldn't be falling. Not now. Not in this condition. Not like an idiot, flailing and struggling for balance.

With a shriek, Franca lost the battle.

THE SCREAM SENT adrenaline shooting through Marshall. Thrusting his phone into his pocket, he yanked open the door.

"Are you okay?" He rushed to kneel beside Franca on the floor, registering the water around her that must have been what sent her tumbling. "Did you hit your head?"

"No, my hip." She levered herself into a sitting position. "Clumsy as usual."

"Careful or you'll slip again." Assessing how best to aid her, Marshall noticed the box she'd knocked to the floor as well as the small stick nearby. The stick that had turned pink.

That was why she'd been in here so long. This was the news they'd both been waiting for. He'd been aware this might happen. Why didn't he feel prepared?

Because such a miracle didn't seem possible.

Franca followed his gaze to the pink stick but didn't comment. No explanation was necessary.

Marshall dragged his attention to the present situation. "While I always enjoy having a nice sit on the floor of the ladies' room, we should get up."

"By all means." When he helped her to her feet,

Franca winced and rubbed her thigh. "Don't worry, it isn't fatal."

"You didn't hurt the…?" His mouth refused to form the word *baby*.

"At this stage, no. I'm one big bundle of insulation."

After wiping the floor with a paper towel to prevent injury to anyone else, Marshall escorted Franca into the hall. "We should talk," he said. "Do some strategic planning."

"I just got the news." She ducked her head. "I'm not ready for this conversation."

"I'm not sure I am, either." Glancing down at her scalp, he noticed a thin line of hair that was a brighter shade than the rest of her strawberry-blond locks. "You should stop dyeing your hair now that you're pregnant."

"Excuse me?" Franca pulled away.

He shouldn't have blurted that. "Sorry."

"Marshall, I didn't mean to snap at you that morning at your place," she said. "I was upset about a lot of things. And I know you're trying to be supportive. But the fact is, your instincts are all wrong."

"I've been told that before." Damn, he was tired of walking on eggshells. "The bottom line is, we're about to become parents."

"Yes, I got that." Franca folded her arms.

Why avoid the obvious? Marshall thought. The right path was clear.

"Marry me," he said.

To HER ASTONISHMENT, Franca almost agreed. Despite the evidence of Marshall's controlling nature—he'd ordered her to stop coloring her hair, for Pete's sake!— she longed to lean on his strength.

What a batty idea. If she miscarried, that would remove the entire reason for his offer. Even if she carried the baby to term, their differences would sooner or later make them both wretched. Franca had witnessed the destruction divorce caused on children and on adults, above all her mother. The best prevention was to avoid marrying the wrong man.

Still, judging by the intensity in Marshall's dark eyes, she believed his proposal was sincere. Marshall had a strong sense of duty. Thank goodness he didn't whip a ring out of his pocket. She wasn't sure what she'd have done—probably fallen over laughing and *really* injured her hip.

"I have to say no." With sadness, she watched his eagerness fade. "While I appreciate your desire to help, I don't need a man to lean on."

"I'm the father," Marshall said quietly. "I should provide for you and the baby."

Franca chose to be realistic. "I'll accept support for the child's sake. As for sharing custody, we can work out the details later."

"Once you recover from the shock, you should reconsider," he said.

"My brain cells are fully functioning." She didn't mean to be hurtful. "Marshall, you're a great guy, but as I said before, we're incompatible. We've always been honest about that."

"People can adjust their expectations," he replied tightly.

"And a few years later, they end up in my office, fighting like cats and dogs," Franca answered. "Now I'm heading home."

"If you have any pain, call me," Marshall said. "Correction: call 911, then me."

"Okay." His concern felt unexpectedly reassuring.

And given her shaky state, Franca was glad when he insisted on walking her out to the nearly empty parking structure.

A little over a month ago, they'd been distant acquaintances howling to music in this same garage, united only by frustration with their individual problems. Now they were bound by a quirk of fate. That, and their own negligence.

As she drove away, Franca checked her rearview mirror. Marshall stood motionless, watching.

If I'd accepted his proposal, we'd be planning our wedding.

Instead, she faced a half-hour drive to a lonely apartment and a cold bed. An apartment filled with memories of a little girl who would never return.

It didn't feel like home at all.

Chapter Eleven

To Marshall, asking advice meant showing weakness. He ought to be able to solve his own problems. But no matter how much research he did on the internet, it failed to produce a workable strategy for persuading Franca to marry him.

By Saturday, he was almost ready to drive to her apartment and demand she reconsider. However, besides the near-certainty of rejection, he had no good counter to her argument that people who married for the wrong reasons ended up hating each other.

Except that they *wouldn't* be marrying for the wrong reasons. A child, and a friendship of many years' standing, formed a basis they could build on. And shuttling between custodial parents was far from an ideal situation for a kid.

And, as if he weren't struggling enough already, the world was suddenly filled with pregnant women and infants in strollers. At the hospital, they jammed the elevators and the hallways. On the street, he passed parents gathering outside shops and urging their toddlers to hurry.

Easy to grasp why patients couldn't compartmentalize their fertility issues. Reminders intruded everywhere.

As a last resort, he might as well seek advice, and how many men had a brother who'd been in basically the same situation? Nick's girlfriend Bethany had become pregnant four years ago and, while Marshall had never met her, he'd heard she, too, had refused to marry the father of her baby.

Nick's experience might offer clues about what *not* to do. Also, his success with Zady indicated he'd learned from his failure.

At the office, Marshall had heard Zady inform the other nurses that she and her sister planned to attend a movie this evening, leaving Nick and Caleb alone at the house. Playing with his nephew would be fun, and after the boy went to bed, the men could talk.

He called Nick. "Sure, stop by," his brother said.

"I'll bring pizza," Marshall offered.

"You hate pizza."

"Correction: I *used* to hate pizza," he said. "You converted me."

"Okay. We usually order from Krazy Kids Pizza," Nick replied. "Pepperoni's a big favorite around here. Wait—you're paying. Make that two large pizzas, one pepperoni and beef, the other mushroom and olive with extra cheese."

"My source tells me that Papa Giovanni's pizza is superior, but otherwise, I agree to your terms," Marshall said.

"Your source?"

"Cole Rattigan." The head of the men's program claimed to have a refined palate.

"I bow to his expertise," Nick said. "Also, Papa Giovanni's is more expensive, so knock yourself out."

A few hours later, Marshall arrived laden with pizza

boxes. Roses edged the front walk of Nick's cozy ranch-style house.

When the door opened, Caleb rushed forward. "Uncle Marsh! Yay!"

"Pizza. Yay," Nick said. "We worked up an appetite playing ball." That accounted for his mussed hair and grass-stained T-shirt.

"Sorry I missed it." Marshall caught his brother's skeptical expression. "Not really."

At the kitchen table, they polished off a good portion of the pizza. A child's card game followed, with Caleb triumphing.

With a little prompting, the three-year-old brushed his teeth and changed into pajamas. To Marshall's pleasure, the boy climbed into his lap and handed him a picture book.

The child dozed off halfway through. Marshall carried him to his pint-size bed, its headboard painted with fairy-tale characters. Nick pulled a patchwork quilt over his son, and they crept out.

"He's fond of you," Nick said. "There's no accounting for taste. Beer?"

"Sure. Thanks."

In the living room, Nick sprawled on the couch and Marshall chose an armchair. "I have to admit, I had a second motive for coming tonight, besides seeing my nephew."

"Seeing your brother?" Nick asked.

"A third motive."

"Shoot."

"I was wondering how you handled it when Caleb's mother refused to marry you," Marshall said. "This isn't idle curiosity."

"Got a girl pregnant, did you?" Nick must have

picked up Marshall's involuntary start, because he hurried to add, "Sorry, man, that was harsh. Am I right?"

Marshall shrugged. "Mind answering the question?"

"I'll start at the beginning."

"Go for it."

Nick and Bethany had met at a party. She'd been pretty, lively and wild. Unattached and blowing off steam after completing his residency, Nick had jumped into an affair.

"We were both careless," he said. "When we found out she was pregnant, she nixed my proposal and insisted on adoption."

"Adoption?" That obviously hadn't happened.

"Her parents talked her out of it because they longed for a grandchild," Nick explained. "Beth still refused to marry me. She preferred living with them."

"Why?"

"Big house. Free babysitting, laundry and housekeeping," Nick said. "Besides, Beth and I weren't in love."

"You stayed involved?" Marshall probed.

"I visited and contributed to Caleb's expenses, as much as I could." Nick hadn't inherited wealth as Marshall had. "After Bethany died in a boating accident last year, I brought him to live with me."

"Yes, I remember." But none of that gave Marshall ideas for how to proceed with Franca. "In retrospect, do you think if you'd tried harder you could have won Beth over?"

"Doubtful, though the romantic approach never hurts." Nick plopped his feet on the coffee table. "How did you propose to your girlfriend—I'm assuming you did, right?"

"It went something like, 'We should get married.'"

"No wonder she said no, Uncle Marsh." At the high-pitched pronouncement from across the room, Marshall's hand jerked, spilling a few drops of beer on his slacks.

"Hey, sport. You're supposed to be in bed," Nick gently scolded his son.

Caleb folded his arms over his teddy-bear print pj's. "Dad, tell him how we did it with Zady."

"We?" Marshall asked.

"It was a joint proposal." Nick grinned. "And you can do it better than me, kid."

"You go down on your knee." Caleb demonstrated. He looked adorably earnest. "You need a ring, too."

"As sparkly as possible," Nick said.

"Yeah." Caleb nodded vigorously. "Like in the movies."

"We'd watched a romantic comedy, which taught us the proper method." Nick grinned. "Okay, killer, back to bed. Uncle Marsh and I are having a grown-up conversation."

Caleb arose with a show of dusting off his pajamas. "Don't forget."

"Thanks for the tip." Marshall listened until he heard his nephew's door close. "I had no idea he could hear us."

"Zady says men's voices carry in this house," Nick admitted. "Let's adjourn to the kitchen."

At the table, they finished their beer with slices of cold pizza. Marshall was glad his brother understood how hunger could strike again so quickly. "So the key is a romantic presentation?"

"Depends on the woman and how she feels about you." Nick's fingers tapped the table. "It's Franca, isn't it?"

"That's private."

"Please remove the stuffing from your shirt and answer again."

"Yes," he said.

"And she turned you down?"

"Let's just say I won't be lining up a best man anytime soon," Marshall replied. "I don't understand women."

"If you did, you'd be the first guy ever," Nick said. "You have to take your cues from her."

"But it makes more sense for her to live at my place. With a baby coming, it's crazy for her to be driving so far every day and living alone," Marshall protested.

"May I speak as a doctor?"

"What else would you speak as?" Grumpily, Marshall added, "Not to mention that I'm one, too."

"You work with men. I work with women," Nick said. "Pregnancy does weird things to their bodies. Their hormones fluctuate, their ankles and breasts swell—drag your mind away from that image, right now—their hearts and lungs work harder, and let's not forget the throwing-up part. All day, not just mornings."

While Marshall had learned all that in medical school, he hadn't considered the impact on Franca's moods. "That sounds seriously unpleasant."

"As I tell my patients' husbands, your job is to be there for her," Nick said. "In your case, you should be more flexible."

"I suck at being flexible."

"Do it anyway."

Marshall reminded himself that he'd come here for counsel. "Your input is appreciated."

"Glad to hear it."

On the way home, Marshall wished for some of the synchronicity that, in his college days, had often landed him face-to-face with Franca. But if he did run into her by accident, how did a man demonstrate flexibility when his gut insisted he was right?

WHILE EVERY OBSTETRICIAN at Safe Harbor was well qualified, Franca wanted to choose one who'd be on her wavelength. She decided on Dr. Nora Franco, whose four-year-old son, Neo, had attended day care with Jazz. She and Nora had broken the ice when, noting the similarity in their names, they'd joked that if Franca married into Nora's husband's family, she'd be Franca Franco.

During one of their chats, Nora had confided that she'd gotten pregnant by accident. Although her policeman boyfriend was now her husband, Franca believed the obstetrician would understand the challenges she faced as a single mom.

Despite a busy schedule, Nora was able to work Franca in late on Monday. After greeting Franca warmly, the tall blonde physician asked a few questions, reviewed her medical history and performed a physical exam.

She confirmed a pregnancy of five weeks' duration, based on the start of Franca's last period. Now she was staring at the computer terminal.

Shifting uneasily on the examining table, Franca tugged her skimpy robe tighter around herself. "Is anything wrong?"

Nora shook her head. "The only thing concerning me is your blood pressure. It's 130 over 80. That stops short of the danger zone, but it's a little higher than your usual pressure, and normally BP drops during early pregnancy. That's because progesterone relaxes the walls of the blood vessels."

"Could this cause problems?" Franca pressed.

"Not unless it worsens significantly. Even then, we

can treat it." Nora wheeled her stool closer. "Are you under stress? Of course an unplanned pregnancy is stressful, but each person reacts differently."

Despite her worries about Jazz and her medical issues, what popped into Franca's head was the bill she'd received for the next three months at her private office. The landlords had raised the rent, and she wasn't sure she could justify the cost.

"I'm weighing whether to continue treating private clients." In fact, she had to rush there in a few minutes to keep an appointment. "But I can't bear to let down people who're depending on me."

"It's wise to reduce any unnecessary strain." Nora regarded her questioningly. "Do you have support from the father?"

That's too personal. "Some. The bottom line is, it's my baby and I'm dealing with it."

"Any close family?"

"Not around here. But I'm fine." She wasn't ready to notify them. Franca didn't wish to upset Gail after what her sister had endured, and as for Mom, her fussing might drive Franca crazy.

More than ever in the ten years since her father's death from heart disease, she wished he were here. A psychologist, Evan Brightman had checked his kids' homework, listened to their problems while smoking his pipe, and cracked jokes at the dinner table. Just a whiff of aromatic smoke could slam Franca's heart with nostalgic longing.

The doctor didn't appear convinced that Franca was fine. However, she moved on. "I estimate your due date as December 15. You should have a baby for Christmas."

Last year's holidays had been joyous, with Jazz's

adoption seemingly a done deal. Franca couldn't bear to imagine what the holidays would be like without her. Was it possible she'd have her precious Baby Bright—short for Baby Brightman—or would she fail to save this child, too?

Nora frowned. "How about sharing what you've been holding back?"

Might as well go for it. "My mother had two miscarriages before carrying to term. My sister, Gail, has lost three pregnancies, and the doctors can't find a reason. I'm afraid I've inherited the same tendency."

"While I don't see any warning signs, let's review common causes of pregnancy loss." Franca was relieved Nora didn't dismiss her concern.

She cited chromosomal abnormalities in the fetus or bacterial infections, but those were usually onetime events, not repetitive. There was no untreated diabetes or substance abuse, either.

"What does that leave?" Franca asked.

"Polycystic ovary syndrome is associated with abnormally high levels of the hormone testosterone. We can test for that," the doctor said. "Another risk is if the mother's immune system attacks the embryo, viewing it as a foreign object. I'll order extra blood work." She tapped notes into the computer.

Franca remembered that she had to rush to meet her client. "Do I have to do the labs today?"

"Tomorrow or Wednesday would be fine." Nora glanced up. "If you suffer cramps or severe abdominal pain and bleeding beyond a little spotting, call me at once."

"By then it will be too late, though, won't it?" Nora sighed, and Franca added, "My sister had heavy bleeding. Fortunately her husband was there."

"Do you live alone?"

"Yes."

"Keep your cell phone within reach," Nora said.

Franca thanked the doctor, scheduled her next checkup and accepted a plastic bag of vitamins and product samples. The drive to her Garden Grove office took forty-five minutes in rush-hour traffic, and she narrowly arrived by six o'clock.

Franca jogged into the one-story white building, where the receptionist was preparing to leave. The woman regarded her apologetically. "Your client just canceled."

"What?" Franca had to pause to catch her breath. "She didn't call my cell."

"She phoned here." The receptionist pulled on a sweater. "People tend to be evasive when they break commitments at the last minute."

"Did she ask for another date?"

"She said you've done such a great job, she and her husband don't need any more counseling."

If the decision was financially motivated, Franca would have offered a discount, but she might not be able to keep the practice open anyway. "Thanks for filling me in," she said. "While I'm here, I should check my mail."

"It's in your drawer. Do you mind locking up? Everyone else is gone."

"No problem."

After the woman left, Franca keyed open her private office. Not so private these days since she only used it some weekends and evenings, and she shared it with another counselor.

In the drawer, she found only flyers and other junk. The rest of the room had an impersonal air. She'd moved most of the toys, books and drawing materials to the medical center.

Nora had been right that she should be reducing her stress levels. Why had she clung to the notion that she was indispensable?

Franca was locking the inner office when a sharp pain in her side sent her doubling over. Groping for support, she banged her leg against a chair.

As she sank onto a couch, she registered that she might be suffering a miscarriage alone in an isolated building. In a panic, Franca took out her phone and instinctively tapped the first number that showed—Marshall's. What was she doing? She should dial 911.

Struggling to end the call, she fumbled the device. As she reached for the symbol to cut off the connection, she heard his voice say, "Franca?"

"I think I'm losing the baby," she blurted.

Chapter Twelve

A dark tide of worry surged through Marshall as he exited the freeway. True, Franca had reported after a moment that she'd experienced a single cramp and suffered no bleeding. But she still might be in danger.

She'd claimed she was well enough to drive the short distance to her apartment. "I overreacted, that's all. I'm sorry for disturbing you."

"For your sake and the baby's, wait for me there." Ultimately, she'd provided the address.

In the clinic parking lot, Marshall broke into a run, his mind conjuring up a horrific scene of Franca collapsed on the floor. Yanking open the door, he was overjoyed to find her on a sofa, calmly leafing through a magazine. "No further problems?"

"Just boredom." A smile softened her mouth. "It was kind of you to rush over, but unnecessary."

"How do you feel?" He ached to touch her.

"Embarrassed," Franca said.

He dropped into a chair. "Are you sure you're both okay?"

"Yes." A pucker formed between her eyebrows. "But if it was over, I imagine you…that you might be… relieved."

"What?" Marshall shot to his feet. How had she developed such a disgusting idea about him? "Do you really have such a low opinion of me?"

Franca's small, warm hand caught his wrist. "Of course not. I misunderstood your reaction to the pregnancy."

"That's one hell of a misunderstanding!"

"You mentioned the morning-after pill." She stroked his arm. "Sit down, Marshall. I'm getting a crick in my neck looking up at you."

He obeyed stiffly. "I brought that up for your sake. I had no idea how *you* felt about having a baby. I still don't."

She wrapped her arms around herself. "While I wouldn't have chosen these circumstances, I love this baby."

Then marry me! However, issuing commands might provoke a fight. How frustrating. When he'd tried to be empathetic and suggested the morning-after pill, she'd assumed he didn't want the baby. If he pressed her to marry him, she'd assume some other wrongheaded thing.

"Now that you can see that I'm fine, I'm heading home," Franca said.

"I'll follow, okay? If you have any problems, flash your lights."

Her lips pressed together. Then, with a sigh, Franca conceded, "That's kind of you."

"I'm on your side," Marshall said. "Whether you believe that or not."

Her gaze searched his face. "You do have your moments."

What did that mean? Marshall refused to prolong their fruitless discussion. "Lead the way, madam."

Franca arose with no sign of pain. Marshall allowed himself to breathe again. She really was okay.

As SHE LED Marshall into her apartment, Franca tried viewing the place from his perspective. Compared to his house, the living room was small, with plain, thrift-store furnishings. "Pretty far from a mansion at the beach," she conceded.

He smiled. "Yes, but it's yours. Did you make the comforter?"

"My mom crocheted it," She fingered the bright colors thrown over the back of the sofa.

"I can't imagine my mother crocheting anything."

She remembered Mildred Davis stalking out of the wedding dinner. "Have you reconciled with her?"

"Afraid not." He studied the scenic photos. "Do these have special meaning for you?"

"My brother shot them near his home in Montana." She stretched, then froze when she felt a twinge in her abdomen.

Fear flooded her, wildly out of proportion. *You are not having a miscarriage.* But the terror she'd experienced at the clinic hadn't entirely dissipated. How desperately she loved Baby Bright, and how helpless she'd been to protect her child.

"What is it?" Marshall caught her shoulder.

"A minor aftershock from the spasm I had earlier. Nothing to worry about."

When he released her, Franca missed his support. Her knees had gone liquid, and she wanted to sit. But sinking into a seat would be like inviting him to stay.

"You're certain?"

She searched for a neutral remark. "I'm just sore

from lying on the examining table at Dr. Franco's office."

"You had an appointment? I presume she's running the appropriate tests." Noting her dubious expression, Marshall elaborated. "When I broke the news to my brother, he reminded me how hard pregnancy is on a woman's body."

He'd told Nick? Franca could have kicked him. "I was hoping to keep this quiet a while longer."

"Sorry. He isn't a blabbermouth, though." Marshall reflected on that. "But I suppose he'll mention it to Zady."

"Who'll spill to her twin."

"Who'll inform her husband and housemates," he conceded.

"Next stop: the internet." Franca's irritation yielded to amusement at how readily she and Marshall fell into their usual banter.

"Are you mad that I spilled the beans?"

"I bow to the inevitable." They ought to figure out how to respond to the inevitable gossip, but she had no energy for strategizing. "Let the chips fall where they may. Our colleagues will move on to fresh gossip soon enough."

Judging by his frown, Marshall hadn't considered how others might react. Then he nodded. "You're right. They'd find out, anyway."

"Exactly." Casual tittle-tattle didn't bother Franca. But if she miscarried, every sideways glance or attempt at consolation would turn a knife in the wound. Just as she was sure it did with her sister.

Restlessly, Franca paced past Jazz's room. Little doll faces and teddy bears peered back as if asking when their mistress was coming home.

Marshall followed her gaze. "The fairy-tale theme reminds me of Caleb's room."

"I'll bet his isn't pink and sparkly."

He smiled. "You must be saving everything until she comes home."

Ouch. "She isn't going to. The DA dropped the case against her mother."

Marshall spoke in a deep rumble. "I know how much you loved her."

Loved her, past tense. Franca almost railed at him for dismissing her grief, almost protested that her love for Jazz would last until the day she died. But he was trying to comfort her, not minimize her loss.

And she was grateful for his presence. Why did she have the urge to strike out at the man who'd run to her side when she called him? *Because it would be too easy to lean on him when ultimately, the only person I can count on is myself.* Doubly so if she miscarried.

"You shouldn't have to carry this burden alone," Marshall told her. "I realize I speak at the risk of getting my head bitten off."

Franca would have laughed if she hadn't hurt so much. "I don't mean to be touchy. But I can handle it. I'm a big girl."

"Not a superhero, though."

"What does that mean?"

"That you can't do everything," he said. "Commuting, working two jobs, living by yourself. All while growing a baby."

"You can't help being bossy, can you?" she protested.

"I'm trying to be flexible, but it goes against my nature." Taking her hands, Marshall chafed them lightly. "Since I'm lousy at it, let me jump in with both feet.

Move in with me. I have plenty of space and I live close to the medical center."

"We'll argue. Like we always do."

"I'm sure you won't hesitate to point out when I'm being a pain in the ass," he said. "Like *you* always do."

Franca had to admit that was true, and that he'd been remarkably patient with her outbursts. "You promise not to resent it when I tell you off?"

"I may growl and sulk, but I'll let it go," he said.

"Growl and sulk," she repeated. "How can a woman refuse such a great offer?"

Was it really a bad idea to move in with him, as long as she knew it wouldn't last? Franca's mother had been crushed by her first husband's abandonment because she'd relied on his support after she'd lost two babies. And Belle had reorganized her class schedule and her future plans trying to please Marshall, only to be tossed aside when she fell short of his expectations.

But forewarned was forearmed, as the old saying went. The man owned a dream house, he cooked breakfast, and he was studying her with enough heat to melt chocolate. Despite all that, Franca might have still resisted if this apartment wasn't so achingly empty and if she hadn't resolved to resign her position at the clinic. With the sense of stepping onto a shifting ice floe, she said, "I'll have my own room?"

She detected a flicker of disappointment in his eyes, but it vanished in a blink. "Of course. You can furnish it with your stuff. I'll put the bed and dresser in the garage."

Replace his gorgeous furniture? "No, we can store *my* old junk." What else should she address? "I'd be happy to pay rent."

"Rent?" His eyebrows shot up. "Not unless you want me to donate it to charity."

She already supported her favorite causes. Besides, having a child wasn't cheap. "I'll buy my own food, drive to work separately, and it's only for the first trimester."

He'd been nodding along until the last part. "Why?"

"By then, I'll find a place of my own nearby." Franca refused to risk letting her emotions tempt her to stay. Better to establish a limit up front.

Marshall released a frustrated breath. "When does the trimester end?"

"The middle of July."

"That's less than two months!"

"Take it or leave it."

A couple of heartbeats passed before he said, "Done."

He'd folded fast, perhaps believing he still had time to change her mind. Well, he'd fail. Meanwhile, moving in with him would solve a lot of problems.

And by July, there might not even be a baby. *Don't worry about that.*

They shook hands and agreed that she'd move in the following weekend. Only after Marshall left did another notion strike Franca.

Despite the dismaying news from her lawyer, she'd kept the apartment intact for her daughter in case things changed unexpectedly. Choosing her future baby's well-being instead felt like she was truly giving up on Jazz.

Any reasonable person would approve of Franca's decision. But that didn't dispel the sense of disloyalty that dogged her.

THE NEXT WEEKEND'S transition went smoothly, to Marshall's satisfaction. That happened partly because he had hired professional movers, and partly because he worked out a floor plan in advance.

With Franca's approval, Jazz's bed and curtains went into the playroom. They could change the pink color scheme later if the baby happened to be a boy. Her brother's photos brightened the upstairs hallway, while her mother's crocheted afghan enlivened the family room.

They had a minor disagreement about her habit of leaving appliances out on the kitchen counter, which he preferred uncluttered. This was resolved when Marshall cleared space for the appliances in the lower cabinets. He conceded that she couldn't reach things higher up, and he certainly didn't want her climbing on a footstool.

Franca's acceptance of his invitation and her willingness to compromise should have been gratifying. Instead, her responses made him uneasy. She was treating him as a roommate, and a temporary one at that. No wonder she didn't bother fighting over minutiae.

How disturbing that she remained cool to him, when awareness of her disturbed his attempts to sleep at night. His skin prickled with longing whenever he heard her stirring down the hall, awakening memories of soaring to the heights with her in the very room where she was sleeping.

During their lovemaking, Marshall had plunged off the emotional deep end, and the resulting cascade threatened his hard-won inner calm. He had to admit, it was wise to withdraw, but not to this extent.

Franca didn't seem to be experiencing any emotional turbulence. On Monday, Marshall had to wake her as she snoozed in complete indifference to her alarm clock's jangling.

"Must be pregnancy hormones," she said over her breakfast cereal.

"You sure you don't want a ride to work?" To hell with what everyone would say when they arrived together. "We can save gas."

"It's only a few miles." Morning light through the French doors cast a rosy glow over her face. "Besides, don't you normally have to be in earlier than me, for surgery?"

She had a point. "Every day but Monday."

"And my Tuesday afternoon counseling group often runs late," Franca said. "Also, it would be a pain to have to coordinate about every last-minute patient or stop at the supermarket. There's also the matter of preserving our privacy."

She was right. But if either of them imagined they could keep their situation secret, Marshall soon learned better.

At work that day, he caught curious glances from Zady. Finally, his nurse poked her head into his private office. "I hope you don't mind, but Nick mentioned... I mean, congratulations!"

"For...?" he asked.

"Fatherhood," she prompted.

He'd forgotten his disclosure to his brother. "Oh. Thanks."

She must have told the other nurses, because he heard them chattering, then fall silent as he approached their station. Marshall was glad to depart for a late-morning meeting to review suite assignments in the new building.

Interior work on the floors would begin soon, with the opening scheduled for late summer. To avoid any further conflict, the administrator had decided that

Marshall should represent the urologists and Dr. Jack Ryder speak for the other specialists as they firmed up specifics.

The two men met in a conference room in the administrator's office. That way, they could call on him should they hit an impasse.

Jack shook hands warily and scanned the tentative floor plan Marshall had prepared on his laptop. The dark-haired obstetrician suggested only one switch, allotting a larger suite to the pediatricians.

"That does reduce the space for urology fellows," Marshall noted as he visualized Jack's suggestion.

"They'll be newcomers," Jack said. "And the pediatricians are crammed into tight quarters right now."

Marshall and Cole Rattigan had labored hard to win fellowship money and attract the best candidates to their program. However, he doubted anyone would reject a fellowship simply because it meant accepting a small office. "That's reasonable."

"By the way, congratulations," Jack said when they'd finished. "I hear you're about to be a dad."

"Thanks." Marshall regarded him questioningly. "Where'd you hear that?"

The other man grinned. "Speaking of being jammed together, I'm in the same suite with your brother."

"Who has a big mouth." Marshall closed his laptop. "I'm surprised you aren't trumpeting the news to all and sundry."

"Why would I do that?"

"Because parenthood is the greatest experience ever," Jack enthused. "My daughter, Rachel, just hit the seven-month mark and watching her develop is a high."

"I'm sure she's a doll." The desire for fatherhood that had grown in Marshall these past few years had taken on almost tangible form since he saw that positive pregnancy test. There'd been distractions—mostly his worry over Franca's health when she feared she was miscarrying—yet day by day, he'd begun to picture his child as a real person, a little boy or girl cradled in his arms. Someone to laugh with, to regale with stories of his childhood and to build a future for.

"It's hard to believe Anya initially wasn't keen on keeping the baby," Jack said. "I had to win her over for Rachel's sake *and* mine."

How amazing that the other man spoke openly about such private matters. Could Jack's experience help him to overcome Franca's resistance? "How did you change her mind?"

"She assumed I'd dump the burden of child rearing on her." The other doctor leaned back with a dreamy expression. "I ran errands to show that I'd be a real partner. What put me over the top was my cooking."

"I fixed an omelet for Franca. She wasn't impressed," Marshall said.

"Think big," Jack advised. "I prepared dinner for Anya and her housemates on a regular basis. They're picky eaters, but I won them over."

"I have no idea how to fix a complicated meal." Nor could he spare the time to take a class.

"There's a ton of recipes on the internet, with step-by-step instructions," Jack said. "Cooking is similar to surgery. If you assemble your tools and ingredients, and follow the directions, you can't go wrong."

"Or if you do, nobody dies."

"Precisely."

Marshall departed with his head buzzing. For maximum impact, he decided to pick a fancy recipe. One of his favorite dishes was chicken mole, a spicy Mexican dish that combined hot peppers with a dash of chocolate.

At lunch, he found a recipe on the internet, along with the pronunciation—*MO-lay*. The long list of ingredients daunted him, but he was willing to go the extra mile to dazzle Franca.

She'd mentioned that she'd be home late tomorrow night. What a perfect opportunity for him to experiment in the kitchen.

As Jack had said, if you followed the recipe, you could hardly go wrong.

Chapter Thirteen

The days had no business passing so rapidly, Franca reflected on Tuesday. True, she'd received positive news: the results of her blood test had come back normal, and a recheck of her blood pressure showed it had dropped slightly. She'd also arranged to leave her old clinic as of June first.

But in her sixth week of pregnancy, this tiny dot within her was growing rapidly, and she felt unprepared for what lay ahead. She hadn't informed her family, because that would require dealing with their reactions. She'd simply sent them her new address, noting that this place was closer to work.

At the hospital, however, secrets didn't stay hidden long. In the cafeteria, Ines and Jeanine flagged her down.

"We heard your news," Ines said over her sandwich. "Congratulations!"

"Is this our fault?" Jeanine asked.

Puzzled, Franca toyed with her chef's salad. "How could my pregnancy be your fault?"

"We figure that's where you went after the wedding," Ines noted.

"We kept talking about how handsome Dr. Davis

was and how somebody ought to—what were the words from Dorothy Parker?" said the taller nurse.

"Somebody ought to be under him," Ines filled in.

"Oh, that." Franca chuckled. "Yes, I took your comments to heart. I went right out and jumped into his bed."

Receiving wide-eyed stares from both women, she realized her attempt at humor had missed the mark. Perhaps because she *had* done just that.

"How was he?" Ines inquired.

Jeanine poked her. "I can't believe you said that!"

Franca popped open her carton of milk. "Use your imagination."

"It's already running wild," Ines said.

"This is none of our business." Jeanine held on to her high moral ground for a few heartbeats before asking, "Are you in love?"

"What kind of question is that?" Heat crept up Franca's neck. Too bad toning down her red hair hadn't reduced her body's tendency to blush.

As for her feelings toward Marshall, she couldn't have described them if she'd wanted to. She'd moved in with the conviction that it was for her health and safety, and that she'd been armored against her susceptibility to him. Yet watching him arrange toys and picture books in the playroom, Franca had been surprised by the tenderness in Marshall's expression.

"I never had toys like this when I was a kid," he'd said when she entered.

"None?" How was that possible in such a wealthy family?

He'd traced a finger down the spine of *Goodnight Moon.* "Just nonfiction books, a microscope, building sets. I intend to do things differently."

"For a lot of us, having a baby is a chance to repeat our childhood and make things turn out right." Immediately, Franca wished she could erase her words. Sometimes a counselor knew too much—and in this case, blurted it out at the wrong moment.

The pain that had flashed across Marshall's face stunned her. Despite her familiarity with his rigid nature, glimpses of vulnerability threatened to suck her in.

He'll be devastated if I miscarry. His gentler side would slam shut, and she'd lose him emotionally, even if he forced himself to stick around from a sense of duty. That would almost be worse than an outright rejection, because postponing the process of healing only encouraged the wound to fester.

But she wasn't going to reveal any of that in this lighthearted conversation with her friends. "How could I be in love with a man who irritates me so much?" Franca countered.

"Dr. Davis may get cranky under pressure," Jeanine acknowledged. "But no guy is a sweetheart all the time."

"My husband can be a real pain," Ines agreed. "He gets over it and so do I."

Franca was weighing how to end this conversation when the nurses solved the problem by noticing they were due back on the job.

"More details later?" Ines prompted as she arose.

"No."

"Spoilsport."

Franca was finishing her salad when Jennifer Martin slipped into the seat opposite her. "Don't worry. I'm not here to pry," the public relations director said. "I witnessed something and I wanted you to know about it."

That sounded ominous. "What is it?"

"We ran into Jazz at the beach on Sunday."

Black hair, blue eyes and a small, worried face filled Franca's mind. "Is she all right?"

"Quieter than usual, but after she and Rosalie started playing, she pepped up," Jennifer said. "They built a sand castle with a little help from Ian. He adores kids." Jennifer's husband, who hosted a video blog called *On the Prowl in OC*, had written several books about fertility treatments and parenthood.

"Did you have a chance to talk to her mother? How'd she strike you?" She feared Bridget might be using drugs again.

"She was with a rough sort of man."

A knot formed in Franca's stomach. "That must be her boyfriend, Axel." Recalling their encounter at the café, she asked, "Did he jerk Jazz around?"

"Not in front of us." Jennifer swallowed. "But when he ordered her to leave the beach, she jumped up in a hurry, like she was afraid of him."

Franca wrapped her arms around herself. "Oh, no."

Jennifer leaned close, shielding their conversation from the busy room. "Bridget was wearing a turtleneck, despite the warm weather. Ian believes he saw a bruise on her neck."

Abused women often wore long sleeves and high collars to hide their injuries. And if Axel was beating Bridget, he might be hurting her daughter, too. "Was Jazz bundled up?"

"No," Jennifer said. "I studied her as closely as I dared without being too obvious. I wish you could get custody."

"Me, too." Franca shook her head regretfully. "I can't do anything without proof." She had to walk a fine line and avoid antagonizing Bridget. If the authorities took the child away from her mother, no matter what the reason, Franca had no legal claim on her.

"I hope I didn't upset you," Jennifer said. "You have to take care of yourself and your baby."

"I will." Still, if she'd measured her blood pressure at that moment, she feared it would have shot through the roof.

That afternoon, Franca was too busy to dwell on what Jennifer had reported. There were job-applicant screenings, educational sessions for patients and endless paperwork to document treatments. The counseling group that met at four o'clock ran late, and afterward, a participant distressed by the topic needed an extra hour of counseling.

Marshall had texted that he planned to cook dinner. Since Franca had made spaghetti last night, that seemed fair enough. What a joy it would be to come home to such a beautiful house and find dinner waiting for her.

Or so she anticipated, until the smell of burned chocolate hit her as she entered from the garage. Had something caught fire? Despite her exhaustion, Franca flew past the laundry room into the kitchen. "Marshall? Are you okay?"

Dismay radiated from the tall man who swiveled toward her. His apron, his face and his shirt sleeves were smeared with goo, while encrusted pans and bowls littered the counter and stove top. Dark glop filled the blender, while the scents of scorched peppers, cloves and anise augmented the pungent chocolate odor.

"What on earth?" Franca had an urge to grab a washcloth and scrub Marshall like a toddler. She doubted he'd appreciate it.

"I had no idea things would burn so quickly," he said.

"If I'd had nurses to hand me stuff like in the operating room, I'm sure I could have pulled it off."

"In other words, you could use a sous-chef." Reassured that nothing was currently on fire, Franca surveyed the mess. It seemed impossible to dirty up this many pots with a single recipe. "What were you making?"

"Chicken mole." He handed her a printout.

Franca scanned it. "There are sixteen, no, seventeen ingredients. That would put me off right there."

"If it were easy, it wouldn't be much of an accomplishment." Marshall stared bleakly around, apparently too overwhelmed to start cleaning.

Franca did her best to hide a smile. Training her attention on the recipe, she noted multiple steps involving browning and blending to create the peppery sauce. "You must have been at this for hours."

"Completely wasted," Marshall said.

"It's a noble failure," she assured him. "You aimed high."

As if taking her words literally, he glanced upward and groaned. A dark brown substance was dripping from the hood above the burners.

"When did you say your cleaning crew comes?" she asked.

He sighed. "I'll ask if they can schedule an extra visit for tomorrow. Franca, I'm sorry. You must be starved, and I was planning something special."

"You were?" She'd assumed he was merely experimenting.

"Jack Ryder suggested…" He broke off.

"What does Jack have to do with this?" The obstetrician had a gung-ho personality, she recalled. That didn't explain this culinary disaster.

"This was how he wooed his wife." Marshall ducked his head.

"By burning down the kitchen?"

"By cooking for her."

"You tackled this recipe for my benefit?" The notion gave Franca a fluttery sensation. "What a sweet thing to do."

"But we have nothing to eat."

She spotted a platter covered by a clean dish towel. "If I read the recipe correctly, the chicken might have escaped damage. Where is it?"

"Right here." Marshall lifted the towel to reveal a pile of poached chicken pieces. Pale and bland without sauce, they should nevertheless be edible. "I forgot about them."

"Is there a salad?" she ventured.

He retrieved a bowl from the refrigerator. "Right here."

"Perfect!"

"That's gracious of you." Marshall stared down at his smudged clothing. "I suppose I should change."

"Let's wash our hands, soak the pans in the sink and call it even."

"You're sure it's legal to leave such a mess?" he asked with an uptick of spirit. "My mother would require smelling salts if anyone left her kitchen in this state."

"It's your house and your rules."

"Our house," he said. She didn't bother to argue.

They set places at the kitchen island, where the chicken proved reasonably tasty. The only disadvantage was that after dinner they had to face the stove.

"From here, it reminds me of a volcano eruption," Marshall observed.

"I'll bet you blew up a few science experiments with

those kits you got as a kid." Franca poured herself a second glass of white grape juice.

He flexed his shoulders, no doubt stiff from hours of chopping and stirring. "I nearly demolished the garage once."

"How old were you?"

"Ten or eleven." He grimaced at the memory. "I wasn't sure my folks would ever forgive me."

"It was their own fault. They should have given you a teddy bear," she said.

"I'd probably have dissected it."

"Like any proper future surgeon." She raised her glass. "Here's to surviving our childhoods."

He clinked with her. "But I'm sure yours was happier than mine, not that this is any sort of contest."

"It *was* happy," Franca said. "Except that… No, I shouldn't complain."

"Complain away." Marshall's steady gaze encouraged her to continue.

"I was the infamous middle child." She tried to avoid clichés, but this one held some truth. "My big sister seemed more accomplished and prettier. My brother became the baby of the family. I tried to win our parents' approval by being a better student and more compliant."

"Did it work?"

"In an offhand way," Franca said. "They praised me, but there was something missing. Until I started working with troubled kids when I was in high school."

"Why did that make a difference?" Marshall asked. "It certainly wouldn't have with my folks."

"My mom identified with my dream of becoming a foster parent. She loved the idea of being surrounded by kids," Franca recalled. "Also, working with youngsters made me want to understand their family dynamics.

That's when I decided to follow in my father's footsteps as a psychologist."

"I imagine he appreciated that."

"Yes, he did."

Rising, Franca stored the leftovers while Marshall called and arranged for the cleaners to arrive the next day. With a sense of skipping school, they left the wrecked kitchen and carried their glasses to the patio.

In the few days since she'd moved in, Franca hadn't had a chance to enjoy the outdoor areas of the house, which included a patch of emerald lawn and a curving flower bed bursting with blooms. Beyond the bluffs, she glimpsed the harbor and the midnight-blue ocean beneath a darkening sky.

In the cool evening air, Franca had an urge to scoot her lounge chair closer to Marshall's. Her hand drifted to her abdomen. How incredible that she carried a part of him merged with a part of her.

"Does it hurt?" He propped up on his elbow to face her.

"No." She peered down at her still-flat stomach. "I was just thinking about how Baby Bright combines both our heritages."

"Cute name."

"Short for Brightman," she explained.

Marshall's expression sobered. "You don't want to give it up for adoption, do you?"

"Certainly not!" she said. "Why?"

"That's what Jack Ryder's wife planned, initially." The glow of outdoor lighting emphasized Marshall's high cheekbones.

"You discussed my pregnancy with him?" In fairness, Franca conceded that plenty of staffers were gabbing about the situation. "Never mind."

"I apologize if I was indiscreet," Marshall said. "I'm a bit overeager."

She couldn't bristle at a guy who'd covered himself in chocolate sauce on her behalf. "I appreciate the good intentions."

Marshall tugged her arm. "Come here. You deserve a massage."

"You're the one who must be sore from all that cooking." She didn't resist, though, when he pulled her onto his lap and his large, skilled hands played over her muscles, releasing the tension.

Awareness of his hard thighs beneath her reawakened sensations she'd tried to drive from her dreams, and desire rushed over her in a heated surge. When Marshall's hands slid around to the front and cupped her exquisitely sensitive breasts, Franca hovered on the edge of surrender.

A gust of sea air snapped her back to reality, though. Embarrassed, she drew his hands away. "I'm tired. I've had a long day."

Marshall cleared his throat. "I didn't mean to go too far."

"It's as much my fault as yours." Shifting position, she cupped his stubbled cheek with her palm. "We've always been attracted to each other."

"You have keen powers of observation." His mouth quirked as he tried to lighten the mood. It looked like it hurt.

Franca could barely keep from kissing this earnest man. It was surprising how appealing she found his smeared face and clothes, sacrificed in an attempt to please her. But she knew how swiftly he could switch gears. "There's a reason we never followed through on it until now." She rose clumsily on stiff knees.

"Fear?" he guessed, catching her hips to aid her balance.

"Or wisdom." Franca eased away. "We have to stay on an even keel for our baby's sake as well as our own."

She could see the struggle as he searched for words. Finally he said, "You're worn out. Go rest."

Franca took her glass inside. What a strange reversal, she thought, that Marshall's emotions had become transparent, while she was the one holding herself in check.

Her maternal hormones must be screwing with them both.

MARSHALL REMAINED SITTING on the edge of the lounge chair, missing Franca's warmth where she'd cuddled against him. How unexpected, that his catastrophe in the kitchen had brought them closer rather than offending her.

He'd moved too fast, though. Lesson learned: relationships progressed best when allowed to unfold gradually. In retrospect, it was clear that after he and Franca had thrown caution aside the night they made love, the experience had driven her to retreat. But although their mutual amusement tonight had furthered their détente, he'd overplayed his hand.

How to proceed? Clearly, his upbringing and instincts weren't up to the task of persuading her to stay. But, by luck, Marshall had stumbled upon helpful advice, first from his brother and then from Jack. While things hadn't played out as anticipated, their suggestions *had* helped.

According to the stories circulating at the hospital, a number of colleagues had won their wives despite initial reluctance. Surely he could glean more useful tips from them. How to do that without baldly declaring himself a hopeless case, he wasn't sure, but he'd stay alert for opportunities.

Marshall had to convince Franca that while they might not be destined to fall madly in love, they could find happiness sharing a partnership as parents and friends.

The sooner, the better.

Chapter Fourteen

Soliciting advice turned out to be a challenge. Neither of the urologists who shared Marshall's suite was married, and he couldn't ask the nurses, who often ate lunch with Franca and would no doubt blab about his clumsy inquiries.

At Thursday night's counseling group, he half expected the men to stand up and accuse him of fraud. After all, he needed advice as much as they did.

However, when he tuned in to the discussion, he was pleased by how much the men had gained from the previous meeting. Several had successfully confronted troublesome relatives, and had an increased sense of teamwork with their wives. Cory reported that not only had his mother-in-law stopped showering them with offensive suggestions, she'd been relieved to learn she didn't have to offer solutions, just sympathy.

Once they wrapped up that topic, Hank Driver brought up another issue: his belief that his wife blamed him for their infertility. It had been his choice to undergo a vasectomy, and the reversal hadn't yet paid off.

Marshall jumped in. "You're convinced she blames you, but she claims she doesn't. Is it possible you blame yourself?"

The detective's forehead furrowed. "You're right. I

do feel like I'm letting her down. Also, I cheated on my previous two wives, which Sarah is aware of because she's a dispatcher in our department. I'd never cheat on *her*, but I'm not sure she trusts me."

"Have you brought that up with her?" Franca asked.

"It never occurred to me," Hank said. "I guess I should."

Being able to contribute to the session cheered Marshall, and he was glad to gain more insight into family dynamics. Still, he hadn't learned anything that would advance his personal quest.

Help came from an unexpected source. On Friday morning, his surgeries ran long. In the cafeteria, he'd barely started to eat when Owen Tartikoff dropped into the vacant seat opposite him.

Marshall's hand jerked, nearly dropping his sandwich. For heaven's sake, the fertility program chief didn't intimidate him. Much.

"How's it going?" The russet-haired doctor had a disconcerting manner of seeming casual while conveying steely resolve.

"We're settling in fine."

The surgeon's cinnamon eyes blinked. "That's an odd way to describe therapy."

Oh, he meant the men's counseling group. "I'd call it productive," Marshall said. "The clients seem to be benefiting."

"How, exactly?"

"I wish I could describe the process to you, because it's very interesting. However, anything revealed in our sessions is confidential."

Owen's fingers drummed on the table. For a guy accustomed to being in charge, having a door slammed in his face must be hard to take. Marshall hoped the surgeon wasn't about to pull rank. As a medical supervisor, he might insist on reading Franca's or Marshall's notes, but that didn't seem right.

He searched for a diversion. "When I spoke of settling in, I was referring to Dr. Brightman and me. You've probably heard the scuttlebutt."

"Yes." Tartikoff leaned back in his chair. "Reminds me of when Bailey and I were housemates while she was pregnant. We fought like cats and dogs for a while."

The distraction appeared to be working. "Your twins are how old?"

That brought out the photos. "Here they are at their third birthday party, in January." The image showed a boy and girl with curly light brown hair, both grinning impishly. "Their names are Julie and Richard. That's for the heroine of the musical *Carousel* and its composer, Richard Rodgers."

Marshall examined the image. "They're quite a pair. You and your wife must be big fans of musicals."

"We sing together. It bridged the gap between us." After a fond gaze at the screen, Owen slipped the phone into his pocket. "That's how I won her over."

Owen had dropped a suggestion right into Marshall's lap. The only problem was that while he could, with an effort, carry a tune, he doubted he'd win Franca's heart by breaking into song.

However, the chocolate-pepper-sauce disaster had amused rather than offended her, hadn't it? "Do you recommend any song in particular?"

"'You'll Never Walk Alone,'" he announced. "That's from *Carousel*, too."

"What about accompaniment?" If success required mastering the guitar, Marshall was lost.

"In my case, there happened to be a pianist handy,"

the other man said. "You could download karaoke music."

"Great idea."

"I figured you for a smart man, and I was right."

How ironic, Marshall mused as they parted. Many of the doctors at Safe Harbor turned themselves inside out trying to score points with the big man. Little did they suspect all it took was agreeing to belt out a tune.

And make a complete fool of yourself.

He decided to start by finding a karaoke-style arrangement in the right key, whatever that was, and hoping for the best.

On Saturday, Franca held her final sessions with private clients: a family of four and a married couple. Although they were sad to learn she was closing her practice, they had progressed enough to continue with another counselor or, if they preferred, on their own.

What an emotional experience, the end of an era. Joining this office five years ago after working at a larger clinic had been a financial risk that had paid off. How exciting and validating to her as a professional, only in her late twenties, to establish her own practice.

Over the years, however, the increasing burden of paperwork along with cuts in insurance payments had taken a toll. When she learned of the opening at Safe Harbor, Franca had leaped at the fresh opportunity.

And now she was cutting the cord on her private practice. It meant saying goodbye to her youthful dreams, even as she embraced new goals.

She'd have liked to confide her mixed reaction to Marshall, but after returning home from surgery, he closeted himself in his study. Despite his occasional openness, he remained opaque in many ways. While she respected his privacy, it reminded her how easily he could withdraw.

By dinner, which they prepared together, they were too tired to do more than chat about the suggestions circulating for the as-yet-unscheduled opening ceremony of the new medical building. On the cafeteria bulletin board, notes had proposed a light-and-sound show and a band playing music from around the world. A few ideas had been hilarious but in poor taste, inspired by the Porvamm's function of providing men's fertility care.

"Giant balloons shaped like the male anatomy?" Franca chuckled as she dished up stir-fry and rice.

"Don't laugh," Marshall grumbled. "When I chose urology as a specialty, I figured there'd be teasing, but I had no idea how many people would consider me a weirdo."

"I can imagine." *Easily.*

"I don't mind the comments at my expense." He doused his rice with soy sauce. "It's poking fun at my patients that bothers me. Those guys go through a lot."

"As I've seen from our group," Franca said. "And you know what? I'm impressed with how protective they are toward their wives."

"Of course." He regarded her steadily. "A man ought to protect the people he cares about."

She had no answer. In truth, his comments spurred her to consider how much he'd changed from the uptight, moralistic young man she'd met in college. Had her fears about him ultimately shutting her out been misplaced? Or had he simply not yet been tested?

They watched a movie that night on the family room's large screen. Although his preference ran to documentaries and science fiction, and hers to roman-

tic comedies and costume dramas, they both enjoyed a
fast-paced thriller with a love story.

Living here was more fun than she'd expected,
Franca conceded as she got ready for bed. She'd been
determined not to drift into a long-term relationship
based on physical attraction and an accidental pregnancy. Was there more than that between her and Marshall, or was proximity clouding her judgment?

Mid-July was only six weeks away. She wished she
had someone to help her gain perspective on the situation. Mentally she considered, and ruled out, everyone
she'd met at the hospital.

On Sunday afternoon, the urge to talk had grown
so strong that after lunch, Franca sat in the kitchen reviewing the names in her phone. In the old days, she'd
have called Belle.

Guilt surged inside her. By sleeping with Marshall,
she'd violated the unwritten girlfriend code. Okay, it
used to be unwritten, until someone posted it on the
internet.

The rules included never canceling important plans
with your friends for a guy, protecting confidences,
showing sympathy rather than saying I told you so and
sticking with a friend at a social event where you'd arrived together. But the most serious commandment was
not dating your close friend's ex.

Since the wedding, Belle had posted charming photos
of her new home in Denver and sung the praises of her
husband. That didn't mean she'd erased Marshall's rejection entirely.

Eventually, Franca would have to fess up, but not
yet. Nor could she use her mother as a sounding board.
Mom would only urge Franca to get married.

That left her sister. In view of Gail's devastating

losses, news of the pregnancy might be painful for her. Yet Franca hadn't talked to her in three months.

If the conversation worked around to pregnancy, fine. If not, they could catch up in other areas. Often, clients who'd suffered trauma commented how hurt they were by friends who avoided them, presumably too uncomfortable to stay in touch. She'd hate for Gail to believe that was the case with her.

Since Marshall was in his study and potentially within earshot, Franca carried her phone outside. The far-off murmur of the surf provided a soothing backdrop.

Tapping her sister's number in Arizona, she perched on a chair. Gail answered on the third ring, "Yes?"

"It's your long-lost sister," Franca said.

"The one with freckles?"

"No, the other one."

They both giggled. Franca's Raggedy Ann coloring was no longer the sore point it used to be. Two years younger than Gail, she'd longed for her big sister's confidence as well as her creamy complexion and chestnut-brown hair. Gail had poked fun at her freckles until one day Franca started to cry. Apologetically, Gail had admitted she envied her little sister's vivid appearance.

"Sorry I haven't called," Gail said. "I've been busy, but that's no excuse."

"Yes, it's entirely your fault," Franca replied. "Except for the part that's my fault."

"Now that we've got the apologies out of the way, tell me how it's going at the hospital. You aren't still on probation, are you?"

"I've passed that stage, thank goodness." Franca relayed her further adventures at Safe Harbor, including the establishment of the men's group. "I'm closing my private practice," she said.

"Wow! I remember how excited you were about having your own office," Gail said. "I got your new home address. Do you have roommates?"

Here goes nothing. "I'm living with a guy."

"Do I hear wedding bells?" Gail asked. "Scratch that. I do *not* want to pry."

"It's too early to answer, anyway."

"Who's the guy?"

She should have prepared herself for that. "Do you remember Marshall Davis?"

"Belle's boyfriend?" Gail let out a whoop. "Have you told her?"

Franca sighed. "No, and I'm a little uncomfortable about it."

"Well, she *is* married."

"Still, it might be a sore point."

"I always thought he and Belle made a handsome couple, but they were shallow, like a set of dolls," Gail said.

"That's interesting." Franca had considered them well-suited. As far as she could tell, they'd never argued, unlike her and Marshall. "How about you? How're things in Phoenix?"

"Hot," Gail said. "Which is great for business, because everybody's air-conditioning needs fixing." Her husband, Tim, repaired heating and cooling systems, while she handled the bookkeeping and scheduled appointments. "How's Jazz? Any chance of getting her back?"

"I'm afraid not." Franca explained about the DA's decision. "Losing her broke my heart. I always dreamed of adopting a foster child but I don't think I can try again. It's too painful."

"Don't give up on your dream," Gail urged.

"At this point, my dream is to have a family." Franca could no longer hold her anxiety in check. "I'm afraid of pregnancy, too. With our family's medical history…" She stopped, distressed at having blundered into sensitive territory.

"I'm well aware of our family's medical history, as you put it," snapped her sister. "To me, it's more personal than that."

"I didn't mean to be tactless."

Franca sensed Gail struggling for control. "Let's not discuss it," she said at last.

"I agree." Franca felt selfish for getting so caught up in her desire to confide that she'd offended her sister. "I'd appreciate your not mentioning Marshall to Mom yet."

"I can protect a confidence." Gail's tone was frosty.

"Give my love to Tim." After they said goodbye, Franca ended the call with a sigh. Instead of reconnecting with her sister, she'd opened a gap between them. And informing Gail about the pregnancy, when she eventually did, would be that much harder.

Her throat tightened. It hurt to keep secrets from the people whose support she valued most.

The scrape of the French door jerked her attention to Marshall, who stood in the opening. "Would you mind coming to my study? I have something to show you."

She could use a change of pace, Franca thought, rising. "What is it?"

"A surprise." With a smile playing around his mouth, he held the door for her.

DURING SURGERY, MARSHALL had the proverbial nerves of steel. Performing a song was entirely different.

He'd arrayed a couple of bouquets around the room to set a romantic scene. It hadn't been easy sneaking them in, but he was satisfied to see they aroused Franca's curiosity. "Pretend it's a bower," he said. "Okay, a bower with exercise equipment."

"I'm afraid to ask what this is about. Why is it so dark in here?"

"Just go with it, okay?" Marshall had tilted the blinds to reduce the light spilling across his monitor. "Hold on a sec."

On the computer, he clicked to the downloaded music. The speaker on this system wasn't great, but it beat the tinny one in his phone.

Marshall pressed start. After a few bars of introduction, he launched into the song. "When you walk through a storm..."

Franca's mouth fell open.

Despite an urge to hide under the desk, Marshall poured his soul into the lyrics about holding up your head and hanging on to hope. A chill ran through him; he wasn't sure whether it sprang from the moving message or from anxiety.

The song reached its crescendo. While practicing, Marshall had murmured the melody and lyrics to keep from being overheard. Singing full-out proved more difficult. Still, he was doing okay until he hit, and shattered, a couple of high notes.

Finally, it was over. Franca stood motionless, staring at him. Stunned, or on the cusp of dissolving into laughter? Should he follow up by presenting her with a bouquet?

That would look ridiculous. *Even more ridiculous that this entire serenade?*

Finally, she spoke. "That was adorable."

"Adorable?" he repeated, unsure how to interpret that remark. "As in cute and childish?"

"It was totally…" She swallowed. "I would never have…"

Marshall ventured closer. "Should I hire an interpreter?"

"It was fine," Franca said. Then she did the one thing he hadn't anticipated.

She broke into tears.

Chapter Fifteen

When Marshall wrapped his arms around Franca, she felt wonderful, and foolish. Why had she searched through her phone for someone to confide in when he'd been here all along?

Planning this wildly out-of-character ballad for her sake. Buying flowers to create a romantic mood. Pushing past his inherent restraint to reach out to her.

Embarrassingly, her tears yielded to sobs. When Marshall guided her to the sofa and onto his lap, she collapsed against him.

"Was I that bad?" he asked.

Laughter battled with her ragged emotions. Franca gulped for air before saying, "Of course not."

Marshall reached for a box of tissues. As Franca accepted one, she thought of how often she'd performed the same kindness for her patients. And how wonderful it was to know that someone cared. Especially when that someone was Marshall.

They both spoke at once. "Why did you...?" And stopped.

Franca leaped into the gap. "Why the serenade?"

Marshall's arms tightened around her. "The advice about cooking brought us closer, so I asked for more suggestions."

"Someone advised you to sing to me?" Franca couldn't imagine who would do such a crazy thing.

He nodded. "Owen Tartikoff."

"*The* Owen Tartikoff?" As if there were more than one. "You're telling me he sang to his wife?"

"He claims he did."

Franca tried to picture the imposing surgeon crooning to his lady love. A hilarious scene, but touching. "What about the choice of music?"

Marshall's cheeks colored. "He suggested it."

"That very song?"

"It worked for him."

Marshall had hit on exactly what she needed through dumb luck rather than insight. But they'd always had a tendency to stumble into the same place, whether physically or emotionally. "It worked for me, too."

"Your turn," Marshall said.

"I have to sing?" Aside from lullabies to an uncritical toddler, Franca hadn't sung since college karaoke parties.

"I meant, to explain. Why are you crying?"

As excuses sprang to mind, Franca realized she'd become accustomed to deflecting difficult questions. Marshall deserved the truth.

Scooting off his lap, she sat beside him on the couch. "I've been talking to my sister."

"Is she okay?"

"Yes, but…" *Just go for it.* "The women in my family have a history of miscarriages."

"You mentioned your mother's troubles," he said.

"Well, she's not the only one who's had difficulties. My sister, Gail, and my aunt had repeated losses, too. Although no cause has been diagnosed, it might be genetic. That would mean I'm at an increased risk of losing the baby."

Marshall stiffened. She could feel him pulling away. "Has your doctor found anything wrong?"

"No. But neither did Gail's."

"That's a serious concern."

"You've been generous, inviting me to move in while I'm pregnant," Franca said. "If I lose the baby…" Well, the rest was obvious.

When she lost the child, she'd lose Marshall, too.

HE UNDERSTOOD NOW why a few abdominal twinges last week had sent Franca into a panic. Also, a miscarriage on top of losing her foster daughter would devastate even the strongest person.

"This is a lot to hold inside," Marshall said.

"As a counselor, I know the importance of sharing one's burdens. But I'm supposed to be a source of support for others," Franca countered.

With his thumb, Marshall wiped moisture from her cheek. "As the father of your baby, I'm on your team."

"If I miscarry, you won't be the father anymore." She drew in a shaky breath.

"You assume that would be the end?" He wished she had more faith in him. "After all these years, I'm not going to stop caring about you."

"If this pregnancy falls apart, I may not be up to attempting another one," Franca said. "Having children is very important to you. And I'm aware that you'd never choose to be a foster parent."

Marshall couldn't deny that children were central to his planned future, and to his happiness. As for fostering, her experience with Jazz had if anything reinforced his aversion to taking in a child who might never bond with him or might ultimately be taken away. That didn't mean he'd abandon Franca.

"We don't have to decide anything yet." Marshall saw no point in battling about something that might not happen. "I'm glad you shared this with me."

She smiled. "That was very sweet, singing to me. You showed me a new side of yourself."

"Let's build on that."

Franca clapped her hands. "I don't believe it! You sound like me during a group session."

"Consider me a convert to therapy." In the interest of truth, Marshall qualified: "To a modest extent."

"All the same, I'm thrilled." Her tears appeared to be forgotten.

"Moving forward," Marshall said, "what shall we burn for dinner?"

"It's only three o'clock."

"We have to plan the menu and hit the supermarket."

"Let's go figure it out."

At the store, Marshall goofed around, loading up the cart with cake mixes and tubs of icing "for all the parties we'll throw." French vanilla, triple chocolate, red velvet—how could he resist?

He didn't specify that those parties might be for children. After all, grown-ups could enjoy them, too.

At home, while Franca napped before it was time to begin cooking, Marshall wandered into the playroom-turned-nursery. Usually when he regarded the princess-pink bedspread, the dolls and the stuffed animals, happiness coursed through him. Today, Franca's disclosure made him keenly aware of the fragility of his dreams.

From atop a toy chest, he picked up a stuffed rabbit with floppy ears. Its button eyes peered at him wistfully.

The little girl it belonged to was gone, and with her a big chunk of Franca's heart. How dreadful if she—and he—had to face another loss.

From the window, Marshall gazed down at the cul-de-sac, serene in the lingering sunlight of early June. A small boy rode his tricycle along the sidewalk under his father's supervision. At another house, two school-age girls sat on the porch with cell phones in hand. Judging by their laughter, they were texting each other.

From the day he'd discovered this house, Marshall had imagined his children growing up in it. When he'd learned Franca was pregnant, he'd thought his dream might finally be coming true.

In this quiet moment, he had to assess the implications of what she'd revealed. While miscarriages weren't uncommon, most couples grieved and then renewed their attempts to have a family. What if Franca couldn't do that?

Below, the boy's mother called him and her husband inside for dinner. Marshall's chest ached with longing to be like that man.

He visualized a Norman Rockwell painting of an idealized family gathered around the table, with just enough mischief to avoid mushiness.

Franca had been right that he sought parenthood to compensate for his own childhood. He yearned for the joy and acceptance he'd missed from his judgmental parents. Yet there'd been love, too.

Too bad you couldn't buy a prepackaged future at the supermarket in the flavor of your choice. Instead, he and Franca would have to make the best of whatever fell into their cart.

If necessary, he'd be willing to adopt a healthy infant, not that he expected the process to be easy. Most importantly, Franca would have to accept him for who he was: a traditional guy whose idea of home didn't include losing control to a system that could destroy your family without warning.

FRANCA AWOKE BATHED in fading light touched with gold as it sifted through the curtains of her bedroom. Marshall's song ran through her head: "You'll Never Walk Alone."

It was reassuring that she truly didn't have to walk alone. Until recently, Franca had steamed ahead, expecting help from no one. But pregnancy, coupled with distance from her family, had left her vulnerable. Things that had never bothered her before, such as the prospect of living alone in an apartment, scared her. In Marshall's house, she felt safe.

The scents of broiling salmon and asparagus floated through the partly open door. Her stomach rumbled.

How luxurious, to sleep while Marshall fixed dinner. Franca washed up and smoothed the wrinkles out of her knit top. While her jeans had grown tight, she was reluctant to invest in maternity clothes just yet.

When she descended the stairs, a thrill of anticipation ran through her as she caught sight of Marshall's lanky form moving about the kitchen. At the doorway, she halted to watch him.

Since college, she'd headed off any potentially serious relationship with a man to concentrate on her career and foster parenthood. She'd volunteered at a home for abused women, and taken in several foster children on an emergency basis before Jazz. She'd believed her lack of enthusiasm for the guys she met indicated she was fine without them.

She'd been deceiving herself. Without realizing it,

she'd compared them to a man who attracted and stimulated her even when he infuriated her. A man they couldn't match and whom she had never expected to grow this close to. *This* man.

His lazy smile enveloped her. "Welcome, beautiful dreamer."

"Is that your next song?"

"There's a song called 'Beautiful Dreamer'?"

"You bet. Let's search for the lyrics," she said. "*After* we eat."

"Everything's ready." With a few strides, Marshall reached the kitchen table—more comfortable than the island where they usually ate—and pulled out a chair for her.

He'd already set their places, Franca noticed. "You'll spoil me."

"That's the idea."

He eased her chair forward, his arms reaching around her and his cheek close to hers. Franca rested her head against his chest and wished she could stay there forever.

Hunger prompted her to straighten. "Okay, Chef Davis. Let's sample your creation." Earlier, she'd planned meals for later in the week while he'd kept tonight's menu to himself. At the market, she'd been too amused by the variety of cake mixes in their cart to pay attention to what else he'd put in.

"Hope you like it," Marshall said.

The salmon and asparagus, served with a salad, were delicious. "I'm glad you didn't give up on Jack Ryder's advice," she said.

"Sorry?"

"About preparing dinner for me."

Marshall paused with his water glass in hand. "I forgot about that. I wasn't trying to impress you."

"Even better."

To her, the meal tasted better than anything she'd eaten in a restaurant. Once they'd finished, he brought out his laptop to search for "Beautiful Dreamer." They listened to the Stephen Foster melody a couple of times, then found karaoke accompaniment and joined in together to sing.

Their voices rang through the house, the blend masking most of the muffed notes, in Franca's opinion. Moving to the family room couch, they relaxed side by side with the laptop on Marshall's knees, and ran through a series of other favorites.

"Be sure to thank Owen Tartikoff for me, if you dare," Franca teased.

"My other source of advice scored a home run, too," he said.

"You mean Jack?"

"No, my brother. He told me to be flexible."

"Amazingly, it worked." Curling against Marshall, Franca tipped up her face to his. He set the laptop aside and drew her into a kiss.

How natural it was to taste his mouth and ruffle his hair. Then to rise and climb the stairs hand in hand.

They made love in his king-size bed, more slowly and gently than before. Her pregnant body had developed a heightened sensitivity, so that simply inhaling the scent of his skin sent her floating to the heights. The climax seemed to last for an hour.

Franca drifted off to sleep, snug and free of cares.

MARSHALL LAY AWAKE musing on this astonishing change in their relationship. Bonding with Franca had combined the best of the old days with their increased maturity.

If he'd had a clue how valuable advice could be, he'd have written to Dear Abby long ago. Maybe he still ought to, regarding how to handle his mother. But the answer was obvious: eventually, he'd have to confront her.

Perhaps she'd soften when she learned she was going to be a grandmother. He wasn't eager to mention that to her, though. If Mildred dismissed this miraculous occurrence with a nasty comment, he might never forgive her.

He was dozing off when, dimly, he heard a phone ringing. Blinking awake in the darkness, Marshall took a few beats to register that it must be Franca's phone. She didn't move. Her hormones must have sent her into an unusually deep sleep.

On the carpet, he scrambled for her jeans and drew the cell from the pocket. The readout said *Unknown Caller.*

Should he answer? When she stirred, he clicked to answer and handed her the device. "It's for you."

Franca held the phone to her ear. "Dr. Brightman." After a moment, she said, "Yes, I know Bridget. Please don't call child services. Where is she?"

Who was calling and what had happened to Bridget? From the bedside table, Marshall took a pad and pen, and jotted the address as Franca spoke it aloud.

She listened with only a few comments such as "Really?" and "I understand," before concluding, "Thank you, Hank. I'll be there as fast as I can. Ten, fifteen minutes at most."

It must be police detective Hank Driver, Marshall registered as Franca climbed out of bed. "What's happened?"

"Bridget's been arrested." Franca grabbed her clothes from the floor. "She asked for me to take Jazz."

Though it would be embarrassing for Hank to see them together, Marshall couldn't let her go alone. "I'll drive, if that's all right."

"Thanks," Franca said, and hurried to the bathroom.

No time to consider how they'd deal with this development. Right now, Marshall's job was to protect Franca, and to stay—he was starting to hate the word—flexible.

Chapter Sixteen

The address Hank had provided lay in the town's northeast quadrant, adjacent to the freeway. En route, Franca couldn't resist pressing her foot against the floor of Marshall's silver sedan, as if to speed it up from the passenger side. It was fortunate that he'd offered to drive, because otherwise she'd have been a danger to herself and others.

He'd leaped into action without comment, calmly but swiftly closing up the house and taking the wheel. She was grateful he didn't speak, because she needed the silence to sort out her turmoil.

According to Hank, Axel had been arrested with stolen items in his car. After obtaining a search warrant for his apartment, police had found enough evidence to put Bridget under suspicion as well. He'd provided no further details, saying the case remained under investigation.

The Safe Harbor police were trained in sensitivity to arrestees' children, Franca was aware. Unless they observed signs of abuse or neglect, they entrusted a child to an alternative caregiver designated by the parent rather than handing them to protective services. Mercifully, Bridget had requested her.

Did Bridget intend for Franca to keep the four-year-old long-term, or was her request a stopgap measure? That might depend on whatever the charges were against Bridget and whether she was released on bail.

How were these events affecting Jazz? Having police officers search her home and confront her mother must be frightening, no matter how sensitively they handled it.

At the apartment complex, Marshall slotted his car into a space marked for visitors. "I'll come in with you."

"Okay." His willingness to stand by her without complaint or criticism was a good start. A good start to what, she had no idea.

In her haste, Franca knocked on the wrong door. Marshall caught up with her. "It's 214, not 114," he said. Since no one answered, she was spared an awkward apology.

With a hand on her spine, he guided her up the outdoor staircase. His strength steadied her.

Hank must have been watching, because the stocky detective opened the door at their approach. "You got here fast." He nodded at Marshall, although the detective must have been surprised to see him. And curious.

"It felt like forever." Stepping past him, Franca took in the cluttered living room, the coffee table covered with beer cans and take-out containers. On the walls, someone had tacked posters of tattooed motorcyclists and video game–style warriors. Bits of paper littered the worn carpet.

Where was Jazz? Franca was about to ask when she spotted Bridget huddled in a chair, her light brown hair askew. "Are you all right?"

"I screwed up." Bridget frowned past her at Marshall. "What's *he* doing here?"

They'd run into each other at the café, Franca recalled. "I hope you don't mind. Dr. Davis was with me when I got the call." She kept her tone professional but gentle. Offending Bridget, especially in her fragile state, might affect her decision about Jazz.

"He's a doctor?" Bridget shrugged. "I guess that's okay."

Marshall seemed about to reply, but apparently thought the better of it. His natural reticence was the perfect attitude in this situation, a counterpoint to Franca's tendency to over-empathize.

"Do you want me to call a lawyer?" she asked.

"I already did." Tears glistened against Bridget's lashes. "That stupid Axel. And stupid me." She said nothing further, probably aware that Hank was listening.

Franca couldn't contain her anxiety any longer. "Where's Jazz?"

"In her room talking to Officer Jorgas," Hank said. "If you'll hang on, I'll check on the child."

Before he could move, however, an inner door flew open and a black-haired sprite darted out. "Mommy Franca!"

Behind her appeared a uniformed police officer, her brown hair pulled into a bun. "She heard their voices. I couldn't stop her."

"It's okay, Jorgas," Hank said.

Everything else vanished from Franca's awareness as she dropped to her knees on the carpet. She barely had time to brace before Jazz flew into her arms.

ON ENTERING, MARSHALL had been struck by the odors of beer and food scraps. While people might suffer financial hardship, they didn't have to live in squalor.

You aren't here to judge. He shifted his attention to

Bridget. Her wilted demeanor formed a contrast to the aggressive manner she'd shown several weeks ago at the café, yet in the jut of her chin he read a touchy pride. He wondered what she and her lout of a boyfriend had been involved in.

In charged a little bundle of fear and joy. Although he couldn't see Franca's expression, he sensed her happiness as she hugged the girl.

A glimpse of Jazz's tearstained face above Franca's shoulder wrenched Marshall's heart. If only he could lower a shining globe of protection around them both.

In her chair, Bridget shivered. When she glanced his way, he ducked his head to hide any hint of criticism. He didn't want to arouse any further resentment from her.

Franca addressed the girl in her arms. "Your mommy's asked me to look after you for a while."

"I have to go with the police," Bridget told her daughter. "I should be able to come get you soon."

That spelled another emotional rollercoaster for Franca, exactly what a pregnant woman didn't need. And more disruption for Jazz.

Marshall's job was to soften the blows. Meanwhile, he forced himself to keep his peace.

"Did I do something wrong?" Jazz asked her mother. Releasing her, Franca straightened.

"Of course not." Bridget reached out for her daughter's hand. "Sweetheart, when grown-ups mess up, it isn't a child's fault."

To Marshall, that seemed like something Franca might say. Perhaps Bridget had learned it from her.

Hank, who'd been talking with the other officer, swung around. At the sudden movement, Jazz shrank against her mother. "Make him go away!"

"He won't hurt you," Bridget said.

The detective squatted down to the child's level. "Hi, Jazz. I'm Hank. You're going home with Dr. Brightman—Mommy Franca," he said. "While we take care of the paperwork, Officer Jorgas will help you pack, okay?"

With a nod, Jazz went into the bedroom, followed by the uniformed woman. Hank addressed Bridget. "Please fill in Dr. Brightman about your daughter's schedule, medical issues and habits."

"She's more familiar with those than me," the woman said. "Just show me where to sign."

Watching as Hank handled the paperwork, Marshall admired his patience. This was a far cry from the way TV shows portrayed law enforcement. The detective even checked that Franca had brought a car seat. Fortunately, she'd put one in Marshall's car before they left.

It was late by the time they hit the road. Franca sat in the rear next to Jazz, who drooped against her. The little girl hadn't responded when Franca had introduced her to Marshall. He must seem like one more faceless adult drifting through her turbulent world. She had a lot to process, and was obviously exhausted.

When they reached his driveway, Jazz stared at the house in confusion. "Is this a hotel?"

"No, honey, it's our new home," Franca said.

"Oh."

After parking in the garage, Marshall rounded the car to Jazz's side. "Shall I carry her?"

"Who're you?" Jazz demanded.

"This is my friend Marshall, remember?" Franca unbuckled the child. "He's a doctor."

Jazz scowled. "I want him to leave."

"He lives here, too," Franca said.

Marshall held the car door for them. "I'm glad you're staying with us."

Scrambling out of the seat, Jazz refused to meet his gaze. "Let's get you to bed." Holding the child's hand, Franca took her inside. Marshall followed with the suitcase, a doll and a stuffed animal.

He wondered how the house appeared to Jazz. Big and strange, no doubt. And from her past experience, she knew not to consider it permanent.

His emotions were being tugged in opposite directions. While he could hardly wait for life to return to normal—the new normal in which he and Franca were lovers—he understood how upsetting it would be for Franca when and if her daughter left. Also, now that he'd visited the unkempt apartment on top of having met the brutish Axel, it troubled him to picture Jazz living under those circumstances.

"Are you hungry?" Franca asked.

The girl's dark hair shook no.

Upstairs in the playroom, Marshall set down the suitcase. Surely Jazz would relax when she found her familiar items arrayed around the space.

Instead, her body went rigid. "Why is my stuff here?" Her voice trembled. "I want to go home!"

Which home did she mean? Apparently Franca understood, because she answered, "When I moved here, I brought your stuff with me."

"I want my room!"

Franca knelt beside her. "Honey, I live here now. This is a much nicer place. And tomorrow you can go to the hospital day care and play with your old friends. They miss you."

That did the trick. "Okay."

"Anything else I can do?" Marshall asked.

"No, thanks. You've been great." Franca's weary

smile reminded him of the tender moments that had been interrupted.

"See you in a few minutes?" In front of Jazz, he stopped short of inviting her to his bedroom, but surely she'd be happier sleeping in his arms. And they could talk about the evening's events.

"It may take a while for Jazz to get settled."

"Of course." He said good-night and went out.

In his suite, Marshall left the door ajar and sat down to read a medical journal. But he couldn't focus on the words as he listened to noises from down the hall. Franca's soothing tones accompanied their movements as she showed the newcomer to the bathroom and took out sheets and towels.

Would Bridget drag her daughter back and forth as she went through the legal process? It wasn't fair to treat Franca as a free babysitter or subject a child to such uncertainty.

The memory of that sour-smelling apartment twisted inside him. Taking in a foster child hadn't been part of his plan, but he could never send Jazz back to that place. Marshall forced his attention on to an article about new techniques in freezing and thawing ovarian tissue. It offered the potential to preserve fertility for women facing chemotherapy.

A shriek yanked him from his reading. Leaping up, Marshall broke into a run.

FRANCA WAS WELL aware that she ought to remain calm and reassuring, no matter what the provocation. That didn't offset her physical exhaustion or today's emotional strain.

After reading a picture book aloud, she could barely stay awake. She was tucking Jazz into bed when, for the thousandth time, the little girl demanded to go "home" to their old apartment.

"This is home now," Franca snapped.

"I won't sleep here!" The tantrum reminded her of Jazz's toddler days. "Take me to my mommy."

"Not tonight." Franca barely refrained from pointing out that Bridget was no doubt at the police station this very minute.

"I hate you!" the little girl lashed out, and swung her doll by the leg.

When pain flared, Franca screamed. Instantly, she saw Jazz's horror at inflicting injury on Franca. Then she heard heavy footsteps racing toward the playroom.

Marshall. He'd been a pillar of strength for her, but to Jazz, he was a large, menacing stranger.

Whatever he said or did now would make all the difference.

THE SIGHT OF Franca's bleeding forehead sent rage jolting through Marshall. "What the hell?"

On the bed, Jazz stuck out her lower lip. "My dolly hit her."

He took in the plastic figure the girl was clutching by its leg. "That's a lie. *You* hit her."

"Marshall, she's been through a lot." Franca's warning tone did nothing to assuage his anger.

"Don't make excuses for her." Oddly, he heard his father's voice infusing his, as if he were repeating words heard long ago, although he didn't recall Upton Davis ever yelling at him. To Jazz, he roared, "Shame on you!"

Her glare matched his. "Leave me alone. You're a meanie!"

Franca's hand on his elbow tempered Marshall's fury as her earlier words sank in. What did he expect from a kid who'd had such a rough upbringing? More quietly, he said, "Apologize."

"No!"

Franca's grip became insistent. "I'd like to speak to you outside."

His jaw clenched, Marshall accompanied her to the hall. She shut the door and led him far enough away that their voices shouldn't carry.

"I snapped at her, and she reached her breaking point," Franca said.

"That's no excuse for hitting you."

"It isn't serious."

"It could have been." While Marshall didn't wish to exaggerate, neither would he tolerate an out-of-control child who, at age four, was beyond the toddler stage. "What if she had kicked you in the stomach?"

"She didn't."

In view of the blood welling along the cut in Franca's forehead, that failed to reassure him. "You're in denial about how vulnerable you are. While I understand that she has to stay here for now, she's big enough to harm you and the baby. Think about the future."

She stiffened, and when she tried to speak, no words emerged. Maybe she was gripped by mixed emotions, too. Being struck must have shocked her almost as much as him.

"Let's treat that cut." In the bathroom, Marshall took antiseptic and an adhesive bandage from the medicine cabinet. After washing his hands, he cleaned the area around the injury and applied the bandage.

"Will I live?" Franca asked wryly.

"Hopefully for many years." She still hadn't responded to his comments. "What are you thinking?" he asked.

"That what you and I share is precious, but I love Jazz." She swallowed. "Don't force me to choose."

"I hope it won't come to that." How could he risk alienating Franca? Also, she'd be in even more danger isolated with this unruly girl.

Marshall understood the necessity of making allowances for a child in crisis. Nevertheless, he refused to abandon his basic values regarding his family, and those didn't include tolerating physical violence. If Jazz behaved this way now, how much worse might she become around a baby, a rival for Franca's affection?

"It may not be our decision if her mother gets out on bail," he said.

"I realize that." Franca folded her arms. "Marshall, there's a lot about you that's terrific."

"Hold on to that thought." He didn't ask about the "but" implied in her statement. No sense revisiting the fact that she considered him insensitive and unbending when he was only doing his best for her.

She nodded, acquiescing. "I'd better go reassure Jazz that I'm not angry."

Although dubious about the risk of another tantrum, Marshall had to trust her judgment. "Call me if you need me. I promise to hang on to my temper."

"Will do."

They kissed lightly and held each other. Then she returned to the playroom.

Filled with apprehension, he went to bed alone.

"ARE YOU OKAY, Mommy Franca?" Huddling beneath the covers, Jazz studied her anxiously.

"Dr. Marshall fixed me up." Franca sat on the edge of the bed.

"My dolly was bad." Blue eyes watched for her response.

Marshall hadn't been entirely wrong, Franca conceded. Jazz had picked up bad habits, such as blaming others for her actions.

"Sweetheart, your dolly didn't hit me. You did," she said. "Even when you're frustrated, it's wrong to hurt others."

Jazz hugged her knees and stared fiercely at the wall.

"When you get mad at your friends, you can't hit them." At day care, Jazz could be expelled if she lashed out physically.

"I won't."

"Now will you apologize?" Franca asked.

Jazz bit her lip before saying, "What's *apologize* mean?"

She must have refused as a reflex. "It means saying you're sorry."

"I'm sorry, Mommy." The girl threw her arms around Franca and snuggled close. In a way, it reminded her of hugging Marshall a few minutes ago.

She treasured his kindness, yet she couldn't expect him to change his basic attitude toward parenting. Nor was it possible to transform a troubled child with a snap of her fingers. How could she care so deeply for two people who were utterly incompatible?

If push came to shove, Franca had to choose the one who needed her most. And that was the child whose arms were wrapped around her right now.

Her heart ached.

Chapter Seventeen

In the morning, Jazz demanded doughnuts for breakfast, which was what Bridget had been feeding her.
When Franca refused, the little girl knocked over her
glass of milk.

Franca's throat tightened at the sight of Marshall's
scowl. *Not another showdown, please.*

Jazz righted the glass and mopped at the spilled milk
with her napkin. "I'm sorry."

"Apology accepted," he replied.

That wasn't easy for Marshall to say, Franca guessed.
She was glad Jazz now understood what an apology was
and when to offer one.

While he cleaned up, the little girl ate her oatmeal
and fruit without further protest. She got dressed for
day care promptly, too.

Franca wasn't naive enough to believe the storms had
ended. She was grateful for the break, though. *Take one
day at a time,* she repeated silently.

At the hospital, eager greetings from friends brought
out Jazz's sunny side. Later, Franca got good news when
she had her blood pressure checked. Despite recent
events, it was within acceptable levels.

Her nausea remained mild and she'd gained a healthy,
modest amount of weight. Her assistant, Maggie, who'd

been thrilled to learn of the pregnancy, recommended a visit to the Baby Bump for maternity clothes.

"It's early," Franca responded as she headed into her office. "I still fit into my looser stuff."

"You'll be sticking out to here before you know it. I did with my daughter." Maggie had both a seven-year-old daughter and a teenage stepson.

"You did a fine job of dropping the weight," Franca replied. At nearly thirty, Maggie had a great figure.

"I could still lose a few pounds." The assistant shrugged. "Don't worry. I'm not jumping into some diet fad."

Franca was pleased at having ducked the subject. No sense buying a bunch of clothes she'd have to donate to the thrift store if she miscarried.

She had to stop thinking that way. A negative mindset might affect her health. Also, she faced more urgent matters.

Shortly after lunch came the nervously anticipated call from Bridget. "You're out on bail?" Franca asked, after assuring her that Jazz was fine.

"The judge released me on my own recognizance."

"I'm glad to hear it." In her office chair, Franca tried to prepare for a demand to hand over the girl. She hoped Bridget grasped how hard it was on the child to be dragged back and forth. "I don't want to pry, but are the charges against you serious?"

Bridget didn't flare up. Instead, she spoke candidly. "Axel got caught stealing packages off people's porches. When the cops searched his car, they found fake IDs and other stuff." She sucked in a deep breath. "We were stealing people's identities online. I was dumb to let him talk me into this, but we were broke. Anyway, my lawyer says I might be able to cut a deal by testifying against him."

What did this mean for Jazz? Franca wondered. "A deal would let you avoid prison?"

"That's up to the DA."

"What about Axel?"

"That's the scary part," Bridget said. "If he finds out I'm a witness, there's no predicting what he'll do."

Franca shuddered at the idea of that abusive man on the loose. "Isn't he still in jail?"

"His gang buddies might raise bail for him," Bridget said. "I'm staying at a women's shelter in case he gets out. Will you hold on to my daughter a while longer?"

"Of course." Although Marshall might not like this, he'd indicated he would let Jazz stay, at least temporarily. "Have you considered the long term, though? I'm not trying to push you."

The silence on the other end worried her. At last Bridget spoke. "I figured it would be easy to raise her now that she's older, but she can be stubborn. Let me think it over, okay?"

"Sure."

"Oh, I have a new phone number." To prevent Axel from harrassing her, Franca presumed. "Ready?"

"Yes." As Bridget recited the number, Franca entered it in her cell.

"I'll be in touch soon. Tell Jazz I love her."

"You bet."

Swiveling her chair, Franca stared out the window. From five stories up on a clear June day, she had a view over the bluffs to the Pacific Ocean. Her thoughts were far from peaceful, however.

If Axel were freed, Bridget might take her daughter and disappear, before or after the trial. Or she might agree to relinquish her permanently, in which case Franca would gain a daughter and lose the man she loved.

She dreaded both possibilities.

AFTER FRANCA TEXTED that Jazz would be staying a few more days, Marshall resolved to make the best of the situation. If he tried hard enough, perhaps he'd break through the little girl's shell and find the kind of loving spirit he treasured in Caleb and Linda. Her apology at breakfast had been a good sign.

That evening, he offered to babysit while Franca shopped for maternity clothes. Jazz raised such a ruckus, however, that Franca took her along.

"I'm the only stable person in her life," she explained when he questioned her decision.

"Aren't you teaching her that it pays to throw a tantrum?" he asked.

"Give the kid a break. She's having a rough time."

So was Franca, he observed. However, arguing was pointless.

At the office the next day, Zady asked Marshall to bring Franca and Jazz to a start-of-summer party she and Nick were throwing for Caleb that Saturday. "We've invited his grandparents and a bunch of his friends."

"Terrific." Surely Jazz would enjoy a party, and seeing Marshall with Caleb might reassure Jazz that he wasn't an ogre. "I have surgery that morning, so I'll be late."

"Oh, it doesn't start till noon. Nick works the overnight shift on Fridays and he sleeps in."

"That'll be fine."

That evening, before Marshall could convey the invitation, Jazz refused to sit down to dinner. "I want a new dress!" She stamped her foot.

"A girl at day care wore a pink dress similar to one she used to have," Franca told him. "I gather it got stained and Bridget tossed it out." To Jazz, she said, "When I have a chance, I'll sew one for you. We can pick out the fabric together."

"I want it now!"

"No, honey. Let's eat."

It took ten minutes of stomping and pouting before the girl accepted defeat. During dinner, Marshall remained on edge in case Jazz knocked over her glass or otherwise created an uproar.

However, she behaved, and went to bed calmly. "She's behaved well this evening," Franca said. "Maybe I should slip out and buy her the dress."

"You've got to be kidding." Noting the concern on her heart-shaped face, Marshall understood the impulse to indulge someone you loved. But he didn't believe that was the way to raise a child.

"I suppose you're right." Franca curled beside him on the family-room sofa, her cheek on his shoulder.

Remembering Zady's invitation, Marshall repeated it to her. "It should be fun."

"I'd love to go." Franca sighed. "I suspect a party is more than Jazz can handle at this stage, though. Any frustration will throw her off the rails."

Reluctantly, he agreed, and texted their regrets.

Franca arranged for Jennifer Martin to babysit Jazz at her house during Thursday evening's group session. The little girl jumped at the idea, excited about playing with Jennifer's daughter, Rosalie. Her friend, being a year older, attended kindergarten rather than day care.

At the session, the group received the happy news

that Hank Driver's wife was pregnant. "Also, we're communicating better now," the detective said. "She *does* trust me not to cheat, but she appreciated my reassurances." He added that he'd decided to leave the men's group. He and his wife planned to join one as a couple.

After the session, he shook hands with Marshall and Franca. "How's the little girl doing?"

"Pretty well," Marshall said.

"I appreciate your calling me," Franca put in.

"This kind of situation is tough on kids." Hank broke off as another client came up to talk to them. They had no chance to ask the detective anything more about the case.

At home, a weary Jazz let Marshall carry her into the house. In his arms, she felt small and helpless, her face soft as she dozed.

"Jennifer said she and Rosalie had a ball," Franca told him on the way upstairs. He'd waited in the car while she went into Jennifer's house to pick up Jazz.

Marshall gazed down at the child cradled against him. Perhaps he could grow to love her.

On Friday afternoon, Cole Rattigan took Marshall on a private tour of the remodeled Portia and Vincent Adams Memorial Medical Building across the drive from the hospital. The new features included a curving front portico and a graceful, high-ceilinged lobby.

The upper stories housed labs and operating suites for the men's program. Despite the lack of carpet and furnishings, the two floors of office space were invitingly spacious.

"It's on track to be finished ahead of schedule," the eminent surgeon said as they descended in the whisper-quiet elevator. "We decided to move up the official opening." He provided a date near the end of June.

"Isn't that rather soon? There's a lot of interior work unfinished."

"We won't be able to move in by the opening." The doctor finger-combed his overgrown brown hair. "But many staff members schedule vacations during July and August, and we'd like a full complement at the ceremony."

"That makes sense." Marshall recalled the suggestions he'd read on the bulletin board. "Will there be a band? A light-and-sound show?" *Or weird-shaped balloons?*

"Still to be determined." Cole smiled. "Speeches! You can count on plenty of those."

As they left the building, it occurred to Marshall that while seeking advice, he'd never asked how Cole had won his wife, Stacy, who'd been his surgical nurse. According to the grapevine, she'd been pregnant with triplets but had initially rejected Cole's proposal. "May I ask a personal question?"

"Shoot," Cole responded cheerfully.

"You've heard that Franca and I are having a baby?"

"Congratulations!"

"She refuses to marry me," Marshall admitted. "I could use ideas."

"You're asking me?" Despite being nearly forty, Cole radiated a gleeful innocence. "I'm honored."

"Any tips from your experience?"

The surgeon paused on the sidewalk. "Stace considered me clueless on how to be a husband, and she had a point."

"How'd you fix that?"

"It was a steep learning curve," the other doctor said. "I just kept plugging away at figuring out what she expected from me. I also had to accept that being a god figure in the OR didn't mean I was one at home."

"So I've discovered."

"By the way," Cole said. "If Owen Tartikoff suggests singing to her, ignore him."

"Why?"

"He has a fantastic voice," Cole explained. "Most of us are less gifted."

"Too late."

But the surgeon's remarks echoed in Marshall's mind. He *was* growing more aware of Franca's emotions and views, and she seemed to be opening up to him. Perhaps eventually she'd accept him as being husband material, too.

It would be easier if Jazz's mom reclaimed her, yet the prospect troubled him. The child he'd carried to her room last night deserved a mother *and* a father, and showed signs of beginning to accept him. Once she adapted to their routine, she might not be so high-strung.

At the end of the day, he was walking to his car when Zady phoned. "I'm picking up Caleb at day care. You should get over here."

In the background, he heard a little girl screaming, "Take me home! Our real home, not that new house!"

He heard Franca's voice responding. While he couldn't discern the words, her tone was ragged.

"I'll be right there." He thanked his sister-in-law and reversed direction toward the hospital.

The day care center lay on the ground floor adjacent to the cafeteria. Near the entrance, Franca knelt beside the howling preschooler. The center's director, Maureen Arthur, watched with folded arms, her glasses halfway down her nose.

"We'll go out to dinner," Franca coaxed. "How about Waffle Heaven?"

"No!" the red-faced girl cried. "I won't go!"

"You're bribing her with junk food?" Marshall asked.

Franca shot him a mind-your-own-business glare. "Waffle Heaven has salads."

"You're rewarding misbehavior," he said. As a psychologist, surely she knew that, but he supposed stress and emotions had the power to short-circuit rational thought.

The day care director nodded.

"Go away!" Jazz yelled at Marshall. "I hate you!"

So much for warming toward him. It hurt to discover that while he'd believed they were making progress, the little girl still viewed him as the enemy.

"We could eat at Krazy Kids Pizza," Franca offered.

"It's best not to negotiate," Maureen told her gently. "When a child throws a tantrum, try to distract her."

Or give her a swat on the bottom. That was what his parents would have done. Still, spanking a child who might have witnessed her mother being abused seemed like a bad idea.

"Maybe I have a toy in here." Franca dug through her purse.

"I don't want a toy!"

Marshall addressed the child in a level tone. "This is a hospital. There are sick people here and your screaming hurts their ears."

Jazz appeared to be weighing his comment. Mercifully, she stopped shouting.

Franca's cell jingled. Plucking it from her purse, she scanned the readout. "Oh, dear. This is important."

"Dr. Davis and I will handle this," the director assured her.

"Thanks." Franca retreated to a secluded corner.

"Can I see them?" Jazz asked.

Marshall focused on the child. "See who?"

"The sick people."

"When you're sick, do you want strangers coming in your room?" he asked.

"I guess not."

"It appears you have this under control," Maureen murmured. "You have a father's instincts, Dr. Davis."

The compliment pleased him enormously. If only Franca had heard it, but she was absorbed in her conversation.

"WHEN I WAS growing up, I kept running away from foster homes," Bridget said to Franca over the phone. "I had this fantasy about living with my mother. When I finally found her, though, she was a mess. Like I am now."

"That must have been awful." Franca nearly held her breath, afraid Bridget would retract what she'd said moments earlier: that she'd decided to let Franca adopt Jazz after all.

"I can't handle being tied down with a kid. Maybe some moms can do that at twenty-three, but not me." Bridget coughed. "And I'm scared."

"Is Axel out of jail?"

"No, but I saw one of his gang buddies near the shelter." Her voice trembled. "The address is supposed to be secret but... Maybe he was just in the neighborhood by accident."

"Did he recognize you?"

"I can't take that chance. I moved to another shelter, but what if he finds me again? This is no way to raise a kid." Bridget went on to say that as soon as her legal troubles were resolved, if she didn't land in prison, she planned to leave the area and start over. "I don't want to haul Jazz halfway across the country. She deserves a real home."

Unexpectedly, doubts gripped Franca. How was she to raise two children alone, especially with Jazz lashing out? Well, she'd manage. She would never break her commitment to the little girl.

"I can set up an appointment with Edmond." He'd been invaluable during their previous adoption proceedings.

"I like him," Bridget agreed. "The sooner you can set it up, the better. And bring Jazz, will you? I want to assure her I love her, that this is for her sake."

"Of course. Let me call you back."

To Franca's relief, she reached the attorney, who set a meeting for midday Saturday at his private office. After notifying Bridget, Franca clicked off with the most turbulent feelings she'd ever experienced.

She stiffened her resolve. There was no turning back from the path she'd set herself on, regardless of the fallout.

Now she had to break the news to Marshall.

Chapter Eighteen

When Franca told him what had happened, Marshall was glad for her sake and for Jazz's. Unless the girl's unstable mother reneged again, Franca would finally get what she'd yearned for since that night when they had both howled their distress into the cavernous parking structure.

Yet an icy rock formed in his chest during Franca's summary of Bridget's remarks. Marshall could summon only rote responses—"I see" and "Uh-huh." Even if his coldness disappointed her, how could he explain his reaction when he didn't understand it himself?

A grumbling Jazz stopped playing with a tablet the day care director had lent her. "I'm hungry."

"We all are," he said. And tired, and standing in a corridor within earshot of passersby. "Krazy Kids Pizza has play equipment." Marshall often drove past the place on Safe Harbor Boulevard. "Let's stop there for dinner."

"I thought you objected to bribing a child with junk food," Franca remarked.

"Since she's no longer throwing a tantrum, this isn't a bribe," Marshall said. "It's an executive decision."

"Might as well," she conceded. "I'm in no mood to cook."

Since they'd arrived in separate cars, he didn't get to listen while Franca broke the good news to Jazz.

At the box-shaped restaurant, its interior teeth-achingly bright with primary colors, the little girl clung to Franca's hand. If she was bursting with excitement or consumed by fear, Marshall couldn't tell. Perhaps, like him, she was struggling to adjust to this development.

The pizza lived up to its bad reputation: overly sweet tomato sauce and thin toppings on a cardboard crust. Jazz loved it. After downing two slices along with a few sips of juice, she dashed off to the welter of tunnels and platforms.

His legs cramped beneath the red table, Marshall squinted in the lingering sunshine. They'd chosen an outdoor spot to be near the play equipment. It was also near exhaust fumes and traffic noise, although those shortcomings didn't appear to bother their fellow diners. Young couples, middle-aged duos and grandparents chatted, played with their phones and watched the kids clambering about.

Other people had a quality that Marshall seemed to lack: the ability to accept life with all its flaws. After surviving the ups and downs of the past weeks, he'd hit a brick wall. It would be dishonest to pretend he could tolerate a household without boundaries, or that he was the right father for a troubled child.

Across the table sat the woman he'd struggled not to love for fifteen years—and fallen for anyway. Despite everything that had occurred between them, though, he couldn't be the man she needed, and she didn't love him the way he was, with all *his* flaws.

They ought to be discussing the future. But the fact that they wouldn't share it weighed on Marshall so heavily he could hardly breathe.

FRANCA SEARCHED IN vain for a hint of the warmth she believed lay beneath Marshall's hard surface. Where was the man who'd carried a sleeping Jazz into the house with tenderness transforming his face?

Whatever love he was capable of had evidently reached its limits. She'd never understood how he could have thrown away his relationship with Belle after behaving as if he meant to marry her. And for such a petty reason as having to drop a class.

She'd hoped, foolishly, that he'd changed. Now, confronted by the reality of raising a difficult child, he'd closed up like a fortress.

Still, they couldn't simply walk away from the situation. "We have to make some decisions," she said.

Marshall roused from his reverie. "Let's start with the fact that you shouldn't be alone while you're pregnant."

"That's all you care about, my pregnancy? Not Jazz?" It was hard to accept his indifference to the little girl, who was giggling as she played hide-and-seek with another youngster. But it reminded Franca of the fragility of the thread that linked her to Marshall, a thread that would snap if she miscarried. "I'll buy a medical alert system."

"That isn't enough, although I'll be happy to pay for one." He spoke stiffly, as if addressing a not-very-cooperative patient. "We can work out an arrangement for you both to live at my house."

"What kind of arrangement?"

"We'll establish rules that Jazz has to abide by, with consequences if she doesn't," Marshall said. "That may seem strict, but if she can't accept discipline, she'll pose a danger to you and our baby."

This was wrong on many levels. Franca started with

the most offensive one. "You act as if she's a juvenile delinquent who should be sentenced to jail. A four-year-old accepting discipline—what does that even mean? Marching in lockstep and never having a meltdown? And what do you suppose it will do to her self-esteem to live with a man who views her as his baby's enemy, who dotes on his child but cracks down on her?"

"That's not what I meant." His jaw tightened until she wondered how he could force out the words. "A child has to respect authority. If she doesn't obey her parents, she'll never succeed in school or in society."

If she doesn't obey like a well-trained puppy, she'll never succeed? Incredible. He was ready to write off a preschooler as a hopeless case on the basis of a few temper tantrums. "Jazz is my responsibility," Franca said. "I'll make the rules for her."

"She should be *our* responsibility."

"Not as long as your idea of parenting borders on medieval." This discussion was about to degenerate into a nasty argument. Time to call it quits. "Jazz and I will leave as soon as I can rent a place."

His chest heaved. "If you insist, I can't stop you. But what about after the baby's born? We'll be sharing custody, I presume."

"I can't plan that far ahead." Especially since, like her mother and sister, she might not make it past the first trimester. "We'll deal with how to co-parent the baby later."

They didn't realize Jazz had returned to the table until she asked, "What baby?" As the girl reached for her unfinished juice, Franca chided herself for not paying closer attention.

Marshall ducked his head. "Little kids, big ears. Reminds me of Caleb."

Franca did her best to answer simply and openly. "I'm pregnant," she told the girl. "If everything goes well, the baby should be born by Christmas."

Jazz paused with the cup in hand. "Where will I sleep?"

"You'll have your own room as soon as I find an apartment. We can't move back to our old place. It's too far from where I work," she said. "And the baby will have a room, too."

Jazz looked confused, understandably. Franca would have preferred to delay the news about her pregnancy.

"We won't live in Marshall's house?"

"It'll be better this way," Franca said. "Then you and he won't fight about things. It'll be fine."

"No!" Judging by her rebellious expression, that juice was about to get tossed.

"Stop!" Marshall barked.

The girl flinched and set the cup on the table. Although the command had achieved the desired result, Jazz's fearful reaction shook Franca.

"Let's go." She didn't add "home," because Marshall's house no longer fit that description.

AWAKENING IN THE middle of the night, Marshall did something he hadn't done since childhood. He went to sit on the top of the stairs and listen.

No house was completely quiet, and in this one he always heard the murmur of the surf from below the bluffs. Also, despite the sturdy construction, the twitter of night birds penetrated the house's walls, along with the distant rumble of trucks along the coast highway.

After a while, those noises faded, and he discerned the creak of a bed as Franca or Jazz shifted around. The soft sigh of breathing drifted to him.

He used to sit this way because he was lonely. His awareness of his parents safely tucked in bed had reminded him that no matter how angry they got, they'd still be there.

Now his loneliness had grown as large and solid as a tumor. He hadn't meant to force Franca to choose between him and Jazz. She was the only woman he'd ever loved and maybe the only one he ever would. He knew she cared for him, too. Sadly, not enough to meet him halfway.

How could he resolve their differences when she was supposed to be the expert on relationships? While the day care director had complimented him on his parenting instincts, Franca disagreed.

Tonight, the house vibrated with her presence. But already, Marshall felt it throbbing with the emptiness to come.

SATURDAY MORNING, FRANCA awoke on the edge of a dream. It faded instantly, but she recalled that it had featured Bridget.

How would the other woman react to seeing her daughter at the law office? Would her unpredictable emotions once again tip in the other direction, like a boat on a stormy ocean?

As she and Jazz ate breakfast with Marshall, Franca had an irrational impulse to lean on his strength. She almost wished he could accompany them to Edmond's for moral support, which was a ridiculous notion. If anything, having him around would probably antagonize Bridget and upset Jazz. Besides, he had several surgeries scheduled today.

The little girl didn't throw a tantrum, for once. Surprisingly, she helped Marshall set the table, and when he poured her milk, she thanked him.

"You're welcome." He regarded the child with an unreadable expression.

Franca couldn't assess what their interaction might mean. She was too worried about what lay ahead.

After Marshall departed, she let Jazz watch cartoons while she reviewed the material she'd saved from the last adoption effort. They had agreed that she would provide Bridget with twice-yearly reports on Jazz's development, including photos. Once Jazz reached high-school age, she could choose whether to have regular visits, assuming that Bridget was available.

Those stipulations seemed fair. They reminded Franca that Bridget could be quite reasonable—under the right circumstances.

The rest of the morning passed slowly. They read picture books and played with dolls and stuffed animals, which Jazz arrayed on the staircase. She objected when Franca instructed her to put them away for lunch.

"They're waiting for Marshall," she said. "He'll carry them to my room."

What an odd thing to say. "We have to clear them away ourselves. He might…" She shouldn't assume he'd be angry. "…trip over them."

"Okay." Jazz addressed her toys as she gathered them in her arms. "You guys be nice. No tantrums."

Was she that frightened of a scolding? The sooner they moved out, the better, Franca thought, and hurried to fix lunch before their appointment.

Except for the two half days a week when he consulted at the hospital, Edmond practiced family law at Geoff Humphreys and Associates. It was located on the ground floor in a strip mall between a dentist's office and a convenience store.

As soon as they parked, Bridget appeared from around a corner. Her flip-flops slapping the sidewalk, she sped over and grabbed Jazz's hand.

"Let's go," she said. "Now!"

The little girl peered up at Franca pleadingly. Despite Franca's attempts to prepare for the worst, she hadn't anticipated this.

The session was over before it had begun.

THE CONCERNS THAT Marshall had suppressed during the morning rushed back as he left the hospital. His instincts urged him to drive to the attorney's office, to lend whatever help he could to Franca.

But if he'd learned anything from her, it was to mistrust his instincts. This morning, Jazz had tried to please him. Was it possible she was changing, or, as Franca seemed to believe, was she simply afraid of him?

For most of his life, Marshall had kept his anxieties to himself, viewing emotion as a weakness. Yet recently, he'd found that when he sought advice, no one scorned him. And in fact, their advice had been useful.

The person who knew him best, in a clear-sighted if not necessarily flattering sense, was his brother. When he reached that conclusion, his car was already headed for Nick's house.

A cluster of balloons tied to the mailbox puzzled him, until he remembered that his brother and Zady were hosting a party. *Great timing, Marshall.*

After wedging his sedan into a spot down the block, Marshall drummed his fingers on the steering wheel. He couldn't leave. He had to talk to his brother.

He pressed Nick's number on his cell. "Can you meet me outside? I need your opinion, and it's urgent."

"My medical opinion?" his brother asked.

"No. Personal."

"I'm your go-to guy on personal matters?" Nick crowed. "Wouldn't miss it for the world."

Leave it to his brother to preen at his expense. If Marshall had anyone else to consult... But he didn't.

As he approached along the sidewalk, Marshall heard the clamor of children's voices from the rear yard. In the living room, the curtains fluttered, marking the presence of additional guests inside.

Nick emerged from a narrow side yard and stopped in the driveway, out of sight of the living room. "Hey, bro. What's up?"

"It's Franca." Hands jammed in his pockets, Marshall sketched the situation about the forthcoming adoption and her plans to move out. "I'm trying to accept Jazz, but how can I when she throws tantrums, and I mean big ones? She whacked Franca in the forehead and drew blood."

"How much?" Nick asked.

Although the sight had jolted Marshall, the cut had healed quickly. "A trace."

His brother leaned against the garage wall, heedless of dirtying his already-soiled T-shirt and jeans. "Caleb was rude to Zady when I took him away from his grandparents. He never hit her, though."

"She might outgrow it." Marshall paused as a motor home rumbled past. "But with a baby coming, how can we risk its safety?"

"You really believe she's that dangerous?" Nick probed.

Marshall hated to think the worst of a small child.

However, he couldn't afford to be naive when he was responsible for protecting his family. "What if Jazz has violent traits that keep re-emerging as she gets bigger? We won't have a chance of curbing them as long as Franca refuses to accept that we have to establish rules. Children have to learn respect and self-control."

"You sound like your parents," his brother said.

"My parents were strict, maybe too strict," Marshall conceded, "but they didn't have to cope with a violent kid."

"That's not true!" said a familiar, dry voice. From the front walkway, Mildred Davis marched into view. Marshall hadn't heard the door open; the motor home must have covered the sound. Her thin face radiating fury, his mother rounded on Nick. "You told me he wouldn't be here."

Her words stung. Why did she dislike him so much?

"He wasn't supposed to be," Nick replied mildly. "Sorry, Aunt Mildred."

"I didn't know you were going to be here, either," Marshall said. "And I don't understand what you mean about violent children."

His mother stared toward a black car at the curb, as if debating whether to ignore him and drive off. Instead, her eyes narrowing, she responded. "You were a selfish little brat when we took you in. You broke my favorite china platter and bit Upton's arm when he gave you a spanking."

He'd bitten his father? "I was, what, two years old?"

"Old enough to respect other people and their property," his mother snarled. "I nearly sent you back to your crazy father and his ditzy wife, but Upton reminded me that you were our nephew. He insisted discipline would bring you around, and it did."

"That's why you were so strict?" He'd assumed it was simply how they'd approached parenting.

"Someone had to keep you on the straight and narrow." Her nostrils flared. "You never appreciated how much we sacrificed."

"Sacrificed?"

"You were a handful when you were small," Mildred said. "You should have been grateful for what we gave you."

"How could I, when you didn't tell me I was adopted?"

"You have no business throwing that in my face!" Pain throbbed beneath her fury. "I knew that as soon as you found out, you'd never see me the same way again. You'd consider me a failure, just as Upton did. I didn't have a career, and I couldn't do the one thing a man wants most from his wife. Well, now you've learned I'm not really your mother, so that's the end of that."

What decades of outdated notions she'd endured about marriage, childbearing and her own self-worth. "Mom, that's not true. There's a lot I'd like to share with you, if you'll let me."

"Share with me?" She spoke the words as if they were an insult.

For heaven's sake, she was about to become a grandmother. "Franca and I are…" His phone shrilled. *Just ignore it.* Except that as a doctor, Marshall had to be available for emergencies. Also, he'd rather not toss out the news of the pregnancy in a rush. "Sorry. Hang on."

His mother tapped her foot in annoyance. Nick gave him a sympathetic look.

The caller was Hank Driver. "I can't reach Franca Brightman," the detective said. "Is she with you?"

"No." She must have muted her phone at the attorney's office. "What's wrong?"

"I just learned that Axel Ryerson is out on bail," he said. "I have reason to believe he's hunting for his girlfriend, and since Franca has the little girl, she could be in danger, too. Any idea where they are?"

"Yes." After providing the attorney's address, Marshall called out, "Sorry, emergency," to his mother and brother, and he ran toward his car.

Chapter Nineteen

The session with the lawyer had accomplished everything Franca had hoped for. Far from intending to cancel the meeting, Bridget had wanted to hurry it along. She'd learned of Axel's release and it had intensified her desire to sign over permanent custody.

"He'll do anything to hurt me, and maybe Jazz, too," she'd said as she'd rushed them inside. "I hid my car around the corner in case he and his friends are cruising the area. I can't risk being spotted out front."

They'd confirmed their previously agreed-upon terms, and Edmond had promised to schedule a court date as soon as possible. The adoption was back on track.

After shaking hands with Edmond, they emerged into the outer office, which was empty on a Saturday afternoon. Bridget peered out through the blinds. "Hold on. There's a silver car driving by that I don't recognize. It's gone behind a pickup and I can't see the driver."

"He might be stopping at the convenience store," Franca pointed out.

"Or not."

Between them, Jazz fidgeted. Earlier, the receptionist had helped entertain her, and after the woman left, the little girl had played on her tablet. However, her patience had clearly frayed.

"Hang on another minute," Franca told her.

"No." Jazz ran toward the exit. "You promised me ice cream."

"Yes, but not yet."

"Someone's getting out of the pickup," Bridget warned. "Damn! It's Axel. How did he know I was here?"

Fear seized Franca as Jazz thrust open the glass door. "Jazz, stop!"

"You can't make me!"

Surely she could outrun a four-year-old. But not in time to catch her before a bulky figure—shaved head, scorpion tattoo—hurtled forward to grab her. "Got you, you little worm."

Jazz screamed. After yelling to Edmond to call the police, the two women raced outside.

"Let her go!" To Franca's dismay, the words squeaked out of her constricted throat.

"Bridget, get in the truck or that's the end of your brat." A knife gleamed in Axel's hand.

"She's not mine anymore. So beat it!" Bridget shouted, and ducked inside the office.

Surely the police would be here any minute. But until then, Franca was alone with Axel and a terrified Jazz. And a wickedly sharp knife.

If only she knew more than rudimentary self-defense. If only she were bigger and stronger or had a gun.

Instead, disbelief held her motionless.

FROM THE FAR side of the pickup, Marshall couldn't see what was happening, but he heard the panic in Franca's voice, followed by Axel's deadly threat. Seizing his flashlight from his car, the only item at hand that might serve as a weapon, he circled the truck.

Before him, Franca stood in Axel's path, her face ashen. Another step and Marshall spotted the shaking child with a knife to her throat. Didn't that bastard understand how easily his hand could slip?

Fury roared in Marshall's ears. Only an awareness of how vulnerable they all were held him in check.

"You're frightening the child," he said.

Axel bared his teeth, his neck swiveling as he took in this new arrival. "What the hell are you gonna do about it?"

"The police are on their way." As if to underscore Franca's words, a siren wailed in the distance.

"You're going back to jail." Since that didn't appear to penetrate the jerk's thick head, Marshall added, "Any idea how prisoners treat an inmate who hurts children?"

When Axel's hand tightened on the knife hilt, Marshall's chest ached. Then the man lowered the knife. "I ain't hurting her."

"Give her to me," Franca commanded.

Stay out of it! But it would be counterproductive to engage in a side argument. Instead, Marshall moved slowly to stand between her and Axel. "This isn't our fight. Just release Jazz."

The man shoved the girl forward. "I don't care about the damn kid anyway." Marshall scooped her up. She huddled against him, shivering.

Holding Jazz and using his body to block any attempt at Franca, Marshall registered Axel glaring toward the law-office window. He half expected the man to try to crash through it, not that that would work outside of the movies. Why didn't he flee? Though, if the man had more sense, he wouldn't be in such a mess in the first place.

A police cruiser swept into the lot, lights flashing. Not far behind followed a second cruiser, then a beige sedan with Hank at the wheel.

"I didn't do nothing!" At a command from the officers, Axel set the knife on the ground and raised his hands.

As the officers secured the scene, Marshall carried Jazz to Franca. When he tried to set the little girl on her feet, however, she clung to him.

"You saved me, Marshall." She hiccuped.

"It's a daddy's job to protect his family," he told her. When he glanced up, he could have sworn tears glittered in Franca's eyes.

After that, they were kept busy providing statements. The female officer who'd been at Bridget's apartment a few days ago spoke to her briefly, disappeared around the building and returned with a small metal box. "Magnetic GPS case."

"That's how he tracked my car!" Bridget said. "That must be what his buddy was doing near the women's shelter."

"Are you okay?" Franca asked.

Bridget stroked Jazz's dark hair. "Yeah, but I'm not proud of myself. You're the one who stayed out here and risked your life. You really are her mom." She regarded Marshall admiringly. "And I'm glad she'll have you for a dad."

"Daddies protect their families," Jazz repeated.

"They sure do," Marshall said.

He still wasn't sure where he stood with Franca. He only knew that, after today, he felt as if Jazz was his daughter, too.

IT WAS LATE afternoon before they arrived home, picking up take-out roast chicken with vegetables and salad on their way. After dinner, Marshall volunteered to bake cupcakes with Jazz.

"Might as well use some of this cake mix." He indicated the row of boxes in the pantry.

"Chocolate!" Jazz peered at the display eagerly, then tempered her demand with, "Or some other kind."

Her old defiance had vanished, although Franca expected it to crop up occasionally. Children didn't transform into angels in a single day.

"Chocolate it is." Marshall removed their paper plates from the table. "Franca, you can be our taste tester."

"That means I get to eat whatever you bake," she told Jazz.

"Cool," the little girl said.

Franca took a seat at the island. She kept reliving the earlier scene, trembling at the memory of how close she and Jazz had come to serious injury or death. Yet the sight of Marshall moving easily about the kitchen reassured her.

His courage and strength had saved them, despite Axel's loud claims to police that he'd never intended to harm anyone. Moreover, much as she might question Marshall's stern approach to discipline, she had to admit that she'd overindulged the little girl. Otherwise, Jazz might not have ignored her command to stay inside.

Sipping a cup of tea, Franca watched Marshall with fresh eyes as he tied aprons around himself and Jazz. She listened as he patiently cautioned about the hot oven and the importance of washing their hands. *Just like a father.*

If only doubt didn't still nag inside her. Could she really trust him completely?

He brought a stool so the four-year-old could reach the counter. After they'd cracked the eggs and stirred in the dry mix and water, he helped her position the hand mixer. Although Franca considered the child too young to handle the device, she resisted the urge to intervene.

Jazz held the mixer fairly steady for a few minutes. When her hand wobbled, Marshall praised her and gently took charge of the mixer to finish the job. The girl beamed with pride.

As they lined cupcake pans with fluted papers, she peppered him with questions. "Will you teach the baby to bake, too?"

"Not for a few years," Marshall said. "By then, you might be big enough to teach her. Or him."

"I'll be the big sister, right?"

"You bet."

Amused as Franca was by this exchange, she wasn't sure they should let Jazz assume the baby was a sure thing. The week's events had pushed the pregnancy to the back of her mind. Now, she touched her palm to her midsection, and her abdomen felt larger and firmer than she recalled. She was, she realized, entering the ninth week. According to the material Dr. Franco had provided, Baby Bright was an inch long, its hands meeting over the heart.

Would there truly be a new baby to hold and love? No use worrying about it now. They'd had enough scares for today.

With Marshall's help, Jazz began spooning batter into the papers. "Are you the baby's daddy?" she asked.

"Yes."

The child stared up at him. "Are you my daddy, too?"

"I want to be," Marshall said. "And watch that spoon. You're dripping."

"Oops."

He reached for a paper towel. "Allow me to demonstrate the fine art of mopping up."

"What's *demonstrate*?"

"It means *to show*. As in, let me demonstrate how to hug." Putting down the towel, he gathered her against him. Jazz giggled.

Franca's heart squeezed. Was it possible they could bond into a family?

"Can I live in your house?" Jazz asked. "If I promise no more tantrums?"

Marshall finished cleaning the spilled batter. "None?"

"Mostly none."

He planted a kiss atop her head. "I don't expect you to be perfect. I wasn't so perfect myself when I was a kid. But I figured you weren't happy here."

"Yes, I am," Jazz said.

"Why were you so determined to go home?"

"I thought you'd kick me out," she said.

"Why would I do that?"

"'Cause I'm bad a lot."

"Not bad. Just naughty. You can learn to do better, like I did."

Jazz clutched her hands together. "And you might take my toys."

"Wow, I'd have to be a mean guy to do that." Opening the oven, Marshall slid in the trays of cupcakes. "You were making a preemptive strike? That means you pushed me away before I could do it to you."

The little girl nodded.

"I wouldn't throw you out over a few tantrums," Marshall said as he set the timer. "Or for any reason, because, remember, daddies protect their families. Good daddies do."

"Unfortunately, not all men are good," Franca said. Bridget had described how Jazz's father had sent them packing when the child was a toddler, only allowing them to throw a few items into a suitcase. Afterward, Bridget and Jazz dropped in and out of shelters and friends' homes, often with little notice. Jazz must have had to leave toys behind more than once.

"So can I stay?" she asked.

Marshall's eyes met Franca's. How could she respond? She wanted for them to stay, too, yet a long-term commitment meant relying on Marshall to have truly changed from the rigid man she'd known years ago. Despite all the promising signs, how could she be sure?

"The grown-ups will talk about this later," he told Jazz. "Please don't worry, okay?"

"Okay."

While the cupcakes were baking, Jazz climbed into Marshall's lap and he read one of her favorite picture books. Then the three of them enjoyed the chocolate treats, barely cooled long enough to hold icing.

Marshall stored the remainder in a plastic container. "We can have them for breakfast," Jazz announced.

"We'll eat cereal and fruit for breakfast," Marshall corrected. "And save our cupcakes for dessert tomorrow night."

She folded her arms. "I want another one now."

"You've had three. Any more and you'll be sick."

Jazz grabbed her half-full glass of milk. "Give me another cupcake!"

For a frozen moment, both adults regarded her indecisively. Aware that the child must be exhausted, Franca had an impulse to spring to her defense before Marshall could react. But he was right.

She closed her hand over Jazz's on the glass. "You've had a rough day, but if this is how you repay Marshall for baking with you, why should he ever agree to make cupcakes again?"

"You're mean!" Jazz replied.

Marshall sat down across from them. "No, she's a mommy who loves you and wants what's best for you. She also deserves your respect. We would never call you names and you shouldn't call us mean or bad either."

Jazz heaved an exaggerated sigh. "Boy, you're *both* saying the same stuff. I give up."

Franca's gaze connected with Marshall's. "That's because we're a team," she said.

Astonishingly, she realized it was true.

HE *HAD* TO win over Franca, Marshall reflected as they descended the stairs after tucking Jazz into bed. He yearned to be both her husband and Jazz's father. But if he said or did the wrong thing, he might drive her away.

I nearly sent you back to your crazy father and his ditzy wife. His mother's words, almost forgotten in the rush of the day's events, popped into his mind. Jolted, he missed his footing and had to grab the banister.

"Are you okay?" Behind him, Franca touched his shoulder in concern. "Confronting an armed man is a traumatic experience. It must be catching up with you."

"Among other things." Reaching the bottom of the stairs, he gestured toward the living room. "Mind joining me in here? There's something I want to share."

"Of course."

Early-evening light drifted through the front windows, augmented by the glow of etched-glass lamps. Marshall had furnished the room elegantly but comfortably with armchairs and a sofa grouped around a patterned rug.

He chose the couch. Franca perched on a chair.

From habit, he sought to phrase his thoughts cautiously. Oh, to hell with caution. He'd lay everything out and if she rejected him, at least he'd done his best.

"I ran into my mother today," he began.

"Where?"

"At Nick's." *Don't stop to explain the details.* "She vented about what a little monster I used to be and how they had to crack down on me."

"How cruel," Franca said. "I can't imagine you were ever difficult."

"Apparently I was a destructive toddler," Marshall said. "That's why they were so strict."

"From everything I've heard, they overdid it."

Her sympathy encouraged him. "I've always believed that there was something fundamentally wrong with me," Marshall said. "That when I'm most myself, I don't deserve to be loved."

"That's awful!"

"The only way I could deserve love was to be perfect," he went on. "Now I understand where that stems from."

"What a burden to carry." Franca leaned forward.

Even if what he was about to say offended her, Marshall couldn't stop. "You said once that my instincts were all wrong. Well, I may have a gift for putting my foot in my mouth, but my instincts *aren't* all wrong. To raise children together, we have to find a balance between my strictness and your nurturing." He halted, his throat tightening, awaiting her reaction.

"You're right." At close range, the pupils of Franca's eyes seemed unusually large. "At Edmond's office, Jazz defied me and ran outside. If you'd been there and ordered her to stop, she'd have obeyed."

She understood. Finally, they'd reached common ground.

Then she averted her gaze. "What's bothering you?" Marshall refused to let her withhold anything. They'd come too far. "Whatever it is, please trust me with it."

Franca took a deep breath. "It isn't really my business, but…"

"Go for it."

"Why did you dump Belle?"

Marshall blinked. "What?"

"I never understood how you could love a woman for years and then dump her because she fell short of your expectations," she said. "So what if she couldn't keep up with her increased class load?"

"You believe I dropped her because she wasn't brilliant enough?"

"That's basically what she told me." Franca clenched her hands in her lap.

Marshall had used her grades as an excuse to avoid hurting Belle's feelings. Instead, by disguising the truth, he'd misled her, and consequently Franca.

"It was her idea to graduate early and move to Boston," he said. "I realized I didn't want her to. I wasn't in love with her and never had been, but it would have been cruel to say that. So when she began struggling academically, it seemed the perfect reason to split. I claimed we both needed to concentrate on our studies."

Franca swallowed. "You weren't in love with her, ever?"

"The woman I really belonged with was you," Marshall admitted. "Only, at that age, I wasn't ready for such an intense relationship."

Franca appeared to be reflecting, perhaps replaying events in light of what he'd just disclosed. "The first time I saw you, at that party, I thought you were coming over to talk to me," she said.

"I was," he admitted. "Then you got klutzy and I could hear my parents announcing you weren't my type."

"They had a lot of nerve." Smiling, she noted, "I mean their alter egos."

"Air people," Marshall said. "That's my name for those voices in our heads."

"Air people," Franca repeated. "I like that."

"I'm sorry for hurting Belle," he said. "I'm not sure she ever really loved me, either, though. How could she, when I never showed her who I was inside?"

Franca considered this for a moment. "My sister described you and Belle as a handsome couple, but shallow."

"Your sister's a perceptive woman. Especially the handsome part." He sobered. Without realizing it, he'd withheld something, too. "Franca, you're the right woman for me, but I can't be a perfect guy. I am who I am. I'm stricter than you, with a different viewpoint on some issues. I'm willing to work things out, but we can't sustain a relationship where I have to walk on eggshells."

Franca sat silent as his words sank in. Maybe he'd gone too far. He'd had no choice, though.

At last she spoke. "You told Jazz you don't expect her to be perfect. I don't expect that of you, either."

Then she did something utterly unexpected. She got down on her knees and asked, "Marshall Davis, will you marry me?"

Chapter Twenty

When Marshall proposed to her weeks ago, Franca had been wary. She'd been convinced Jazz and the baby depended on her alone to shoulder the responsibility for them, and had viewed Marshall's rigidity as a threat.

But since then he'd opened up emotionally, overcoming the restraint that had served as his survival mechanism all his life. And although he might have been unfair to Belle in some ways, he'd been young and inexperienced—and had done his best to spare her.

She loved this man. He'd let her view his scarred soul, and had accepted her despite *her* flaws. He'd matured into a partner Franca could count on. The confrontation with Axel had proved that.

She no longer believed he'd run out on her if she miscarried. After all, she'd been honest about her family's history, and it hadn't fazed him. And now he'd accepted Jazz as his child, too.

Yet his answer to her proposal was taking an awfully long time. "Marshall?"

The corners of his mouth twitched. "It's my understanding that a proposal should be accompanied by a ring and preferably flowers."

Was he mocking her? "I beg your pardon?"

"I love you," he said.

"And I love you." She'd made that clear, hadn't she?

"Now as to this proposal business, let's improvise." Pushing the coffee table aside, he knelt facing her. "Since neither of us was clever enough to buy a ring, we'll have to create our own."

Franca's uncertainty vanished as he reached out. Although it required a bit of scooting, soon they'd encircled each other in their arms.

His masculine scent, a hint of aftershave lotion with an undertone of surgical soap, buoyed her. How exhilarating to be sheltered and loved. "This is the best kind of ring," she whispered.

When his lips touched hers, Franca forgot everything but her precious connection with this tender, wonderful man.

"The best kind of circle, indeed," Marshall said when the kiss ended. "As long as we don't topple over."

Franca smiled. "It feels heavenly, no matter how awkward we look."

"No one's watching," he assured her. "Except for that security camera over there."

"What!" She stared upward. "I don't see it."

"Oh. Guess I forgot to have it installed."

Torn between laughing and poking him in the ribs, Franca lost her balance and would have collapsed except for his support. It seemed a symbolic start to their future together.

"We can shop for rings tomorrow," he said. "Whatever style you choose."

"I'll enjoy that." They moved to sit side by side on the couch. She stroked his cheek, and he drew her against his shoulder.

As she relaxed, Franca recalled their earlier topic. "You didn't finish telling me about your mom. Did she explain why she cut you off when you found out you were adopted?"

"In a way." Marshall's deep voice vibrated through her. "She's convinced my father considered her a failure because she couldn't have kids. And she assumed that once I learned she wasn't my birth mother, I'd cast her off."

"A preemptive strike, like Jazz?" Franca murmured.

He rested his cheek on her head. "That's right."

What a dark place Mildred Davis must inhabit, where her self-worth depended on two men whose love she didn't trust. "I hate to think how sad her own childhood must have been that she had such a low opinion of herself even into adulthood."

"I'm not sure how to break through that," Marshall said. "But I want her to enjoy being a grandmother. She's earned that chance."

"You didn't tell her I'm pregnant?"

"Not yet," he said. "But I will."

"Speaking of children," Franca said, "shall we see if Jazz is still awake? Regardless of what she said to you, I'm sure she's worried."

"Absolutely."

The moment they entered the playroom, the girl sat bolt upright, dark hair wild around her face. "Oh, it's you!" She held out her arms. "I was afraid it was that bad man."

Franca should have anticipated that the trauma would linger in Jazz's mind. She hurried over. "We're here because something great has happened."

Marshall pulled up a chair, since the bed was too small for them both to sit on the edge. "Franca and I are getting married. You'll be our daughter and we'll live here forever."

"With the baby, too?"

"You bet," he said.

"Yay!" After hugging them both, Jazz asked, "Can I sleep with you guys tonight?"

Franca wasn't sure how to answer. Like her, Marshall must have been looking forward to making love again.

"Will that help you feel safe?" he asked.

Jazz nodded vigorously.

"Just for tonight," Marshall warned. "So you won't be scared." He glanced at Franca and mouthed, "Okay?"

"There's nothing more important than our little girl," she confirmed. "But it's only for tonight."

"Okay, Mommy and Daddy." Jazz scrambled out of bed.

They walked down the hall hand in hand.

THE NEXT DAY, the three of them went to Nick and Zady's house to bring them and Caleb up to date. Later, while Marshall and Jazz played a game with their hosts, Franca slipped out to the patio and placed the first of several important calls.

Her mom responded with excitement when Franca gave her the news about the baby. Then she asked, "Have you mentioned this to Gail yet?"

"No. I'm nervous about that," Franca admitted, stretching her legs.

"She'll be delighted for you," her mother insisted. "Don't put it off."

"I won't." As soon as they finished, she inhaled the fresh air, perfumed with jasmine from bushes surrounding the small yard. Then she pressed her sister's name in the phone.

After exchanging greetings, Gail said, "Have you talked to Mom?"

"I just did," Franca answered, puzzled.

"So she broke the news."

"Uh...what news?"

"She didn't share that I'm four months pregnant?" Usually, their mother would have spread the word near and far.

Four months meant her sister was well into the second trimester. "That's terrific! I guess she figured you'd rather break it to me yourself." Might as well go for it. "Marshall and I are engaged."

"Congratulations!"

"And I get to adopt Jazz after all. We saw the lawyer yesterday."

"Fantastic!"

"And I'm nine weeks pregnant."

There was a stunned silence. Then: "Our kids will be almost the same age. And Glenn's, too."

"That *is* a bonus." Although the three cousins would live in different states, they'd spend many holidays together as a family.

"What aren't you saying?" Gail pressed.

No use avoiding the subject. "I'm worried about the pregnancy. Not that there's anything wrong, according to my doctor."

"Because of our family medical history, which I was so rude about when you brought it up?" Gail said. "I've never reached the fourth month before. My doctor says the miscarriages might have been a fluke, or a problem that self-corrected."

"I feel as if a curse has been lifted," Franca ventured.

"Me, too. We can both hope for the best."

A few minutes later, she completed the family notifications. Her brother congratulated her and added that his wife's pregnancy was progressing well, also. He, too, was thrilled that the three cousins would be close in age.

After she clicked off, Franca wished she could stop there. However, she had to place one more call. *Just get it over with.*

Belle answered on the second ring. "Franca! I was about to call you. I have fantastic news."

Franca broke into laughter. "You can't be!"

"I can't be what?"

But she'd known the instant she heard the joy in Belle's voice. "You're pregnant."

"How did you guess?" Without waiting, her friend said, "I'm two months along. I'd have called you sooner but you were so sad about losing Jazz."

"I haven't lost her," Franca said. "Her birth mother changed her mind."

"That's great!"

"And I'm pregnant."

"Oh." Belle seemed to be searching for polite phrasing. "Is there a father? I mean, in the picture?"

"Yes, and we're getting married." *Now for the hard part.* "It's Marshall."

A pause. Then a disbelieving, "Marshall *Davis*?"

"We ran into each other at the hospital where we're both on staff," Franca explained. "He's changed over the years." She had no idea what to add, except, "I hope this isn't uncomfortable for you. I want us to stay friends." While she didn't believe Belle would hold a grudge, she might not be able to help feeling betrayed.

"Good," Belle said. "It's way overdue."

"What?"

Her friend must have shifted the phone, because there was a moment's static before she continued, "I sensed he was drawn to you, only I was too selfish to call him on it because I was afraid I'd lose him. Well, I lost him anyway. Seeing you alone year after year, I kept wondering about what might have been."

"If Marshall and I had had a relationship in college, we'd have ended up hating each other," Franca told her.

"Really?"

"We had a lot to work out even now," she assured her friend. "You're truly okay with this?"

"It stings," Belle admitted. "For me, Marshall was a romantic dream. But the truth is, I have the best possible husband. When he looks at me, there's no other woman lurking behind his eyes."

"You deserve that, and more." It was brave of Belle to be honest, and generous of her to understand.

"You do, too."

Now they could move on. "I just talked to my brother and sister. They're both expecting babies within a few months of mine, and yours."

"This will be quite a Christmas!"

"It sure will."

At last the calls were over, the old hurts healed. Yet there remained one family member to bring into the happy circle.

When they got home, Marshall tried calling his mother, but reached only her voice mail. He composed an email apologizing for running off abruptly at Nick's house, and then explained about the confrontation at the lawyer's office. He informed her of the engagement, the pregnancy and Jazz's forthcoming adoption. Seeking neutral ground, he invited her to join them for the opening ceremony of the new medical building, and to go out to dinner with them afterward.

After proofreading the email for him, Franca hoped the prospect of becoming a grandmother would overcome Mildred's reticence. Also, Marshall had emphasized in the email that he considered himself just as much a father to his adoptive daughter as to the baby Franca was carrying. He hoped his mother would grasp the message that it didn't matter how a child came into the family.

Her response arrived later that evening. He forwarded the email to Franca.

I'm pleased that both my nephews have found brides and that you'll be able to experience fatherhood, Mildred wrote. Since you will have a baby of your own, perhaps raising an adopted child won't be as difficult as it was for me. That part of my life is behind us. I'm sure you'll understand why I don't belong at this ceremony or at your family dinner.

"She's sticking to her guns." The sorrow on Marshall's face resonated inside Franca. "We'll invite her to other events, of course, but she seems resolved to regard me as nothing more than a nephew. I'm honestly not sure she ever loved me."

Was that true? To Franca, the words "I don't belong at this ceremony" indicated pain rather than rejection. Still, Marshall might be right.

Yet the separation troubled her. Later, while checking her own mail, Franca decided that, as the woman's future daughter-in-law, she ought to write to her and add her insights. As to whether her words would make a difference, Franca figured it was a long shot. After asking Marshall to be sure he didn't object, she composed a message and hit Send.

Then she went upstairs with her future husband to put their daughter to bed. And, finally, to make love again.

Chapter Twenty-One

Banners and a band ushered invitees into the elegant lobby of the Portia and Vincent Adams Memorial Medical Building. Its acquisition and renovation had been a long, difficult, even tragic process, involving the bankruptcy of the former dental building's owners, a competitive sale when it seemed unaffordable and then a financial commitment by the wealthy Adams couple just before their deaths in a car crash.

Marshall had only joined the staff last fall. Yet stepping inside with Franca and Jazz, he felt his heart expand with warmth and pride. Not only did his professional future lie within these walls, but the crowd filling the folding chairs included warm, familiar faces. Nick, Zady and Caleb had saved seats for them. Jennifer Martin, who as public relations director was helping run the event, left her five-year-old daughter with them—much to Jazz's joy—while her husband assisted with the sound equipment.

People stopped by to say hello, people with whom he had formed connections. They included Zady's twin sister, Zora, and her husband, Lucky, as well as other urologists and nurses.

Throughout his education and training, Marshall had isolated himself from those around him. Many had considered him cold and snobbish, while the truth was that he'd longed to be a part of their easy camaraderie. How had this happened, that in the span of a few months he'd bridged the gaps of a lifetime?

When his hand covered Franca's, she tipped him an understanding smile. On his other side, Jazz was giggling as she chatted with her little friend Rosalie. Then she rested her cheek against Marshall's arm.

He belonged here. The awareness lifted his spirits as high as the bright clusters of Mylar balloons.

Yet a heaviness dragged him down to earth, because a key person was missing. How could a man accept that his own mother didn't love him? Mildred Davis *was* his mother—except that, apparently, she no longer wished to be.

At the front, Owen Tartikoff and Cole Rattigan took places of honor alongside the Adamses' daughters, both of whom were in their early teens, and their grandmother. After the band finished a rousing number, the hospital administrator rose to speak.

A powerfully built fellow who inspired confidence, Dr. Mark Rayburn uttered a few words of welcome before unveiling a statue commissioned for the building. The bronze figure of a man in slacks and a sport coat, lovingly holding a baby in the crook of his arm, occupied one end of a park-style bench. The bronze sculpture was so realistic that Marshall imagined visitors sitting next to the man before realizing he wasn't an actual person.

Applause surged, and the artist took a bow. Mark proceeded to thank the Adams girls and their grandmother for the bequest from the Vince and Portia Adams estate, stirring an ovation.

Next up was Owen Tartikoff. The surgeon energized the people in the lobby with his description of the growth of the Safe Harbor fertility program and its cutting-edge successes.

He introduced Cole Rattigan as head of the men's program. What a contrast, Marshall thought: where Owen was forceful and commanding, Cole was reticent and self-deprecating.

"I'm surprised they let me speak in public," he told the crowd. "The last time I lectured, I mentioned declining sperm levels worldwide and the media claimed I'd predicted the end of life on earth. Reporters were camped out on my doorstep for weeks."

Laughter rippled through the room. Marshall recalled reading about that episode a few years ago and pitying the doctor whose remarks had been sensationalized.

Cole summarized the issues facing infertile men, tossed out a few statistics and concluded, "The key to any program is its personnel. We're bringing on board distinguished younger surgeons and there's one in particular I'd like to introduce who's been intimately involved in the planning of this building. Dr. Marshall Davis, please come up and say a few words."

The old fear of making a fool of himself held Marshall motionless. Then Jazz said, "That's you, Daddy."

"It sure is." Loud clapping, led by Franca, propelled him to the podium. En route, he quickly considered what he might say. He might list the fellowships they'd secured, or review the discussions the staff had had about allocating office space. But why risk boring the audience to death?

At the microphone, Marshall plunged right in. "I've never terrified the public like my distinguished colleague Dr. Rattigan, but the public used to terrify me.

I had a fear of public speaking because I feared if I said the wrong thing, the audience would rise up and mock me en masse."

Sympathetic murmurs greeted this admission. On his brother's lips, he read the words, "You're kidding!" Apparently Nick hadn't suspected what lay behind his mask.

"This hospital is about creating families," Marshall said. "For the community, for our patients and for our staff. To my astonishment, it brought me together with my brother and with an old friend who's soon to be my wife, Dr. Franca Brightman."

More clapping followed, with a notable clatter from his office's nurses. Ines poked two fingers in her mouth as if to produce a wolf whistle, until Jeanine knocked her hand away.

"As many of you know, my fiancée and I are setting an example of how to form a family, both by having a baby and by adopting our adorable foster daughter, Jazz." He grinned down at Franca, who resembled a fertility goddess in her forest-green maternity dress. Jazz wiggled happily in her chair.

He was about to wrap up his remarks when a movement near the entrance caught his attention. The rail-thin figure of Mildred Davis, clad in a gray suit that matched her upswept hair, edged inside.

Should he acknowledge her? At his brother's wedding, she hadn't hesitated to stalk from the banquet hall in front of everyone. A rebuff here would be embarrassing and hurtful. But she'd come, hadn't she?

Trust your instincts.

"Very importantly, let me thank the woman who raised me to be a man of accomplishment, whose rock-solid adherence to her principles taught me to stand by what I believe in and fight for it." Marshall regarded her directly. "My mother, Mildred Davis."

In her stunned expression, he read the same fear that he used to experience, of being ridiculed. Then Franca and Nick rose to their feet, turned toward her and cheered. The rest of the audience joined in enthusiastically.

Tears ran down his mother's cheeks. He didn't recall ever seeing her cry before.

To hell with decorous behavior. Down the aisle Marshall went, greeting his mother with a hug. Barely reaching his chest, she responded with a powerful grip of her own.

"Well, I can't top that," Mark Rayburn said from the stage. "I now declare the Portia and Vincent Adams Memorial Medical Building open!"

The band broke into "Happy Days Are Here Again." Around the room, chairs scraped and clothing rustled as people prepared to leave.

"I'm proud of you," his mother said. "By the way, you're marrying the right woman."

"I know, Mom." Marshall released her. "What changed your mind about today?"

Mildred glanced past him, as if to be sure they weren't overheard. "Franca emailed to say how much you love me, that every memory you have of growing up involves Upton and me as your parents."

"She wrote all that?" He'd assumed Franca was sending a simple courtesy note.

"She explained how hard it was for you to accept her foster child, but that you'd eventually forged a bond as strong as any parent's. And she urged me to be a part of your family, in any role I choose."

"That sounds like quite an email."

"It inspired me to take out our old scrapbooks, the ones we made after vacations and holidays." His mother had spent many hours assembling beautiful, quilted volumes of photos and memorabilia. "I'd forgotten how happy we were. I realized that I'd become locked into my anger, even when it was counterproductive. I'm afraid I'm not a very flexible person."

"Me, either," Marshall said. "I'm working on it, though." Franca and the others were approaching, with Jazz trotting ahead. "Here comes your granddaughter."

"I always envied my friends who were grandmothers," Mildred admitted. She hugged the little girl without reserve, and Franca, as well.

"You'll join us for dinner, won't you?" Franca asked.

"If I'm still invited."

"Absolutely," Marshall said.

"Don't worry about the cost," Nick added. "My brother's paying."

"I certainly am." Marshall offered his mother and his fiancée each an arm. Caleb crooked his elbow for Jazz, who gave him a dazzling smile.

As they emerged into the summer evening, he heard the others making various restaurant suggestions. Since it didn't matter to him where they ate, he let the names flow by: Papa Giovanni's, Fu Manchu's, Salads and More, Krazy Kids Pizza, Waffle Heaven.

How ironic that, for all these years, he and Franca had avoided involvement because of their contrasting personalities, Marshall mused. Thanks to her, he'd found the acceptance and the love he'd always craved.

Opposites could not only attract, they could bring out

the best in each other. He and Franca and their family members were the living proof.

Now if they could only agree on where to eat dinner...

* * * * *

MY FUNNY VALENTINE

Debbie Macomber

One

Dianne Williams had the scenario all worked out. She'd be pushing her grocery cart down the aisle of the local grocery store and gazing over the frozen-food section when a tall, dark, handsome man would casually stroll up to her and with a brilliant smile say, "Those low-cal dinners couldn't possibly be for you."

She'd turn to him and suddenly the air would fill with the sounds of a Rimsky-Korsakov symphony, or bells would chime gently in the distance—Dianne didn't have that part completely figured out yet—and in that instant she would know deep in her heart that this was the man she was meant to spend the rest of her life with.

All right, Dianne was willing to admit, the scenario was childish and silly, the kind of fantasy only a teenage girl should dream up. But reentering the dating scene after umpteen years of married life created problems Dianne didn't even want to consider.

Three years earlier, Dianne's husband had left her and the children to find himself. Instead he found a SYT (sweet young thing), promptly divorced Dianne and moved across the country. It hurt; in fact, it hurt more than anything Dianne had ever known, but she was a survivor, and always had been. Perhaps that was the reason Jack didn't seem to suffer a single pang of guilt about abandoning her to raise Jason and Jill on her own.

Her children, Dianne had discovered, were incredibly resilient. Within a year of their father's departure, they were urging her to date. Their father did, they reminded Dianne with annoying frequency. And if it wasn't her children pushing her toward establishing a new relationship, it was her own dear mother.

When it came to locating Mr. Right for her divorced daughter, Martha Janes knew no equal. For several months, Dianne had been subjected to a long parade of single men. Their unmarried status, however, seemed their sole attribute.

After dinner with the man who lost his toupee on a low-hanging chandelier, Dianne had insisted enough was enough and she would find her own dates.

This proved to be easier said than done. Dianne hadn't gone out once in six months. Now, within the next week, she needed a man. Not just any man, either. One who was tall, dark and handsome. It would be a nice bonus if he was exceptionally wealthy, too, but she didn't have time to be choosy. The Valentine's dinner at the Port Blossom Community Center was Saturday night. *This* Saturday night.

From the moment the notice was posted six weeks earlier, Jason and Jill had insisted she attend. Surely their mother could find a date given that much time! And someone handsome to boot. It seemed a matter of family honor.

Only now the dinner was only days away and Dianne was no closer to achieving her goal.

"I'm home," Jason yelled as he walked into the house. The front door slammed in his wake, hard enough to shake the kitchen windows. He threw his books on the counter, moved directly to the refrigerator, opened the door and stuck the upper half of his fourteen-year-old body inside.

"Help yourself to a snack," Dianne said, smiling and shaking her head.

Jason reappeared with a chicken leg clenched between his teeth like a pirate's cutlass. One hand was filled with a piece of leftover cherry pie while the other held a platter of cold fried chicken.

"How was school?"

He shrugged, set down the pie and removed the chicken leg from his mouth. "Okay, I guess."

Dianne knew what was coming next. It was the same question he'd asked her every afternoon since the notice about the dinner had been posted.

"Do you have a date yet?" He leaned against the counter as his steady gaze pierced her. Her son's eyes could break through the firmest resolve, and cut through layers of deception.

"No date," she answered cheerfully. At least as cheerfully as she could under the circumstances.

"The dinner's this Saturday night."

As if she needed reminding. "I know. Stop worrying, I'll find someone."

"Not just anyone," Jason said emphatically, as though he were speaking to someone with impaired hearing. "He's got to make an impression. Someone decent."

"I know, I know."

"Grandma said she could line you up with—"

"No," Dianne interrupted. "I categorically refuse to go on any more of Grandma's blind dates."

"But you don't have the time to find your own now. It's—"

"I'm working on it," she insisted, although she knew she wasn't working very hard. She *was* trying to find someone to accompany her to the dinner, only she'd never dreamed it would be this difficult.

Until the necessity of attending this affair had been forced upon her, Dianne hadn't been aware of how limited her choices were. In the past couple of years, she'd met few single men, apart from the ones her mother had thrown at her. There were a couple of unmarried men at the office where she was employed part-time as a bookkeeper. Neither, however, was anyone she'd seriously consider dating. They were both too suave, too urbane—too much like Jack. Besides, problems might arise if she were to mingle her social life with her business one.

The front door opened and closed again, a little less noisily this time.

"I'm home!" ten-year-old Jill announced from the entryway. She dropped her books on the floor and marched toward the kitchen. Then she paused on the threshold and planted both hands on her hips as her eyes sought out her brother. "You better not have eaten all the leftover pie. I want some, too, you know."

"Don't grow warts worrying about it," Jason said sarcastically. "There's plenty."

Jill's gaze swiveled from her brother to her mother. The level of severity didn't diminish one bit. Dianne met her daughter's eye and mouthed the words along with her.

"Do you have a date yet?"

Jason answered for Dianne. "No, she doesn't. And she's got five days to come up with a decent guy and all she says is that she's working on it."

"Mom..." Jill's brown eyes filled with concern.

"Children, please."

"Everyone in town's going," Jill claimed, as if Dianne wasn't already aware of that. "You've *got* to be there, you've just got to. I told all my friends you're going."

More pressure! That was the last thing Dianne needed. Nevertheless, she smiled serenely at her two children and assured them they didn't have a thing to worry about.

An hour or so later, while she was making dinner, she could hear Jason and Jill's voices in the living room. They were huddled together in front of the television, their heads close together. Plotting, it looked like, charting her barren love life. Doubtless deciding who their mother should take to the dinner. Probably the guy with the toupee.

"Is something wrong?" Dianne asked, standing in the doorway. It was unusual for them to watch television this time of day, but more unusual for them to be so chummy. The fact that they'd turned on the TV to drown out their conversation hadn't escaped her.

They broke guiltily apart.

"Wrong?" Jason asked, recovering first. "I was just talking to Jill, is all. Do you need me to do something?"

That offer alone was enough evidence to convict them both. "Jill, would you set the table for me?" she asked, her gaze lingering on her two children for another moment before she returned to the kitchen.

Jason and Jill were up to something. Dianne could only guess what. No doubt the plot they were concocting included their grandmother.

Sure enough, while Jill was setting the silverware on the kitchen table, Jason used the phone, stretching the cord as far as it would go and mumbling into the

mouthpiece so there was no chance Dianne could over-
hear his conversation.

Dianne's suspicions were confirmed when her
mother arrived shortly after dinner. And within minutes, Jason and Jill had deserted the kitchen, saying
they had to get to their homework. Also highly suspi-
cious behavior.

"Do you want some tea, Mom?" Dianne felt obliged
to ask, dreading the coming conversation. It didn't take
Sherlock Holmes to deduce that her children had called
their grandmother hoping she'd find a last-minute date
for Dianne.

"Don't go to any trouble."

This was her mother's standard reply. "It's no trouble," Dianne said.

"Then make the tea."

Because of her evening aerobics class—W.A.R. it
was called, for Women After Results—Dianne had
changed and was prepared to make a hasty exit.

While the water was heating, she took a white ce-
ramic teapot from the cupboard. "Before you ask, and
I know you will," she said with strained patience, "I
haven't got a date for the Valentine's dinner yet."

Her mother nodded slowly as if Dianne had just announced something of profound importance. Martha
was from the old school, and she took her time getting
around to whatever was on her mind, usually preceding
it with a long list of questions that hinted at the subject.
Dianne loved her mother, but there wasn't anyone on
this earth who could drive her crazier.

"You've still got your figure," Martha said, her expression serious. "That helps." She stroked her chin a
couple of times and nodded. "You've got your father's
brown eyes, may he rest in peace, and your hair is nice

and thick. You can thank your grandfather for that. He had hair so thick—"

"Ma, did I mention I have an aerobics class tonight?"

Her mother's posture stiffened. "I don't want to bother you."

"It's just that I might have to leave before you say what you're obviously planning to say, and I didn't want to miss the reason for your unexpected visit."

Her mother relaxed, but just a little. "Don't worry. I'll say what must be said and then you can leave. Your mother's words are not as important as your exercise class."

An argument bubbled up like fizz from a can of soda, but Dianne successfully managed to swallow it. Showing any sign of weakness in front of her mother was a major tactical error. Dianne made the tea, then carried the pot over to the table and sat across from Martha.

"Your skin's still as creamy as—"

"Mom," Dianne said, "there's no need to tell me all this. I know my coloring is good. I also know I've still got my figure and that my hair is thick and that you approve of my keeping it long. You don't need to sell me on myself."

"Ah," Martha told her softly, "that's where you're wrong."

Dianne couldn't help it—she rolled her eyes. When Dianne was fifteen her mother would have slapped her hand, but now that she was thirty-three, Martha used more subtle tactics.

Guilt.

"I don't have many years left."

"Mom—"

"No, listen. I'm an old woman now and I have the

right to say what I want, especially since the good Lord may choose to call me home at any minute."

Stirring a teaspoon of sugar into her tea offered Dianne a moment to compose herself. Bracing her elbows on the table, she raised the cup to her lips. "Just say it."

Her mother nodded, apparently appeased. "You've lost confidence in yourself."

"That's not true."

Martha's smile was meager at best. "Jack left you, and now you think there must be something wrong with you. But, Dianne, what you don't understand is that he would've gone if you were as beautiful as Marilyn Monroe. Jack's leaving had nothing to do with you and everything to do with Jack."

This conversation was taking a turn Dianne wanted to avoid. Jack was a subject she preferred not to discuss. As far as she could see, there wasn't any reason to peel back the scars and examine the wound at this late date. Jack was gone. She'd accepted it, dealt with it, and gone on with her life. The fact that her mother was even mentioning her ex-husband had taken Dianne by surprise.

"My goodness," Dianne said, checking her watch. "Look at the time—"

"Before you go," her mother said quickly, grabbing her wrist, "I met a nice young man this afternoon in the butcher's shop. Marie Zimmerman told me about him and I went to talk to him myself."

"Mom—"

"Hush and listen. He's divorced, but from what he said it was all his wife's fault. He makes blood sausage and insisted I try some. It was so good it practically melted in my mouth. I never tasted sausage so good. A man who makes sausage like that would be an asset to any family."

Oh, sweet heaven. Her mother already had her married to the guy!

"I told him all about you and he generously offered to take you out."

"Mother, *please.* I've already said I won't go out on any more blind dates."

"Jerome's a nice man. He's—"

"I don't mean to be rude, but I really have to leave now, or I'll be late." Hurriedly, Dianne stood, collected her coat, and called out to her children that she'd be back in an hour.

The kids didn't say a word.

It wasn't until she was in her car that Dianne realized they'd been expecting her to announce that she finally had a date.

Two

"Damn," Dianne muttered, scrambling through her purse for the tenth time. She knew it wasn't going to do the least bit of good, but she felt compelled to continue the search.

"Double damn," she said as she set the bulky leather handbag on the hood of her car. Raindrops spattered all around her.

Expelling her breath, she stalked back into the Port Blossom Community Center and stood in front of the desk. "I seem to have locked my keys in my car," she told the receptionist. "Along with my cell."

"Oh, dear. Is there someone you can get in touch with?"

"I'm a member of the auto club so I can call them for help. I also want to call home and say I'll be late. So if you'll let me use the phone?"

"Oh, sure." The young woman smiled pleasantly, and lifted the phone onto the counter. "We close in fifteen minutes, you know."

A half hour later, Dianne was leaning impatiently against her car in the community center parking lot when a red tow truck pulled in. It circled the area, then eased into the space next to hers.

The driver, whom Dianne couldn't see in the dark, rolled down his window and stuck out his elbow. "Are you the lady who phoned about locking her keys in the car?"

"No. I'm standing out in the rain wearing a leotard for the fun of it," she muttered.

He chuckled, turned off the engine and hopped out of the driver's seat. "Sounds like this has been one of those days."

She nodded, suddenly feeling a stab of guilt at her churlishness. He seemed so friendly.

"Why don't you climb in my truck where it's nice and warm while I take care of this?" He opened the passenger-side door and gestured for her to enter.

She smiled weakly, and as she climbed in, said, "I didn't mean to snap at you just now."

He flashed her a grin. "No problem." She found herself taking a second look at him. He was wearing gray-striped coveralls and the front was covered with grease stains. His name, Steve, was embroidered in red across the top of his vest pocket. His hair, which was neatly styled, appeared to have been recently cut. His eyes were a warm shade of brown and—she searched for the right word—gentle, she decided.

After ensuring that she was comfortable in his truck, Steve walked around to the driver's side of her compact car and used his flashlight to determine the type of lock.

Dianne lowered the window. "I don't usually do things like this. I've never locked the keys in my car before—I don't know why I did tonight. Stupid."

He returned to the tow truck and opened the passenger door. "No one can be smart all the time," he said cheerfully. "Don't be so hard on yourself." He moved the seat forward a little and reached for a toolbox in the space behind her.

"I've had a lot on my mind lately," she said.

Straightening, he looked at her and nodded sympathetically. He had a nice face too, she noted, easy on the eyes. In fact, he was downright attractive. The coveralls didn't detract from his appeal, but actually suggested a certain ruggedness. He was thoughtful and friendly just when Dianne was beginning to think there wasn't anyone in the world who was. But then, standing in the dark and the rain might make anyone feel friendless, even though Port Blossom was a rural community with a warm, small-town atmosphere.

Steve went back to her car and began to fiddle with the lock. Unable to sit still, Dianne opened the truck door and climbed out. "It's the dinner that's got me so upset."

"The dinner?" Steve glanced up from his work.

"The Valentine's dinner the community center's sponsoring this Saturday night. My children are forcing me to go. I don't know for sure, but I think they've got money riding on it, because they're making it sound like a matter of national importance."

"I see. Why doesn't your husband take you?"

"I'm divorced," she said bluntly. "I suppose no one expects it to happen to them. I assumed after twelve years my marriage was solid, but it wasn't. Jack's remarried now, living in Boston." Dianne had no idea why she was rambling on like this, but once she'd opened her mouth, she couldn't seem to stop. She didn't usually relate the intimate details of her life to a perfect stranger.

"Aren't you cold?"

"I'm fine, thanks." That wasn't entirely true—she

was a little chilled—but she was more worried about not having a date for the stupid Valentine's dinner than freezing to death. Briefly she wondered if Jason, Jill and her mother would accept pneumonia as a reasonable excuse for not attending.

"You're sure? You look like you're shivering."

She rubbed her palms together and ignored his question. "That's when my mother suggested Jerome."

"Jerome?"

"She seems to think I need help getting my feet wet."

Steve glanced up at her again, clearly puzzled.

"In the dating world," Dianne explained. "But I've had it with the dates she's arranged."

"Disasters?"

"Encounters of the worst kind. On one of them, the guy set his napkin on fire."

Steve laughed outright at that.

"Hey, it wasn't funny, trust me. I was mortified. He panicked and started waving it around in the air until the maitre d' arrived with a fire extinguisher and chaos broke loose."

Dianne found herself smiling at the memory of the unhappy episode. "Now that I look back on it, it was rather amusing."

Steve's gaze held hers. "I take it there were other disasters?"

"None I'd care to repeat."

"So your mother's up to her tricks again?"

Dianne nodded. "Only this time my kids are involved. Mom stumbled across this butcher who specializes in...well, never mind, that's not important. What is important is if I don't come up with a date in the next day or two, I'm going to be stuck going to this stupid dinner with Jerome."

"It shouldn't be so bad," he said. Dianne could hear the grin in his voice.

"How generous of you to say so." She crossed her arms over her chest. She'd orbited her vehicle twice before she spoke again.

"My kids are even instructing me on the kind of man they want me to date."

"Oh?"

Dianne wasn't sure he'd heard her. Her lock snapped free and he opened the door and retrieved her keys, which were in the ignition. He handed them to her, and with a thank-you, Dianne made a move to climb into her car.

"Jason and Jill—they're my kids—want me to go out with a tall, dark, handsome—" She stopped abruptly, thrusting out her arm as if to keep her balance.

Steve looked at her oddly. "Are you all right?"

Dianne brought her fingertips to her temple and nodded. "I think so..." She inhaled sharply and motioned toward the streetlight. "Would you mind stepping over there for a minute?"

"Me?" He pointed to himself as though he wasn't sure she meant him.

"Please."

He shrugged and did as she requested.

The idea was fast gaining momentum in her mind. He was certainly tall—at least six foot three, which was a nice complement to her own slender five ten. And he was dark—his hair appeared to be a rich shade of mahogany. As for the handsome part, she'd noticed that right off.

"Is something wrong?" he probed.

"No," Dianne said, grinning shyly—although what

she was about to propose was anything but shy. "By the way, how old are you? Thirty? Thirty-one?"

"Thirty-five."

"That's good. Perfect." A couple of years older than she was. Yes, the kids would approve of that.

"Good? Perfect?" He seemed to be questioning her sanity.

"Married?" she asked.

"Nope. I never got around to it, but I came close once." His eyes narrowed suspiciously.

"That's even better. I don't suppose you've got a jealous girlfriend—or a mad lover hanging around looking for an excuse to murder someone?"

"Not lately."

Dianne sighed with relief. "Great."

"Your car door's open," he said, gesturing toward it. He seemed eager to be on his way. "All I need to do is write down your auto club number."

"Yes, I know." She stood there, arms folded, studying him in the light. He was even better-looking than she'd first thought. "Do you own a decent suit?"

He chuckled as if the question amused him. "Yes."

"I mean something really nice, not the one you wore to your high-school graduation."

"It's a really nice suit."

Dianne didn't mean to be insulting, but she had to have all her bases covered. "That's good," she said. "How would you like to earn an extra hundred bucks Saturday night?"

"I beg your pardon?"

"I'm offering you a hundred dollars to escort me to the Valentine's dinner here at the center."

Steve stared at her as though he suspected she'd escaped from a mental institution.

"Listen, I know this is a bit unusual," Dianne rushed on, "but you're perfect. Well, not perfect, but you're exactly the kind of man the kids expect me to date, and frankly I haven't got time to do a whole lot of recruiting. Mr. Right hasn't showed up, if you know what I mean."

"I think I do."

"I need a date for one night. You fit the bill and you could probably use the extra cash. I realize it's not much, but a hundred dollars sounds fair to me. The dinner starts at seven and should be over by nine. I suspect fifty dollars an hour is more than you're earning now."

"Ah…"

"I know what you're thinking, but I promise you I'm not crazy. I've got a gold credit card, and they don't issue those to just anyone."

"What about a library card?"

"That, too, but I do have a book overdue. I was planning to take it back tomorrow." She started searching through her purse to prove she had both cards before she saw that he was teasing her.

"Ms. …."

"Dianne Williams," she said stepping forward to offer him her hand. His long, strong fingers wrapped around hers and he smiled, studying her for perhaps the first time. His eyes softened as he shook her hand. The gesture, though small, reassured Dianne that he was the man she wanted to take her to this silly dinner. Once more she found herself rushing to explain.

"I'm sure this all sounds crazy. I don't blame you for thinking I'm a nutcase. But I'm not, really I'm not. I attend church every Sunday, do volunteer work at the grade school, and help coach a girls' soccer team in the fall."

"Why'd you pick me?"

"Well, that's a bit complicated, but you have nice eyes, and when you suggested I sit in your truck and get out of the rain—actually it was only drizzling—" she paused and inhaled a deep breath "—I realized you were a generous person, and you just might consider something this..."

"...weird," he finished for her.

Dianne nodded, then looked him directly in the eye. Her defenses were down, and there was nothing left to do but admit the truth.

"I'm desperate. No one but a desperate woman would make this kind of offer."

"Saturday night, you say?"

The way her luck was running, he'd suddenly remember he had urgent plans for the evening. Something important like dusting his bowling trophies.

"From seven to nine. No later, I promise. If you don't think a hundred is enough..."

"A hundred's more than generous."

She sagged with relief. "Does this mean you'll do it?"

Steve shook his head slowly, as though to suggest he ought to have it examined for even contemplating her proposal.

"All right," he said after a moment. "I never could resist a damsel in distress."

Three

"Hello, everyone!" Dianne sang out as she breezed in the front door. She paused just inside the living room and watched as her mother and her two children stared openly. A sense of quiet astonishment pervaded the room. "Is something wrong?"

"What happened to you?" Jason cried. "You look awful!"

"You look like Little Orphan Annie, dear," her mother said, her hand working a crochet hook so fast the yarn zipped through her fingers.

"I phoned to tell you I'd be late," Dianne reminded them.

"But you didn't say anything about nearly drowning. What happened?"

"I locked my keys in the car—I already explained that."

Jill walked over to her mother, took her hand and led her to the hallway mirror. The image that greeted Dianne was only a little short of shocking. Her long thick hair hung in limp sodden curls over her shoulders. Her mascara, supposedly no-run, had dissolved into black tracks down her cheeks. She was drenched to the skin and looked like a prize the cat had dragged onto the porch.

"Oh, dear," she whispered. Her stomach muscles tightened as she recalled the odd glances Steve had given her, and his comment that it must be "one of those days." No wonder!

"Why don't you go upstairs and take a nice hot shower?" her mother said. "You'll feel worlds better."

Humbled, for more reasons than she cared to admit, Dianne agreed.

As was generally the rule, her mother was right. By the time Dianne reappeared a half hour later, dressed in her terry-cloth robe and fuzzy pink slippers, she felt considerably better.

Making herself a cup of tea, she reviewed the events of the evening. Even if Steve had agreed to attend the Valentine's dinner out of pity, it didn't matter. What did matter was the fact that she had a date. As soon as she told her family, they'd stop hounding her.

"By the way," she said as she carried her tea into the living room, "I have a date for Saturday night."

The room went still. Even the television sound seemed to fade into nothingness. Her two children and her mother did a slow turn, their faces revealing their surprise.

"Don't look so shocked," Dianne said with a light, casual laugh. "I told you before that I was working on it. No one seemed to believe I was capable of finding a date on my own. Well, that isn't the case."

"Who?" Martha demanded, her eyes disbelieving.

"Oh, ye of little faith," Dianne said, feeling only a small twinge of guilt. "His name is Steve Creighton."

"When did you meet him?"

"Ah..." Dianne realized she wasn't prepared for an

inquisition. "A few weeks ago. We happened to bump into each other tonight, and he asked if I had a date for the dinner. Naturally I told him I didn't and he suggested we go together."

"Steve Creighton." Her mother repeated the name slowly, rolling the syllables over her tongue, as if trying to remember where she'd last heard it. Then she shook her head and resumed crocheting.

"You never said anything about this guy before." Jason's gaze was slightly accusing. He sat on the carpet, knees tucked under his chin.

"Of course I didn't. If I had, all three of you would be bugging me about him, just the way you are now."

Martha gave her ball of yarn a hard jerk. "How'd you two meet?"

Dianne wasn't ready for this line of questioning. She'd assumed letting her family know she had the necessary escort would've been enough to appease them. Silly of her.

They wanted details. Lots of details, and the only thing Dianne could do was make them up as she went along. She couldn't very well admit she'd only met Steve that night and was so desperate for a date that she'd offered to pay him to escort her to the dinner.

"We met, ah, a few weeks ago in the grocery store," she explained haltingly, averting her gaze. She prayed that would satisfy their curiosity. But when she paused to sip her tea, the three faces were riveted on her.

"Go on," her mother urged.

"I… I was standing in the frozen-food section and… Steve was there, too, and…he smiled at me and introduced himself."

"What did he say after that?" Jill wanted to know, eager for the particulars. Martha shared her granddaughter's interest. She set her yarn and crochet hook aside, focusing all her attention on Dianne.

"After he introduced himself, he said surely those low-cal dinners couldn't be for me—that I looked perfect just the way I was." The words fell stiffly from her lips. She had to be desperate to divulge her own fantasy to her family like this.

All right, she *was* desperate.

Jill's shoulders rose with an expressive sigh. "How romantic!"

Jason, however, was frowning. "The guy sounds like a flake to me. A real man doesn't walk up to a woman and say something stupid like that."

"Steve's very nice."

"Maybe, but he doesn't sound like he's got all his oars in the water."

"I think he sounds sweet," Jill countered, immediately defending her mother by championing Steve. "If Mom likes him, then he's good enough for me."

"There are a lot of fruitcakes out there." Apparently her mother felt obliged to tell her that.

It was all Dianne could do not to remind her dear, sweet mother that she'd arranged several dates for her with men who fell easily into that category.

"I think we should meet him," Jason said, his eyes darkening with concern. "He might turn out to be a serial murderer or something."

"Jason—" Dianne forced another light laugh "—you're being silly. Besides, you're going to meet him Saturday night."

"By then it'll be too late."

"Jason's got a point, dear," Martha said. "I don't think it would do any harm to introduce your young man to the family before Saturday night."

"I... He's probably busy... He's working all sorts of weird hours and..."

"What does he do?"

"Ah..." She couldn't think fast enough to come up with a lie and had to admit the truth. "He drives a truck."

Her words were followed by a tense silence as her children and mother exchanged meaningful looks. "I've heard stories about truck drivers," Martha said, pinching her lips tightly together. "None I'd care to repeat in front of the children, mind you, but...stories."

"Mother, you're being—"

"Jason's absolutely right. I insist we meet this Steve. Truck drivers and cowboys simply aren't to be trusted."

Dianne rolled her eyes.

Her mother forgave her by saying, "I don't expect you to know this, Dianne, since you married so young."

"You married Dad when you were eighteen— younger than I was when I got married," Dianne said, not really wanting to argue, but finding herself trapped.

"Yes, but I've lived longer." She waved her crochet hook at Dianne. "A mother knows these things."

"Grandma's right," Jason said, sounding very adult. "We need to meet this Steve before you go out with him."

Dianne threw her hands in the air in frustration. "Hey, I thought you kids were the ones so eager for me to be at this dinner!"

"Yes, but we still have standards," Jill said, now siding with the others.

"I'll see what I can do," Dianne mumbled.

"Invite him over for dinner on Thursday night," her mother said. "I'll make my beef Stroganoff and bring over a fresh apple pie."

"Ah...he might be busy."

"Then tell him Wednesday night," Jason advised in a voice that was hauntingly familiar. It was the same tone Dianne used when she meant business.

With nothing left to do but agree, Dianne said, "Okay. I'll try for Thursday." Oh, Lord, she thought, what had she got herself into?

She waited until the following afternoon to contact Steve. He'd given her his business card, which she'd tucked into the edging at the bottom of the bulletin board in her kitchen. She wasn't pleased about having to call him. She'd need to offer him more money if he agreed to this dinner. She couldn't very well expect him to come out of the generosity of his heart.

"Port Blossom Towing," a crisp female voice answered.

"Ah...this is Dianne Williams. I'd like to leave a message for Steve Creighton."

"Steve's here." Her words were followed by a click and a ringing sound.

"Steve," he answered distractedly.

"Hello." Dianne found herself at a loss for words. She'd hoped to just leave a message and ask him to return the call at his convenience. Having him there, on the other end of the line, when she wasn't expecting it left her at a disadvantage.

"Is this Dianne?"

"Yes. How'd you know?"

He chuckled softly, and the sound was pleasant and warm. "It's probably best if I don't answer that. Are you checking up to make sure I don't back out of Saturday night? Don't worry, I won't. In fact, I stopped off at the community center this morning and picked up tickets for the dinner."

"Oh, you didn't have to do that, but thanks. I'll reimburse you later."

"Just add it to my tab," he said lightly.

Dianne cringed, then took a breath and said, "Actually, I called to talk to you about my children."

"Your children?"

"Yes," she said. "Jason and Jill, and my mother, too, seem to think it would be a good idea if they met you. I assured them they would on Saturday night, but apparently that isn't good enough."

"I see."

"According to Jason, by then it'll be too late, and you might turn out to be a serial murderer or something. And my mother found the fact that you drive a truck worrisome."

"Do you want me to change jobs, too? I might have a bit of a problem managing all that before Saturday night."

"Of course not. Now, about Thursday—that's when they want you to come for dinner. My mother's offered to fix her Stroganoff and bake a pie. She uses Granny Smith apples," Dianne added, as though that bit of information would convince him to accept.

"Thursday night?"

"I'll give you an additional twenty dollars."

"Twenty dollars?" He sounded insulted, so Dianne raised her offer.

"All right, twenty-five, but that's as high as I can go. I'm living on a budget, you know." This fiasco was quickly running into a big chunk of cash. The dinner tickets were thirty each, and she'd need to reimburse Steve for those. Plus, she owed him a hundred for escorting her to the silly affair, and now an additional twenty-five if he came to dinner with her family.

"For twenty-five you've got yourself a deal," he said at last. "Anything else?"

Dianne closed her eyes. This was the worst part. "Yes," she said, swallowing tightly. The lump in her throat had grown to painful proportions. "There's one other thing. I… I want you to know I don't normally look that bad."

"Hey, I told you before—don't be so hard on yourself. You'd had a rough day."

"It's just that I don't want you to think I'm going to embarrass you at this Valentine's dinner. There may be people there you know, and after I made such a big deal over whether you had a suit and everything, well, I thought you might be more comfortable knowing…" She paused, closed her eyes and then blurted, "I've decided to switch brands of mascara."

His hesitation was only slight. "Thank you for sharing that. I'm sure I'll sleep better now."

Dianne decided to ignore his comment since she'd practically invited it. She didn't understand why she should find herself so tongue-tied with this man, but then again, perhaps she did. She'd made a complete idiot of herself. Paying a man to escort her to a dinner wasn't exactly the type of thing she wanted to list on a résumé.

"Oh, and before I forget," Dianne said, determined to put this unpleasantness behind her, "my mother and the kids asked me several questions about…us. How we met and the like. It might be a good idea if we went over my answers so our stories match."

"You want to meet for coffee later?"

"Ah…when?"

"Say seven, at the Pancake Haven. Don't worry, I'll buy."

Dianne had to bite back her sarcastic response. Instead she murmured, "Okay, but I won't have a lot of time."

"I promise not to keep you any longer than necessary."

Four

"All right," Steve said dubiously, once the waitress had poured them each a cup of coffee. "How'd we meet?"

Dianne told him, lowering her voice when she came to the part about the low-cal frozen dinners. She found it rather humiliating to have to repeat her private fantasy a second time, especially to Steve.

He looked incredulous when she'd finished. "You've got to be kidding."

Dianne took offense at his tone. This was *her* romantic invention he was ridiculing, and she hadn't even mentioned the part about the Rimsky-Korsakov symphony or the chiming bells.

"I didn't have time to think of anything better," Dianne explained irritably. "Jason hit me with the question first thing and I wasn't prepared."

"What did Jason say when you told him that story?"

"He said you sounded like a flake."

"I don't blame him."

Dianne's shoulders sagged with defeat.

"Don't worry about it," Steve assured her, still frowning. "I'll clear everything up when I meet him

Thursday night." He said it in a way that suggested the task would be difficult.

"Good—only don't make me look like any more of a fool than I already do."

"I'll try my best," he said with the same dubious inflection he'd used when they'd first sat down.

Dianne sympathized. This entire affair was quickly going from bad to worse, and there was no one to fault but her. Who would've dreamed finding a date for the Valentine's dinner would cause so many problems?

As they sipped their coffee, Dianne studied the man sitting across from her. She was somewhat surprised to discover that Steve Creighton looked even better the second time around. He was dressed in slacks and an Irish cable-knit sweater the color of winter wheat. His smile was a ready one and his eyes, now that she had a chance to see them in the light, were a deep, rich shade of brown like his hair. The impression he'd given her of a considerate, generous man persisted. He must be. No one else would have agreed to this scheme, at least not without a more substantial inducement.

"I'm afraid I might've painted my kids a picture of you that's not quite accurate," Dianne admitted. Both her children had been filled with questions about Steve when they'd returned from school that afternoon. Jason had remained skeptical, but Jill, always a romantic—Dianne couldn't imagine where she'd inherited that!—had bombarded her for details.

"I'll do my best to live up to my image," Steve was quick to assure her.

Placing her elbows on the table, Dianne brushed a thick swatch of hair away from her face and tucked it behind her ear. "Listen, I'm sorry I ever got you involved in this."

"No backing out now—I've laid out cold hard cash for the dinner tickets."

Which was a not-so-subtle reminder that she owed him for those. She dug through her bag and brought out her checkbook. "I'll write you a check for the tickets right now."

"I'm not worried." He dismissed her offer with a wave of his hand.

Nevertheless, Dianne insisted. If she paid him in increments, she wouldn't have to think about how much this fiasco would end up costing her. She had the distinct feeling that by the time the Valentine's dinner was over, she would've spent as much as if she'd taken a Hawaiian vacation. Or gone to Seattle for the weekend, anyway.

After adding her signature, with a flair, to the bottom of the check, she kept her eyes lowered and said, "If I upped the ante ten dollars do you think you could manage to look…besotted?"

"Besotted?" Steve repeated the word as though he'd never heard it before.

"You know, smitten."

"Smitten?"

Again he made it sound as though she were speaking a foreign language. "Attracted," she tried for the third time, loud enough to catch the waitress's attention. The woman appeared and splashed more coffee into their nearly full cups.

"I'm not purposely being dense," he said. "I'm just not sure what you mean."

"Try to look as though you find me attractive," she said, leaning halfway across the table and speaking in a heated whisper.

"I see. So that's what 'besotted' means." He took another sip of his coffee, and Dianne had the feeling he did so in an effort to hide a smile.

"You aren't supposed to find that amusing." She took a gulp of her own drink and nearly scalded her mouth. Under different circumstances she would've grimaced with pain, or at least reached for the water glass. She did none of those things. A woman has her pride.

"Let me see if I understand you correctly," Steve said matter-of-factly. "For an extra ten bucks you want me to look 'smitten.'"

"Yes," Dianne answered with as much dignity as she could muster, which at the moment wasn't a lot.

"I'll do it, of course," Steve said, grinning and making her feel all the more foolish, "only I'm not sure I know how." He straightened, squared his shoulders and momentarily closed his eyes.

"Steve?" Dianne whispered, glancing around, hoping no one was watching them. He seemed to be attempting some form of Eastern meditation. She half expected him to start chanting. "What are you doing?"

"Thinking about how to look smitten."

"Are you making fun of me?"

"Not at all. If you're willing to offer me an extra ten bucks, it must be important to you. I want to do it right."

Dianne thought she'd better tell him. "This isn't for me," she said. "It's for my ten-year-old daughter, who happens to have a romantic nature. Jill was so impressed with the story of how we supposedly met, that I… I was kind of hoping you'd be willing to…you know." Now that she was forced to spell it out, Dianne wasn't certain of anything. But she knew one thing—suggesting he look smitten with her had been a mistake.

"I'll try."

"I'd appreciate it," she said.

"How's this?" Steve cocked his head at a slight angle, then slowly lowered his eyelids until they were half closed. His mouth curved upward in an off-center smile while his shoulders heaved in what Dianne suspected was meant to be a deep sigh of longing. As though in afterthought, he pressed his open hands over his heart while making soft panting sounds.

"Are you doing an imitation of a Saint Bernard?" Dianne snapped, still not sure whether he was laughing at her. "You look like a…a dog. Maybe Jason's right and you really are a flake."

"I was trying to look besotted," Steve said. "I thought that was what you wanted." As if it would improve the image, he cocked his head the other way and repeated the performance.

"You're making fun of me, and I don't appreciate it one bit." Dianne tossed her napkin on the table and stood. "Thursday night, six o'clock, and please don't be late." With that she slipped her purse strap over her shoulder and stalked out of the restaurant.

Steve followed her to her car. "All right, I apologize. I got carried away in there."

Dianne nodded. She'd gone a little overboard herself, but not nearly as much as Steve. Although she claimed she wanted him to give the impression of being attracted to her for Jill's sake, that wasn't entirely true. Steve was handsome and kind, and to have him looking at her with his heart in his eyes was a fantasy that was strictly her own.

Admitting that, even to herself, was a shock. The walls around her battered heart had been reinforced by three years of loneliness. For reasons she couldn't really explain, this tow-truck driver made her feel vulnerable.

"I'm willing to try again if you want," he said. "Only…"

"Yes?" Her car was parked in the rear lot where the lighting wasn't nearly as good. Steve's face was hidden in the shadows, and she couldn't tell if he was being sincere or not.

"The problem," he replied slowly, "comes from the fact that we haven't kissed. I don't mean to be forward, you understand. You want me to wear a certain look, but it's a little difficult to manufacture without having had any, er, physical closeness."

"I see." Dianne's heart was pounding hard enough to damage her rib cage.

"Are you willing to let me kiss you?"

It was a last resort and she didn't have much choice. But she didn't have anything to lose, either. "If you insist."

With a deep breath, she tilted her head to the right, shut her eyes and puckered up. After waiting what seemed an inordinate amount of time, she opened her eyes. "Is something wrong?"

"I can't do it."

Embarrassed in the extreme, Dianne set her hands on her hips. "What do you mean?"

"You look like you're about to be sacrificed to appease the gods."

"I beg your pardon!" Dianne couldn't believe she was hearing him correctly. Talk about humiliation— she was only doing what he'd suggested.

"I can't kiss a woman who acts like she's about to undergo the most revolting experience of her life."

"You're saying I'm...oh...oh!" Too furious to speak, Dianne gripped Steve by the elbow and jerked him over to where his tow truck was parked, a couple of spaces down from her own car. Hopping onto the running board, she glared down at him. Her higher vantage point made her feel less vulnerable. Her eyes flashed with anger; his were filled with mild curiosity.

"Dianne, what are you doing now?"

"I'll have you know I was quite a kisser in my time."

"I don't doubt it."

"You just did. Now listen and listen well, because I'm only going to say this once." Waving her index finger under his nose, she paused and lowered her hand abruptly. He was right, she hadn't been all that thrilled to fall into this little experiment. A kiss was an innocent-enough exchange, she supposed, but kissing Steve put her on the defensive. And that troubled her.

"Say it."

Self-conscious now, she shifted her gaze and stepped off the running board, feeling ridiculous.

"What was so important that you were waving your finger under my nose?" Steve pressed.

Since she'd made such a fuss, she didn't have any alternative but to finish what she'd begun. "When I was in high school...the boys used to like to kiss me."

"They still would," Steve said softly, "if you'd give them a little encouragement."

She looked up at him and had to blink back unexpected tears. A woman doesn't have her husband walk out on her and not find herself awash in pain and self-doubt. Once she'd been confident; now she was dubious and insecure.

"Here," Steve said, holding her by the shoulders. "Let's try this." Then he gently, sweetly slanted his mouth over hers. Dianne was about to protest when their lips met and the option to refuse was taken from her.

Mindlessly she responded. Her arms slid around his middle and her hands splayed across the hard muscles of his back. And suddenly, emotions that had been simmering just below the surface rose like a tempest within her, and her heart went on a rampage.

Steve buried his hands in her hair, his fingers twisting and tangling in its thickness, bunching it at the back of her head. His mouth was soft, yet possessive. She gave a small, shocked moan when his tongue breached the barrier of her lips, but she adjusted quickly to the deepening quality of his kiss.

Reluctantly, Steve eased his mouth from hers. For a long moment, Dianne didn't open her eyes. When she finally did, she found Steve staring down at her.

He blinked.

She blinked.

Then, in the space of a heartbeat, he lowered his mouth back to hers.

Unable to stop, Dianne sighed deeply and leaned into his strength. Her legs felt like mush and her head was spinning with confusion. Her hands crept up and closed around the folds of his collar.

This kiss was long and thorough. It was the sweetest kiss Dianne had ever known—and the most passionate.

When he lifted his mouth from hers, he smiled tenderly. "I don't believe I'll have any problem looking besotted," he whispered.

Five

"Steve's here!" Jason called, releasing the living-room curtain. "He just pulled into the driveway."

Jill's high-pitched voice echoed her brother's. "He brought his truck. It's red and—"

"—wicked," Jason said, paying Steve's choice of vehicles the highest form of teenage compliment.

"What did I tell you," Dianne's mother said, as she briskly stirred the Stroganoff sauce. "He's driving a truck that's red and wicked." Her voice rose hysterically. "The man's probably a spawn of the devil!"

"Mother, 'wicked' means 'wonderful' to Jason."

"I've never heard anything so absurd in my life."

The doorbell chimed just then. Unfastening the apron from around her waist and tossing it aside, Dianne straightened and walked into the wide entryway. Jason, Jill and her mother followed closely, crowding her.

"Mom, please," Dianne pleaded, "give me some room here. Jason. Jill. Back up a little, would you?"

All three moved several paces back, allowing Dianne some space. But the moment her hand went for the doorknob, they crowded forward again.

"Children, Ma, please!" she whispered frantically. The three were so close to her she could barely breathe.

Reluctantly Jason and Jill shuffled into the living room and slumped onto the sofa near the television set. Martha, however, refused to budge.

The bell chimed a second time, and after glaring at her mother and receiving no response, Dianne opened the door. On the other side of the screen door stood Steve, a huge bouquet of red roses in one hand and a large stuffed bear tucked under his other arm.

Dianne stared as she calculated the cost of long-stemmed roses, and a stuffed animal. She couldn't even afford carnations. And if he felt it necessary to bring along a stuffed bear, why hadn't he chosen a smaller, less costly one?

"May I come in?" he asked after a lengthy pause.

Her mother elbowed Dianne in the ribs and smiled serenely as she unlatched the lock on the screen door.

"You must be Steve. How lovely to meet you," Martha said as graciously as if she'd always thought the world of truck drivers.

Holding the outer door for him, Dianne managed to produce a weak smile as Steve entered her home. Jason and Jill had come back into the hallway to stand next to their grandmother, eyeing Dianne's newfound date with open curiosity. For all her son's concern that Steve might turn out to be an ax-murderer, one look at the bright-red tow truck and he'd been won over.

"Steve, I'd like you to meet my family," Dianne said, gesturing toward the three.

"So, you're Jason," Steve said, holding out his hand. The two exchanged a hearty handshake. "I'm pleased to meet you. Your mother speaks highly of you."

Jason beamed.

Turning his attention to Jill, Steve held out the over-size teddy bear. "This is for you," he said, giving her the stuffed animal. "I wanted something extra-special for Dianne's daughter, but this was all I could think of. I hope you aren't disappointed."

"I *love* teddy bears!" Jill cried, hugging it tight. "Did Mom tell you that?"

"Nope," Steve said, centering his high-voltage smile on the ten-year-old. "I just guessed."

"Oh, thank you, thank you." Cuddling the bear, Jill raced up the stairs, giddy with delight. "I'm going to put him on my bed right now."

Steve's gaze followed her daughter, and then his eyes briefly linked with Dianne's. In that split second, she let him know she wasn't entirely pleased. He frowned slightly, but recovered before presenting the roses to Dianne's mother.

"For me?" Martha brought her fingertips to her mouth as though shocked by the gesture. "Oh, you shouldn't have! Oh, my heavens, I can't remember the last time a man gave me roses." Reaching for the corner of her apron, she discreetly dabbed her eyes. "This is such a treat."

"Mother, don't you want to put those in water?" Dianne said pointedly.

"Oh, dear, I suppose I should. It was a thoughtful gesture, Steve. Very thoughtful."

"Jason, go help your grandmother."

Her son looked as though he intended to object, but changed his mind and obediently followed Martha into the kitchen.

As soon as they were alone, Dianne turned on Steve. "Don't you think you're laying it on a little thick?" she whispered. She was so furious she was having trouble speaking clearly. "I can't afford all this!"

"Don't worry about it."

"I am worried. In fact I'm experiencing a good deal of distress. At the rate you're spending my money, I'm going to have to go on an installment plan."

"Hush, now, before you attract everyone's attention."

Dianne scowled at him. "I—"

Steve placed his fingers over her lips. "I've learned a very effective way of keeping you quiet—don't force me to use it. Kissing you so soon after my arrival might create the wrong impression."

"You wouldn't dare!"

The way his mouth slanted upward in a slow smile made her afraid he would. "I was only doing my best to act besotted," he said.

"You didn't have to spend this much money doing it. Opening my door, holding out my chair—that's all I wanted. First you roll your eyes like you're going into a coma and pant like a Saint Bernard, then you spend a fortune."

"Dinner's ready," Martha shouted from the kitchen.

With one last angry glare, Dianne led him into the big kitchen. Steve moved behind Dianne's chair and pulled it out for her. "Are you happy now?" he whispered close to her ear as she sat down.

She nodded, thinking it was too little, too late, but she didn't have much of an argument since she'd specifically asked for this.

Soon the five were seated around the wooden table. Dianne's mother said the blessing, and while she did, Dianne offered up a fervent prayer of her own. She wanted Steve to make a good impression—but not too good.

After the buttered noodles and the Stroganoff had been passed around, along with a lettuce-and-cucumber salad and homemade rolls, Jason embarked on the topic that had apparently been troubling him from the first.

"Mom said you met at the grocery store."

Steve nodded. "She was blocking the aisle and I had to ask her to move her cart so I could get to the Hearty Eater Pot Pies."

Jason straightened in his chair, looking more than a little satisfied. "I thought it might be something like that."

"I beg your pardon?" Steve asked, playing innocent.

Her son cleared his throat, glanced carefully around before answering, then lowered his voice. "You should hear Mom's version of how you two met."

"More noodles?" Dianne said, shoving the bowl toward her son.

Jill looked confused. "But didn't you smile at Mom and say she's perfect just the way she is?"

Steve took a moment to compose his thoughts while he buttered his third dinner roll. Dianne recognized that he was doing a balancing act between her two children. If he said he'd commented on the low-cal frozen dinners and her figure, then he risked offending Jason, who seemed to think no man in his right mind would say something like that. On the other hand, if he claimed otherwise, he might wound Jill's romantic little heart.

"I'd be interested in knowing that myself," Martha added, looking pleased that Steve had taken a second helping of her Stroganoff. "Dianne's terribly close-mouthed about these things. She didn't even mention you until the other night."

"To be honest," Steve said, sitting back in his chair, "I don't exactly recall what I said to Dianne. I remember being irritated with her for hogging the aisle, but when I asked her to move, she apologized and immediately pushed her cart out of the way."

Jason nodded, appeased.

"But when I got a good look at her, I couldn't help thinking she was the most beautiful woman I'd seen in a long while."

Jill sighed, mollified.

"I don't recall any of that," Dianne said, reaching for another roll. She tore it apart with a vengeance and smeared butter on both halves before she realized she had an untouched roll balanced on the edge of her plate.

"I was thinking that after dinner I'd take Jason out for a ride in the truck," Steve said when a few minutes had passed.

"You'd do that?" Jason nearly leapt from his chair in his eagerness.

"I was planning to all along," Steve explained. "I thought you'd be more interested in seeing how all the gears worked than in any gift I could bring you."

"I am." Jason was so excited he could barely sit still.

"When Jason and I come back, I'll take you out for a spin, Dianne."

She shook her head. "I'm not interested, thanks."

Three pairs of accusing eyes flashed in her direction. It was as if she'd committed an act of treason.

"I'm sure my daughter didn't mean that," Martha said, smiling sweetly at Steve. "She's been very tired lately and not quite herself."

Bewildered, Dianne stared at her mother.

"Can we go now?" Jason asked, already standing.

"If your mother says it's okay," Steve said, with a glance at Dianne. She nodded, and Steve finished the last of his roll and stood.

"I'll have apple pie ready for you when you get back," Martha promised, quickly ushering the two out the front door.

As soon as her mother returned to the kitchen, Dianne asked, "What was all that about?"

"What?" her mother demanded, feigning ignorance.

"That I've been very tired and not myself lately?"

"Oh, that," Martha said, clearing the table. "Steve wants to spend a few minutes alone with you. It's only natural. So I had to make some excuse for you."

"Yes, but—"

"Your behavior, my dear, was just short of rude. When a gentleman makes it clear he wants to spend some uninterrupted time in your company, you should welcome the opportunity."

"Mother, I seem to recall your saying Steve was a spawn of the devil, remember?"

"Now that I've met him, I've had a change of heart."

"What about Jerome, the butcher? I thought you were convinced he was the one for me."

"I like Steve better. I can tell he's a good man, and you'd be a fool to let him slip through your fingers by pretending to be indifferent."

"I am indifferent."

With a look of patent disbelief, Martha Janes shook her head. "I saw the way your eyes lit up when Steve walked into the house. You can fool some folks, but you can't pull the wool over your own mother's eyes. You're falling in love with this young man, and frankly, I'm pleased. I like him."

Dianne frowned. If her eyes had lit up when Steve arrived, it was because she was busy trying to figure out a way to repay him for the roses and the teddy bear. What she felt for him wasn't anything romantic. Or was it?

Dear Lord, she couldn't actually be falling for this guy, could she?

The question haunted Dianne as she loaded the dishwasher.

"Steve's real cute," Jill announced. Her daughter would find Attila the Hun cute, too, if he brought her a teddy bear, but Dianne resisted the impulse to say so.

"He looks a little bit like Hugh Jackman, don't you think?" Jill continued.

"I can't say I've noticed." A small lie. Dianne had noticed a lot more about Steve than she was willing to admit. Although she'd issued a fair number of complaints, he really was being a good sport about this. Of course, she was paying him, but he'd gone above and beyond the call of duty. Taking Jason out for a spin in the tow truck was one example, although why anyone would be thrilled to drive around in that contraption was something Dianne didn't understand.

"I do believe Steve Creighton will make you a decent husband," her mother stated thoughtfully as she removed the warm apple pie from the oven. "In fact, I was just thinking how nice it would be to have a summer wedding. It's so much easier to ask relatives to travel when the weather's good. June or July would be perfect."

"Mother, please! Steve and I barely know each other."

"On the contrary," Steve said, sauntering into the kitchen. He stepped behind Dianne's mother and sniffed appreciatively at the aroma wafting from her apple pie. "I happen to be partial to summer weddings myself."

Six

"Don't you think you're overdoing it a bit?" Dianne demanded as Steve eased the big tow truck out of her driveway. She was belted into the seat next to him, feeling trapped—not to mention betrayed by her own family. They had insisted Steve take her out for a spin so the two of them could have some time alone. Steve didn't want to be alone with her, but her family didn't know that.

"Maybe I did come on a little strong," Steve agreed, dazzling her with his smile.

It was better for her equilibrium if she didn't glance his way, Dianne decided. Her eyes would innocently meet his and he'd give her one of those heart-stopping, lopsided smiles, and something inside her would melt. If this continued much longer, she'd be nothing more than a puddle by the end of the evening.

"The flowers and the stuffed animal I can understand," she said stiffly, willing to grant him that much. "You wanted to make a good impression, and that's fine, but the comment about being partial to summer weddings was going too far. It's just the kind of thing my mother was hoping to hear from you."

"You're right."

The fact that he was being so agreeable should have forewarned Dianne that something was amiss. She'd sensed it from the first moment she'd climbed into the truck. He'd closed the door and almost immediately something pulled wire-taut within her. The sensation was peculiar, even wistful—a melancholy pining she'd never felt before.

She squared her shoulders and stared straight ahead, determined not to fall under his spell the way her children and her mother so obviously had.

"As it is, I suspect Mom's been faithfully lighting votive candles every afternoon, asking God to send me a husband. She thinks God needs her help—that's why she goes around arranging dates for me."

"You're right, of course. I should never have made that comment about summer weddings," Steve said, "but I assumed that's just the sort of thing a *besotted* man would say."

Dianne sighed, realizing once again that she didn't have much of an argument. But he was doing everything in his power to make her regret that silly request.

"Hey, where are you taking me?" she asked when he turned off her street onto a main thoroughfare.

Steve turned his smile on her full force and twitched his thick eyebrows a couple of times for effect. "For a short drive. It wouldn't look good if we were to return five minutes after we left the house. Your family—"

"—will be waiting at the front door. They expect me back any minute."

"No, they don't."

"And why don't they?" she asked, growing uneasy. This wasn't supposed to be anything more than a ride around the block, and she'd had to be coerced into even that.

"Because I told your mother we'd be gone for an hour."

"An hour?" Dianne cried, as though he'd just announced he was kidnapping her. "But you can't do that! I mean, what about your time? Surely it's valuable."

"I assumed you'd want to pay me a few extra dollars— after all, I'm doing this to create the right impression. It's what—"

"I know, I know," she interrupted. "You're just acting smitten." The truth of the matter was that Dianne was making a fuss over something that was actually causing her heart to pound hard and fast. The whole idea of being alone with Steve appealed to her too much. *That* was the reason she fought it so hard. Without even trying, he'd managed to cast a spell on her family, and although she hated to admit it, he'd cast one on her, too. Steve Creighton was laughter and magic. Instinctively she knew he wasn't another Jack. Not the type of man who would walk away from his family.

Dianne frowned as the thought crossed her mind. It would be much easier to deal with the hand life had dealt her if she wasn't forced to associate with men as seemingly wonderful as Steve. It was easier to view all men as insensitive and inconsiderate.

Dianne didn't like that Steve was proving to be otherwise. He was apparently determined to crack the hard shell around her heart, no matter how hard she tried to reinforce it.

"Another thing," she said stiffly, crossing her arms with resolve, but refusing to glance in his direction. "You've got to stop being so free with my money."

"I never expected you to reimburse me for those gifts," he explained quietly.

"I insist on it."

"My, my, aren't we prickly. I bought the flowers and the toy for Jill of my own accord. I don't expect you to pick up the tab," he said again.

Dianne didn't know if she should argue with him or not. Although his tone was soft, a thread of steel ran through his words, just enough to let her know nothing she said was going to change his mind.

"That's not all," she said, deciding to drop that argument for a more urgent one. She probably did sound a bit shrewish, but if he wasn't going to be practical about this, *she'd* have to be.

"You mean there's more?" he cried, pretending to be distressed.

"Steve, please," she said, shocked at how feeble she sounded. She scarcely recognized the voice as her own. "You've got to stop being so…so wonderful," she finally said.

He came to a stop at a red light and turned to her, draping his arm over the back of the seat. "I don't think I heard you right. Would you mind repeating that?"

"You can't continue to be so—" she paused, searching for another word "—charming."

"Charming," he echoed. "Charming?"

"To my children and my mother," she elaborated. "The gifts were one thing. Giving Jason a ride in the tow truck was fine, too, but agreeing with my mother about summer weddings and then playing basketball with Jason—none of that was necessary."

"Personally, I would've thought your mother measuring my chest and arm length so she could knit me a sweater would bother you the most."

"That, too!"

"Could you explain why this is such a problem?"

"Isn't it obvious? If you keep doing that sort of thing, they'll expect me to continue dating you after the Valentine's dinner, and, frankly, I can't afford it."

He chuckled at that as if she was making some kind of joke. Only it wasn't funny. "I happen to live on a budget—"

"I don't think we should concern ourselves with that," he broke in.

"Well, I *am* concerned." She expelled her breath sharply. "One date! That's all I can afford and that's all I'm interested in. If you continue to be so...so..."

"Wonderful?" he supplied.

"Charming," she corrected, "then I'll have a whole lot to answer for when I don't see you again after Saturday."

"So you want me to limit the charm?"

"Please."

"I'll do my best," he said, and his eyes sparked with laughter, which they seemed to do a good deal of the time. If she hadn't been so flustered, she might have been pleased that he found her so amusing.

"Thank you." She glanced pointedly at her watch. "Shouldn't we head back to the house?"

"No."

"No? I realize you told my mother we'd be gone an hour, but that really is too long and—"

"I'm taking you to Jackson Point."

Dianne's heart reacted instantly, zooming into her throat and then righting itself. Jackson Point overlooked a narrow water passage between the Kitsap Peninsula and Vashon Island. The view, either at night or during the day, was spectacular, but those who came to appreciate it at night were generally more interested in each other than the glittering lights of the island and Seattle farther beyond.

"I'll take the fact that you're not arguing with me as a positive sign," he said.

"I think we should go back to the house," she stated with as much resolve as she could muster. Unfortunately it didn't come out sounding very firm. The last time she'd been to Jackson Point had been a lifetime ago. She'd been a high-school junior and madly in love for the first time. The last time.

"We'll go back in a little while."

"Steve," she cried, fighting the urge to cry, "why are you doing this?"

"Isn't it obvious? I want to kiss you again."

Dianne pushed her hair away from her face with both hands. "I don't think that's such a good idea." Her voice wavered, just like her teenage son's.

Before she could come up with an argument, Steve pulled off the highway and down the narrow road that led to the popular lookout. She hadn't wanted to think about that kiss they'd shared. It had been a mistake. Dianne knew she'd disappointed Steve—not because of the kiss itself, but her reaction to it. He seemed to be waiting for her to admit how deeply it had affected her, but she hadn't given him the satisfaction.

Now, she told herself, he wanted revenge.

Her heart was still hammering when Steve stopped the truck and turned off the engine. The lights across the water sparkled in welcome. The closest lights were from Vashon Island, a sparsely populated place accessible only by ferry. The more distant ones came from West Seattle.

"It's really beautiful," she whispered. Some of the

tension eased from her shoulders and she felt herself begin to relax.

"Yes," Steve agreed. He moved closer and placed his arm around her shoulder.

Dianne closed her eyes, knowing she didn't have the power to resist him. He'd been so wonderful with her children and her mother—more than wonderful. Now it seemed to be her turn, and try as she might to avoid it, she found herself a willing victim to his special brand of magic.

"You *are* going to let me kiss you, aren't you?" he whispered close to her ear.

She nodded.

His hands were in her hair as he directed his mouth to hers. The kiss was slow, as though he was afraid of frightening her. His mouth was warm and moist over her own, gentle and persuasive. Dianne could feel her bones start to dissolve and knew that if she was going to walk away from this experience unscathed, she needed to think fast. Unfortunately, her mind was already overloaded.

When at last they drew apart, he dragged in a deep breath. Dianne sank back against the seat and noted that his eyes were still closed. Taking this moment to gather her composure, she scooted as far away from him as she could, pressing the small of her back against the door handle.

"You're very good at this," she said, striving to sound unaffected, and knowing she hadn't succeeded.

He opened his eyes and frowned. "I'll assume that's a compliment."

"Yes. I think you should." Steve was the kind of man who'd attract attention from women no matter where he went. He wouldn't be interested in a divorcée and a ready-made family, and there was no use trying to convince herself otherwise. The only reason he'd agreed to take her to the Valentine's dinner was because she'd offered to pay him. This was strictly a business arrangement.

His finger lightly grazed the side of her face. His eyes were tender as he studied her, but he said nothing.

"It would probably be a good idea if we talked about Saturday night," she said, doing her best to keep her gaze trained away from him. "There's a lot to discuss and…there isn't much time left."

"All right." His wayward grin told her she hadn't fooled him. He knew exactly what she was up to.

"Since the dinner starts at seven, I suggest you arrive at my house at quarter to."

"Fine."

"We don't need to go to the trouble or the expense of a corsage."

"What are you wearing?"

Dianne hadn't given the matter a second's thought. "Since it's a Valentine's dinner, something red, I suppose. I have a red-and-white striped dress that will do." It was a couple of years old, but this dinner wasn't exactly the fashion event of the year, and she didn't have the money for a new outfit, anyway.

She looked at her watch, although she couldn't possibly read it in the darkness.

"Is that a hint you want to get back to the house?"

"Yes," she said.

Her honesty seemed to amuse him. "That's what I thought." Without argument, he started the engine and put the truck in Reverse.

The minute they turned onto her street, Jason and Jill came vaulting out the front door. Dianne guessed they'd both been staring out the upstairs window, eagerly awaiting her return.

She was wrong. It was Steve they were eager to see.

"Hey, what took you so long?" Jason demanded as Steve climbed out of the truck.

"Grandma's got the apple pie all dished up. Are you ready?" Jill hugged Steve's arm, gazing anxiously up at him.

Dianne watched the unfolding scene with dismay. Steve walked into her house with one arm around Jason and Jill clinging to the other.

It was as if she were invisible. Neither of her children had said a single word to her!

To his credit, Jason paused at the front door. "Mom, you coming?"

"Just bringing up the rear," she muttered.

Jill shook her head, her shoulders lifting, then falling, in a deep sigh. "You'll have to forgive my mother," she told Steve confidingly. "She can be a real slowpoke sometimes."

Seven

"Oh, Mom," Jill said softly. "You look so beautiful."

Dianne examined her reflection in the full-length mirror. At the last moment, she'd been gripped by another bout of insanity. She'd gone out and purchased a new dress.

She couldn't afford it. She couldn't rationalize that expense on top of everything else, but the instant she'd seen the flowered pink creation in the shop window, she'd decided to try it on. That was her first mistake. Correction: that was just one mistake in a long list of recent mistakes where Steve Creighton was concerned.

The dress was probably the most flattering thing she'd ever owned. The price tag had practically caused her to clutch her chest and stagger backward. She hadn't purchased it impulsively. No, she was too smart for that. The fact that she was nearly penniless and it was only the middle of the month didn't help matters. She'd sat down in the coffee shop next door and juggled figures for ten or fifteen minutes before crumpling up the paper and deciding to buy the dress, anyway. It was her birthday, Mother's Day and Christmas gifts to herself all rolled into one.

"I brought my pearls," Martha announced as she bolted breathlessly into Dianne's bedroom. She was late, which wasn't like Martha, but Dianne hadn't been worried. She knew her mother would be there before she had to leave for the dinner.

Martha stopped abruptly, folding her hands prayerfully and nodding with approval. "Oh, Dianne. You look…"

"Beautiful," Jill finished for her grandmother.

"Beautiful," Martha echoed. "I thought you were going to wear the red dress."

"I just happened to be at the mall and stumbled across this." She didn't mention that she'd made the trip into Tacoma for the express purpose of looking for something new to wear.

"Steve's here," Jason yelled from the bottom of the stairs.

"Here are my pearls," Martha said, reverently handing them to her daughter. The pearls were a family heirloom and worn only on the most special occasions.

"Mom, I don't know…"

"Your first official date with Steve," she said as though that event was on a level with God giving Moses the Ten Commandments. Without further ado, Martha draped the necklace around her daughter's neck. "I insist. Your father insists."

"Mom?" Dianne asked, turning around to search her mother's face. "Have you been talking to Dad again?" Dianne's father had been gone for more than ten years. However, for several years following his death, Martha claimed they carried on regular conversations.

"Not exactly, but I know your father would have insisted, had he been here. Now off with you. It's rude to keep a date waiting."

Preparing to leave her bedroom, Dianne closed her eyes. She was nervous. Which was silly, she told herself. This wasn't a *real* date, since she was paying Steve for the honor of escorting her. She'd reminded herself of that the entire time she was dressing. The only reason they were even attending this Valentine's dinner was because she'd asked him. Not only asked, but offered to pay for everything.

Jill rushed out of the bedroom door and down the stairs. "She's coming and she looks beautiful."

"Your mother always looks beautiful," Dianne heard Steve say matter-of-factly as she descended the steps. Her eyes were on him, standing in the entryway dressed in a dark gray suit, looking tall and debonair.

He glanced up and his gaze found hers. She was gratified to see that his eyes widened briefly.

"I was wrong, she's extra-beautiful tonight," he whispered, but if he was speaking to her children, he wasn't looking at them. In fact, his eyes were riveted on her, which only served to make Dianne more uneasy.

They stood staring at each other like star-crossed lovers until Jill tugged at Steve's arm. "Aren't you going to give my mom the corsage?"

"Oh, yes, here," he said. Apparently he'd forgotten he was holding an octagon-shaped plastic box.

Dianne frowned. They'd agreed earlier that he wasn't going to do this. She was already over her budget, and flowers were a low-priority item, as far as Dianne was concerned.

"It's for the wrist," he explained, opening the box for her. "I thought you said the dress was red, so I'm afraid this might not go with it very well." The corsage was fashioned of three white rosebuds between a froth of red-and-white silk ribbons. Although her dress was several shades of pink, there was a smattering of red in the center of the flowers that matched the color in the ribbon perfectly. It was as if Steve had seen the dress and chosen the flowers to complement it. "It's…"

"Beautiful," Jill supplied once more, smugly pleased with herself.

"Are you ready?" Steve asked.

Jason stepped forward with her wool coat as though he couldn't wait to be rid of her. Steve took the coat from her son's hands and helped Dianne into it, while her son and daughter stood back looking as proud as if they'd arranged the entire affair themselves.

Before she left the house, Dianne gave her children their instructions and kissed them each on the cheek. Jason wasn't much in favor of letting his mother kiss him, but he tolerated it.

Martha continued to stand at the top of the stairs, dabbing her eyes with a tissue and looking down as if the four of them together were the most romantic sight she'd ever witnessed. Dianne sincerely prayed that Steve wouldn't notice.

"I won't be late," Dianne said as Steve opened the front door.

"Don't worry about it," Jason said pointedly. "There's no need to rush home."

"Have a wonderful time," Jill called after them.

The first thing Dianne realized once they were out the door was that Steve's tow truck was missing from her driveway. She looked around, half expecting to find the red monstrosity parked on the street.

With his hand cupping her elbow, he led her instead to a luxury car. "What's this?" she asked, thinking he might have rented it. If he had, she wanted it understood this minute that she had no intention of paying the fee.

"My car."

"Your car?" she asked. He opened the door for her and Dianne slid onto the supple white leather. Tow-truck operators obviously made better money than she'd assumed. If she'd known that, she would've offered him seventy-five dollars for this evening instead of a hundred.

Steve walked around the front of the sedan and got into the driver's seat. They chatted on the short ride to the community center, with Dianne making small talk in an effort to cover her nervousness.

The parking lot was nearly full, but Steve found a spot on the side lot next to the sprawling brick building.

"You want to go in?" he asked.

She nodded. Over the years, Dianne had attended a dozen of these affairs. There was no reason to feel nervous. Her friends and neighbors would be there. Naturally there'd be questions about her and Steve, but this time she was prepared.

Steve came around the car, opened her door and helped her out. She saw that he was frowning.

"Is something wrong?" she asked anxiously.

"You look pale."

She was about to reply that it was probably nerves when he said, "Not to worry, I have a cure for that." Before she'd guessed his intention, he leaned forward and brushed his mouth over hers.

He was right. The instant his lips touched hers, hot color exploded in her cheeks. She felt herself swaying toward him, and Steve caught her gently by the shoulders.

"That was a mistake," he whispered once they'd moved apart. "Now the only thing I'm hungry for is you. Forget the dinner."

"I...think we should go inside now," she said, glancing around the parking lot, praying no one had witnessed the kiss.

Light and laughter spilled out from the wide double doors of the Port Blossom Community Center. The soft strains of a romantic ballad beckoned them in.

Steve took her coat and hung it on the rack in the entry. She waited for him, feeling more jittery than ever. When he'd finished, Steve slipped his arm about her waist and led her into the main room.

"Steve Creighton!" They had scarcely stepped into the room when Steve was greeted by a robust man with a salt-and-pepper beard. Glancing curiously at Dianne, the stranger slapped Steve on the back and said, "It's about time you attended one of our functions."

Steve introduced Dianne to the man, whose name was Sam Horton. The name was vaguely familiar to her, but she couldn't quite place it.

Apparently reading her mind, Steve said, "Sam's the president of the Chamber of Commerce."

"Ah, yes," Dianne said, impressed to meet one of the community's more distinguished members.

"My wife, Renée," Sam said, absently glancing around, "is somewhere in this mass of humanity." Then he turned back to Steve. "Have you two found a table yet? We'd consider it a pleasure to have you join us."

"Dianne?" Steve looked at her.

"That would be very nice, thank you." Wait until her mother heard this. She and Steve dining with the Chamber of Commerce president! Dianne couldn't help smiling. No doubt her mother would attribute this piece of good luck to the pearls. Sam left to find his wife, in order to introduce her to Dianne.

"Dianne Williams! It's so good to see you." The

voice belonged to Beth Martin, who had crossed the room, dragging her husband, Ralph, along with her. Dianne knew Beth from the PTA. They'd worked together on the spring carnival the year before. Actually, Dianne had done most of the work while Beth had done the delegating. The experience had been enough to convince Dianne not to volunteer for this year's event.

Dianne introduced Steve to Beth and Ralph. Dianne felt a small sense of triumph as she noted the way Beth eyed Steve. This man was worth every single penny of the money he was costing her!

The two couples chatted for a few moments, then Steve excused himself. Dianne watched him as he walked through the room, observing how the eyes of several women followed him. He did make a compelling sight, especially in his well-cut suit.

"How long have you known Steve Creighton?" Beth asked the instant Steve was out of earshot. She moved closer to Dianne, as though she was about to hear some well-seasoned gossip.

"A few weeks now." It was clear that Beth was hoping Dianne would elaborate, but Dianne had no intention of doing so.

"Dianne." Shirley Simpson, another PTA friend, moved to her side. "Is that Steve Creighton you're with?"

"Yes." She'd had no idea Steve was so well known.

"I swear he's the cutest man in town. One look at him and my toes start to curl."

When she'd approached Steve with this proposal, Dianne hadn't a clue she would become the envy of her friends. She really *had* got a bargain.

"Are you sitting with anyone yet?" Shirley asked. Beth bristled as though offended she hadn't thought to ask first.

"Ah, yes. Sam Horton's already invited us, but thanks."

"Sam Horton," Beth repeated and she and Shirley shared a significant look. "My, my, you are traveling in elevated circles these days. Well, more power to you. And good luck with Steve Creighton. I've been saying for ages that it's time someone bagged him. I hope it's you."

"Thanks," Dianne said, feeling more than a little confused by this unexpected turn of events. Everyone knew Steve, right down to her PTA friends. It didn't make a lot of sense.

Steve returned a moment later, carrying two slender flutes of champagne. "I'd like you to meet some friends of mine," he said, leading her across the room to where several couples were standing. The circle immediately opened to include them. Dianne recognized the mayor and a couple of others.

Dianne threw Steve a puzzled look. He certainly was a social animal, but the people he knew... Still, why should she be surprised? A tow-truck operator would have plenty of opportunity to meet community leaders. And Steve was such a likable man, who obviously made friends easily.

A four-piece band began playing forties' swing, and after the introductions, Dianne found her toe tapping to the music.

"Next year we should make this a dinner-dance," Steve suggested, smiling down on Dianne. He casually put his hand on her shoulder as if he'd been doing that for months.

"Great idea," Port Blossom's mayor said, nodding. "You might bring it up at the March committee meeting."

Dianne frowned, not certain she understood. It was

several minutes before she had a chance to ask Steve about the comment.

"I'm on the board of directors for the community center," he explained briefly.

"You are?" Dianne took another sip of her champagne. Some of the details were beginning to get muddled in her mind, and she wasn't sure if it had anything to do with the champagne.

"Does that surprise you?"

"Yes. I thought you had to be, you know, a business owner to be on the board of directors."

Now it was Steve's turn to frown. "I am."

"You are?" Dianne asked. Her hand tightened around the long stem of her glass. "What business?"

"Port Blossom Towing."

That did it. Dianne drank what remained of her champagne in a single gulp. "You mean to say you *own* the company?"

"Yes. Don't tell me you didn't know."

She glared up at him, her eyes narrowed and distrusting. "I didn't."

Eight

Steve Creighton had made a fool of her.

Dianne was so infuriated she couldn't wait to be alone with him so she could give him a piece of her mind. Loudly.

"What's that got to do with anything?" Steve asked.

Dianne continued to glare at him, unable to form any words yet. It wasn't just that he owned the towing company or even that he was a member of the board of directors for the community center. It was the fact that he'd deceived her.

"You should've told me you owned the company!" she hissed.

"I gave you my business card," he said, shrugging.

"You gave me your business card," she mimicked in a furious whisper. "The least you could've done was mention it. I feel like an idiot."

Steve was wearing a perplexed frown, as if he found her response completely unreasonable. "To be honest, I assumed you knew. I wasn't purposely keeping it from you."

That wasn't the only thing disturbing her, but the second concern was even more troubling than the first.

"While I'm on the subject, what are you? Some sort of…love god?"

"What?"

"From the moment we arrived all the women I know, and even some I don't, have been crowding around me asking all sorts of leading questions. One friend claims you make her toes curl and another…never mind."

Steve looked exceptionally pleased. "I make her toes curl?"

How like a man to fall for flattery! "That's not the point."

"Then what is?"

"Everyone thinks you and I are an item."

"So? I thought that's what you wanted."

Dianne felt like screaming. "Kindly look at this from my point of view. I'm in one hell of a mess because of you!" He frowned as she went on. "What am I supposed to tell everyone, including my mother and children, once tonight is over?" Why, oh why hadn't she thought of this sooner?

"About what?"

"About you and me," she said slowly, using short words so he'd understand. "I didn't even *want* to attend this dinner. I've lied to my own family and, worse, I'm actually paying a man to escort me. This is probably the lowest point of my life, and all you can do is stand there with a silly grin."

Steve chuckled and his mouth twitched. "This silly grin you find so offensive is my besotted look. I've been practicing it in front of a mirror all week."

Dianne covered her face with her hands. "Now… now I discover that I'm even more of a fool than I realized. You're this upstanding businessman and, worse, a…a playboy."

"I'm not a playboy," he corrected. "And that's a pretty dated term, anyway."

"Maybe—but that's the reputation you seem to have. There isn't a woman at this dinner who doesn't envy me."

All she'd wanted was someone presentable to escort her to this dinner so she could satisfy her children. She lived a quiet, uncomplicated life, and suddenly she was the most gossip-worthy member of tonight's affair.

Sam Horton stepped to the microphone in front of the hall and announced that dinner was about to be served, so would everyone please go to their tables.

"Don't look so discontented," Steve whispered in her ear. He was standing behind her, and his hands rested gently on her shoulders. "The woman who's supposed to be the envy of every other one here shouldn't be frowning. Try smiling."

"I don't think I can," she muttered, fearing she might break down and cry. Being casually held by Steve wasn't helping. She found his touch reassuring and comforting when she didn't want either, at least not from him. She was confused enough. Her head was telling her one thing and her heart another.

"Trust me, Dianne, you're blowing this out of proportion. I didn't mean to deceive you. Let's just enjoy the evening."

"I feel like such a fool," she muttered again. Several people walked past them on their way to the tables, pausing to smile and nod. Dianne did her best to respond appropriately.

"You're not a fool." He slipped his arm around her waist and led her toward the table where Sam and his wife, as well as two other couples Dianne didn't know, were waiting.

Dianne smiled at the others while Steve held out her chair. A gentleman to the very end, she observed wryly. He opened doors and held out chairs for her, and the whole time she was making an idiot of herself in front of the entire community.

As soon as everyone was seated, he introduced Dianne to the two remaining couples—Larry and Louise Lester, who owned a local restaurant, and Dale and Maryanne Atwater. Dale was head of the town's most prominent accounting firm.

The salads were delivered by young men in crisp white jackets. The Lesters and the Atwaters were discussing the weather and other bland subjects. Caught in her own churning thoughts, Dianne ate her salad and tuned them out. When she was least expecting it, she heard her name. She glanced up to find six pairs of eyes studying her. She had no idea why.

She lowered the fork to her salad plate and glanced at Steve, praying he'd know what was going on.

"The two of you make such a handsome couple," Renée Horton said. Her words were casual, but her expression wasn't. Everything about her said she was intensely curious about Steve and Dianne.

"Thank you," Steve answered, then turned to Dianne and gave her what she'd referred to earlier as a silly grin and what he'd said was his besotted look.

"How did you two meet?" Maryanne Atwater asked nonchalantly.

"Ah…" Dianne's mind spun, lost in a haze of half-truths and misconceptions. She didn't know if she dared repeat the story about meeting in the local grocery, but she couldn't think fast enough to come up with anything else. She thought she was prepared, but the moment she was in the spotlight, all her self-confidence deserted her.

"We both happened to be in the grocery store at the same time," Steve explained smoothly. The story had been repeated so often it was beginning to sound like the truth.

"I was blocking Steve's way in the frozen-food section," she said, picking up his version of the story. She felt embarrassed seeing the three other couples listening so intently to their fabrication.

"I asked Dianne to kindly move her cart, and she stopped to apologize for being so thoughtless. Before I knew it, we'd struck up a conversation."

"I was there!" Louise Lester threw her hands wildly in the air, her blue eyes shining. "That was the two of you? I saw the whole thing!" She dabbed the corners of her mouth with her napkin and checked to be sure she had everyone's attention before continuing. "I swear it was the most romantic thing I've ever seen."

"It certainly was," Steve added, smiling over at Dianne, who restrained herself from kicking him in the shin, although it was exactly what he deserved.

"Steve's cart inadvertently bumped into Dianne's," Louise went on, grinning broadly at Steve.

"Inadvertently, Steve?" Sam Horton teased, chuckling loudly enough to attract attention. Crazy though it was, it seemed that everyone in the entire community center had stopped eating in order to hear Louise tell her story.

"At any rate," Louise said, "the two of them stopped to chat, and I swear it was like watching a romantic comedy. Naturally Dianne apologized—she hadn't realized she was blocking the aisle. Then Steve started sorting through the stuff in her cart, teasing her. We all know how Steve enjoys kidding around."

The others shook their heads, their affection for their friend obvious.

"She was buying all these diet dinners," Steve said, ignoring Dianne's glare. "I told her she couldn't possibly be buying them for herself."

The three women at the table sighed audibly. It was all Dianne could do not to slide off her chair and disappear under the table.

"That's not the best part," Louise said, beaming with pride at the attention she was garnering. A dreamy look stole over her features. "They must've stood and talked for ages. I'd finished my shopping and just happened to stroll past them several minutes later, and they were still there. It was when I was standing in the checkout line that I noticed them coming down the aisle side by side, each pushing a grocery cart. It was so cute, I half expected someone to start playing a violin."

"How sweet," Renée Horton whispered.

"I thought so myself and I mentioned it to Larry once I got home. Remember, honey?"

Larry nodded obligingly. "Louise must've told me that story two or three times that night," her husband reported.

"I just didn't know it was you, Steve. Imagine, out of all the people to run into at the grocery store, I happened to stumble upon you and Dianne the first time you met. Life is so ironic, isn't it?"

"Oh, yes, life is very ironic," Dianne said. Steve sent her a subtle smile, and she couldn't hold back an answering grin.

"It was one of the most beautiful things I've ever seen," Louise finished.

* * *

"Can you believe that Louise Lester?" Steve said later. They were sitting in his luxury sedan waiting for their turn to pull out of the crowded parking lot.

"No," Dianne said simply. She'd managed to make it through the rest of the dinner, but it had demanded every ounce of poise and self-control she possessed. From the moment they'd walked in the front door until the time Steve helped her put on her coat at the end of the evening, they'd been the center of attention. And the main topic of conversation.

Like a bumblebee visiting a flower garden, Louise Lester had breezed from one dinner table to the next, spreading the story of how Dianne and Steve had met and how she'd been there to witness every detail.

"I've never been so…" Dianne couldn't think of a word that quite described how she'd felt. "This may have been the worst evening of my life." She slumped against the back of the seat and covered her eyes.

"I thought you had a good time."

"How could I?" she cried, dropping her hand long enough to glare at him. "The first thing I get hit with is that you're some rich playboy."

"Come on, Dianne. Just because I happen to own a business doesn't mean I'm rolling in money."

"Port Blossom Towing is one of the fastest-growing enterprises in Kitsap County," she said, repeating what Sam Horton had been happy to tell her. "What I don't understand is why my mother hasn't heard of you. She's been on the lookout for eligible men for months. It's a miracle she didn't—" Dianne stopped abruptly.

"What?"

"My mother was looking all right, but she was realistic enough to stay in my own social realm. You're a major-league player. The only men my mother knows are in the minors—butchers, teachers, everyday sort of guys."

Now that she thought about it, however, her mother had seemed to recognize Steve's name when Dianne first mentioned it. She probably *had* heard of him, but couldn't remember where.

"Major-league player? That's a ridiculous analogy."

"It isn't. And to think I approached you, offering you money to take me to this dinner." Humiliation washed over her again, then gradually receded. "I have one question—why didn't you already have a date?" The dinner had been only five days away, so surely the most eligible bachelor in town, a man who could have his choice of women, would've had a date!

He shrugged. "I'm not seeing anyone."

"I bet you got a good laugh when I offered to pay you." Not to mention the fact that she'd made such a fuss over his owning a proper suit.

"As a matter of fact, I was flattered."

"No doubt."

"Are you still upset?"

"You could say that, yes." *Upset* was putting it mildly.

Since Dianne's house was only a couple of miles from the community center, she reached for her purse and checkbook. She waited until he pulled into the driveway before writing a check and handing it to him.

"What's this?" Steve asked.

"What I owe you. Since I didn't know the exact cost of Jill's stuffed animal, I made an educated guess. The cost of the roses varies from shop to shop, so I took an average price."

"I don't think you should pay me until the evening's over," he said, opening his car door.

As far as Dianne was concerned, it had been over the minute she'd learned who he was. When he came around to her side of the car and opened her door, she said, "Just what are you planning now?" He led her by the hand to the front of the garage, which was illuminated by a floodlight. They stood facing each other, his hands on her shoulders.

She frowned, gazing up at him. "I fully intend to give you your money's worth," he replied.

"I beg your pardon?"

"Jason, Jill and your mother."

"What about them?"

"They're peering out the front window waiting for me to kiss you, and I'm not going to disappoint them."

"Oh, no, you don't," she objected. But the moment his eyes held hers, all her anger drained away. Then, slowly, as though he recognized the change in her, he lowered his head. Dianne knew he was going to kiss her, and in the same instant she knew she wouldn't do anything to stop him...

Nine

"You have the check?" Dianne asked once her head was clear enough for her to think again. It was a struggle to pull herself free from the magic Steve wove so easily around her.

Steve pulled the check she'd written from his suit pocket. Then, without ceremony, he tore it in two. "I never intended to accept a penny."

"You have to! We agreed—"

"I want to see you again," he said, clasping her shoulders firmly and looking intently at her.

Dianne was struck dumb. If he'd announced he was an alien, visiting from the planet Mars, he couldn't have surprised her more. Not knowing what to say, she eyed him speculatively. "You're kidding, aren't you?"

A smile flitted across his lips as though he'd anticipated her reaction. The left side of his mouth rose slightly higher in that lazy, off-center grin of his. "I've never been more serious in my life."

Now that the shock had worn off, it took Dianne all of one second to decide. "Naturally, I'm flattered—but no."

"No?" Steve was clearly taken aback, and he needed a second or two to compose himself. "Why not?"

"After tonight you need to ask?"

"Apparently so," he said, stepping away from her a little. He paused and shoved his fingers through his hair with enough force to make Dianne flinch. "I can't believe you," he muttered. "The first time we kissed I realized we had something special. I thought you felt it, too."

Dianne couldn't deny it, but she wasn't about to admit it, either. She lowered her gaze, refusing to meet the hungry intensity of his eyes.

When she didn't respond, Steve continued, "I have no intention of letting you out of my life. In case you haven't figured it out yet—and obviously you haven't—I'm crazy about you, Dianne."

Unexpected tears clouded her vision as she gazed up at him. She rubbed her hands against her eyes and sniffled. This wasn't supposed to be happening. She wanted the break to be clean and final. No discussion. No tears.

Steve was handsome and ambitious, intelligent and charming. If anyone deserved an SYT, it was this oh-so-eligible bachelor. She'd been married, and her life was complicated by two children and a manipulative mother.

"Say something," he demanded. "Don't just stand there looking at me with tears in your eyes."

"Th-these aren't tears. They're…" Dianne couldn't finish as fresh tears scalded her eyes.

"Tomorrow afternoon," he said, his voice gentle. "I'll stop by the house, and you and the kids and I can all go to a movie. You can bring your mother, too, if you want."

Dianne managed to swallow a sob. "That's the lowest, meanest thing you've ever suggested."

He frowned. "Taking you and the kids to a movie?"

"Y-yes. You're using my own children against me and that's—"

"Low and mean," he finished, scowling more fiercely. "All right, if you don't want to involve Jason and Jill, then just the two of us will go."

"I already said no."

"Why?"

Her shoulders trembled slightly as she smeared the moisture across her cheek. "I'm divorced." She said it as if it had been a well-kept secret and no one but her mother and children were aware of it.

"So?" He was still scowling.

"I have children."

"I know that, too. You're not making a lot of sense, Dianne."

"It's not that—exactly. You can date any woman you want."

"I want to date *you*."

"No!" She was trembling from the inside out. She tried to compose herself, but it was hopeless with Steve standing so close, looking as though he was going to reach for her and kiss her again.

When she was reasonably sure she wouldn't crumble under the force of her fascination with him, she looked him in the eye. "I'm flattered, really I am, but it wouldn't work."

"You don't know that."

"But I do, I do. We're not even in the same league, you and I, and this whole thing has got completely out of hand." She stood a little straighter, as though the extra inch in height would help. "The deal was I pay you to escort me to the Valentine's dinner—but then I had to go and complicate matters by suggesting you look smitten with me and you did such a good job of it that you've convinced yourself you're attracted to me and you aren't. You couldn't be."

"Because you're divorced and have two children," he repeated incredulously.

"You're forgetting my manipulative mother."

Steve clenched his fists at his sides. "I haven't forgotten her. In fact, I'm grateful to her."

Dianne narrowed her eyes. "Now I *know* you can't be serious."

"Your mother's a real kick, and your kids are great, and in case you're completely blind, I think you're pretty wonderful yourself."

Dianne fumbled with the pearls at her neck, twisting the strand between her fingers. The man who stood before her was every woman's dream, but she didn't know what was right anymore. She knew only one thing. After the way he'd humiliated her this evening, after the way he'd let her actually pay him to take her to the Valentine's dinner, make a total fool of herself, there was no chance she could see him again.

"I don't think so," she said stiffly. "Goodbye, Steve."

"You really mean it, don't you?"

She was already halfway to the front door. "Yes."

"All right. Fine," he said, slicing the air with his hands. "If this is the way you want it, then fine, just fine." With that he stormed off to his car.

Dianne knew her family would give her all kinds of flack. The minute she walked in the door, Jason and Jill barraged her with questions about the dinner. Dianne was as vague as possible and walked upstairs to her room, pleading exhaustion. There must have been something in her eyes that convinced her mother and children to leave her alone, because no one disturbed her again that night.

She awoke early the next morning, feeling more than a little out of sorts. Jason was already up, eating a huge bowl of cornflakes at the kitchen table.

"Well," he said, when Dianne walked into the kitchen, "when are you going to see Steve again?"

"Uh, I don't know." She put on a pot of coffee, doing her best to shove every thought of her dinner companion from her mind. And not succeeding.

"He wants to go out on another date with you, doesn't he?"

"Uh, I'm not sure."

"You're not sure?" Jason asked. "How come? I saw you two get mushy last night. I like Steve. He's fun."

"Yes, I know," she said, standing in front of the machine while the coffee dripped into the glass pot. Her back was to her son. "Let's give it some time. See how things work out," she mumbled.

To Dianne's relief, he seemed to accept that and didn't question her further. That, however, wasn't the case with her mother.

"So talk to me," Martha insisted later that day, working her crochet hook as she sat in the living room with Dianne. "You've been very quiet."

"No, I haven't." Dianne didn't know why she denied it. Her mother was right, she had been introspective.

"The phone isn't ringing. The phone should be ringing."

"Why's that?"

"Steve. He met your mother, he met your children, he took you out to dinner…"

"You make it sound like we should be discussing wedding plans." Dianne had intended to be flippant, but the look her mother gave her said she shouldn't joke about something so sacred.

"When are you seeing him again?" Her mother tugged on her ball of yarn when Dianne didn't immediately answer, as if that might bring forth a response.

"We're both going to be busy for the next few days."

"Busy? You're going to let busy interfere with love?"

Dianne ignored the question. It was easier that way. Her mother plied her with questions on and off for the rest of the day, but after repeated attempts to get something more out of her daughter and not succeeding, Martha reluctantly let the matter drop.

Three days after the Valentine's dinner, Dianne was shopping after work at a grocery store on the other side of town—she avoided going anywhere near the one around which she and Steve had fabricated their story—when she ran into Beth Martin.

"Dianne," Beth called, racing down the aisle after her. Darn, Dianne thought. The last person she wanted to chitchat with was Beth, who would, no doubt, be filled with questions about her and Steve.

She was.

"I've been meaning to phone you all week," Beth said, her smile so sweet Dianne felt as if she'd fallen into a vat of honey.

"Hello, Beth." She made a pretense of scanning the grocery shelf until she realized she was standing in front of the disposable-diaper section. She jerked away as though she'd been burned.

Beth's gaze followed Dianne's. "You know, you're not too old to have more children," she said. "What are you? Thirty-three, thirty-four?"

"Around that."

"If Steve wanted children, you could—"

"I have no intention of marrying Steve Creighton," Dianne answered testily. "We're nothing more than friends."

Beth arched her eyebrows. "My dear girl, that's not what I've heard. All of Port Blossom is buzzing with talk about the two of you. Steve's been such an elusive bachelor. He dates a lot of women, or so I've heard, but from what everyone's saying, and I do mean *everyone*, you've got him hooked. Why, the way he was looking at you on Saturday night was enough to bring tears to my eyes. I don't know what you did to that man, but he's yours for the asking."

"I'm sure you're mistaken." Dianne couldn't very well announce that she'd paid Steve to look besotted. He'd done such a good job of it, he'd convinced himself and everyone else that he was head over heels in love with her.

Beth grinned. "I don't think so."

As quickly as she could, Dianne made her excuses, paid for her groceries and hurried home. Home, she soon discovered, wasn't exactly a haven. Jason and Jill were waiting for her, and it wasn't because they were eager to carry in the grocery sacks.

"It's been three days," Jill said. "Shouldn't you have heard from Steve by now?"

"If he doesn't phone you, then you should call him," Jason insisted. "Girls do that sort of thing all the time now, no matter what Grandma says."

"I..." Dianne looked for an escape. Of course there wasn't one.

"Here's his card," Jason said, taking it from the corner of the bulletin board. "Call him."

Dianne stared at the raised red lettering. Port

Blossom Towing, it said, with the phone number in large numbers below. In the corner, in smaller, less-pronounced lettering, was Steve's name, followed by one simple word: *owner.*

Dianne's heart plummeted and she closed her eyes. He'd really meant it when he said he had never intentionally misled her. He assumed she knew, and with good reason. The business card he'd given her spelled it out. Only she hadn't noticed...

"Mom." Jason's voice fragmented her introspection.

She opened her eyes to see her son and daughter staring up at her, their eyes, so like her own, intent and worried.

"What are you going to do?" Jill wanted to know.

"W.A.R."

"Aerobics?" Jason said. "What for?"

"I need it," Dianne answered. And she did. She'd learned long ago that when something was weighing on her, heavy-duty exercise helped considerably. It cleared her mind. She didn't enjoy it, exactly; pain rarely thrilled her. But the aerobics classes at the community center had seen her through more than one emotional trauma. If she hurried, she could be there for the last session of the afternoon.

"Kids, put those groceries away for me, will you?" she said, heading for the stairs, yanking the sweater over her head as she raced. The buttons on her blouse were too time-consuming, so she peeled that over her head the moment she entered the bedroom, closing the door with her foot.

In five minutes flat, she'd changed into her leotard, kissed the kids and was out the door. She had a small attack of guilt when she pulled out of the driveway and glanced back to see both her children standing on the porch looking dejected.

The warm-up exercises had already begun when Dianne joined the class. For the next hour she leapt, kicked, bent and stretched, doing her best to keep up with everyone else. By the end of the session, she was exhausted—and no closer to deciding whether or not to phone Steve.

With a towel draped around her neck, she walked out to her car. Her cardiovascular system might've been fine, but nothing else about her was. She searched through her purse for her keys and then checked her coat pocket.

Nothing.

Dread filled her. Framing the sides of her face with her hands, she peered inside the car. There, innocently poking out of the ignition, were her keys.

Ten

"Jason," Dianne said, closing her eyes in thanks that it was her son who'd answered the phone and not Jill. Her daughter would have plied her with questions and more advice than "Dear Abby."

"Hi, Mom. I thought you were at aerobics."

"I am, and I may be here a whole lot longer if you can't help me out." Without a pause, she continued, "I need you to go upstairs, look in my underwear drawer and bring me the extra set of car keys."

"They're in your underwear drawer?"

"Yes." It was the desperate plan of a desperate woman. She didn't dare contact the auto club this time for fear they'd send Port Blossom Towing to the rescue in the form of one Steve Creighton.

"You don't expect me to paw through your, uh, stuff, do you?"

"Jason, listen to me, I've locked my keys in the car, and I don't have any other choice."

"You locked your keys in the car? *Again?* What's with you lately, Mom?"

"Do we need to go through this now?" she demanded. Jason wasn't saying anything she hadn't already said to herself a hundred times over the past few minutes. She was so agitated it was a struggle not to break down and weep.

"I'll have Jill get the keys for me," Jason agreed, with a sigh that told her it demanded a good deal of effort, not to mention fortitude, for him to comply with this request.

"Great. Thanks." Dianne breathed out in relief. "Okay. Now, the next thing you need to do is get your bicycle out of the garage and ride it down to the community center."

"You mean you want me to *bring* you the keys?"

"Yes."

"But it's raining!"

"It's only drizzling." True, but as a general rule Dianne didn't like her son riding his bike in the winter.

"But it's getting dark," Jason protested next.

That did concern Dianne. "Okay, you're right. Call Grandma and ask her to come over and get the keys from you and then have her bring them to me."

"You want me to call Grandma?"

"Jason, are you hard of hearing? Yes, I want you to call Grandma, and if you can't reach her, call me back here at the community center." Needless to say, her cell phone was locked in the car. *Again.* "I'll be waiting." She read off the number for him. "And listen, if my car keys aren't in my underwear drawer, have Grandma bring me a wire clothes hanger, okay?"

He hesitated. "All right," he said after another burdened sigh. "Are you sure you're all right, Mom?"

"Of course I'm sure." But she was going to remember his attitude the next time he needed her to go on a Boy Scout campout with him.

Jason seemed to take hours to do as she'd asked.

Since the front desk was now busy with the after-work crowd, Dianne didn't want to trouble the staff for the phone a second time to find out what was keeping her son.

Forty minutes after Dianne's aerobic class was over, she was still pacing the foyer of the community center, stopping every now and then to glance outside. Suddenly she saw a big red tow truck turn into the parking lot.

She didn't need to be psychic to know that the man driving the truck was Steve.

Mumbling a curse under her breath, Dianne walked out into the parking lot to confront him.

Steve was standing alongside her car when she approached. She noticed that he wasn't wearing the gray-striped coveralls he'd worn the first time they'd met. Now he was dressed in slacks and a sweater, as though he'd come from the office.

"What are you doing here?" The best defense was a good offense, or so her high-school basketball coach had advised her about a hundred years ago.

"Jason called me," he said, without looking at her.

"The traitor," Dianne muttered.

"He said something about refusing to search through your underwear and his grandmother couldn't be reached. And that all this has to do with you going off to war."

Although Steve was speaking in an even voice, it was clear he found the situation comical.

"W.A.R. is my aerobics class," Dianne explained stiffly. "It means Women After Results."

"I'm glad to hear it." He walked around to the passenger side of the tow truck and brought out the instrument he'd used to open her door the first time. "So," he said, leaning against the side of her compact, "how have you been?"

"Fine."

"You don't look so good, but then I suppose that's because you're a divorced woman with two children and a manipulative mother."

Naturally he'd taunt her with that. "How kind of you to say so," she returned with an equal dose of sarcasm.

"How's Jerome?"

"Jerome?"

"The butcher your mother wanted to set you up with," he answered gruffly. "I figured by now the two of you would've gone out." His words had a biting edge.

"I'm not seeing Jerome." The thought of having to eat blood sausage was enough to turn her stomach.

"I'm surprised," he said. "I would've figured you'd leap at the opportunity to date someone other than me."

"If I wasn't interested in him before, what makes you think I'd go out with him now? And why aren't you opening my door? That's what you're here for, isn't it?"

He ignored her question. "Frankly, Dianne, we can't go on meeting like this."

"Funny, very funny." She crossed her arms defiantly.

"Actually I came here to talk some sense into you," he said after a moment.

"According to my mother, you won't have any chance of succeeding. I'm hopeless."

"I don't believe that. Otherwise I wouldn't be here." He walked over to her and gently placed his hands on her shoulders. "Maybe, Dianne, you've been fine these past few days, but frankly I've been a wreck."

"You have?" As Dianne looked at him she thought

she'd drown in his eyes. And when he smiled, it was all she could do not to cry.

"I've never met a more stubborn woman in my life."

She blushed. "I'm awful, I know."

His gaze became more intent as he asked, "How about if we go someplace and talk?"

"I...think that would be all right." At the moment there was little she could refuse him. Until he'd arrived, she'd had no idea what to do about the situation between them. Now the answer was becoming clear...

"You might want to call Jason and Jill and tell them."

"Oh, right, I should." How could she have forgotten her own children?

Steve was grinning from ear to ear. "Don't worry, I already took care of that. While I was at it, I phoned your mother, too. She's on her way to your house now. She'll make the kids' dinner." He paused, then said, "I figured if I was fortunate enough, I might be able to talk you into having dinner with me. I understand Walker's has an excellent seafood salad."

If he was fortunate enough, he might be able to talk her into having dinner with him? Dianne felt like weeping. Steve Creighton was the sweetest, kindest, handsomest man she'd ever met, and *he* was looking at *her* as if he was the one who should be counting his blessings.

Steve promptly opened her car door. "I'm going to buy you a magnetic key attachment for keeping a spare key under your bumper so this doesn't happen again."

"You are?"

"Yes, otherwise I'll worry about you."

No one had ever worried about her, except her immediate family. Whatever situation arose, she handled. Broken water pipes, lost checks, a leaky roof—nothing

had ever defeated her. Not even Jack had been able to
break her spirit, but one kind smile from Steve Creighton and she was a jumble of emotions. She blinked back
tears and made a mess of thanking him, rushing her
words so that they tumbled over each other.

"Dianne?"

She stopped and bit her lower lip. "Yes?"

"Either we go to the restaurant now and talk, or I'm
going to kiss you right here in this parking lot."

Despite everything, she managed to smile. "It
wouldn't be the first time."

"No, but I doubt I'd be content with one kiss."

She lowered her lashes, thinking she probably
wouldn't be, either. "I'll meet you at Walker's."

He followed her across town, which took less than
five minutes, and pulled into the empty parking space
next to hers. Once inside the restaurant, they were
seated immediately by a window overlooking Sinclair
Inlet.

Dianne had just picked up her menu when Steve said,
"I'd like to tell you a story."

"Okay," she said, puzzled. She put the menu aside.
Deciding what to eat took second place to listening to
Steve.

"It's about a woman who first attracted the attention of a particular man at the community center about
two months ago."

Dianne took a sip of water, her eyes meeting his
above the glass, her heart thumping loudly in her ears.
"Yes…"

"This lady was oblivious to certain facts."

"Such as?" Dianne prompted.

"First of all, she didn't seem to have a clue how attractive she was or how much this guy admired her. He

did everything but stand on his head to get her attention, but nothing worked."

"What exactly did he try?"

"Working out at the same hours she did, pumping iron—and looking exceptionally good in his T-shirt and shorts."

"Why didn't this man say something to…this woman?"

Steve chuckled. "Well, you see, he was accustomed to women giving him plenty of attention. So this particular woman dented his pride by ignoring him, then she made him downright angry. Finally it occurred to him that she wasn't *purposely* ignoring him—she simply wasn't aware of him."

"It seems to me this man is rather arrogant."

"I couldn't agree with you more."

"You couldn't?" Dianne was surprised.

"That was when he decided there were plenty of fish in the sea and he didn't need a pretty divorcée with two children—he'd asked around about her, so he knew a few details like that."

Dianne smoothed the pink linen napkin across her lap. "What happened next?"

"He was sitting in his office one evening. The day had been busy and one of his men had phoned in sick, so he'd been out on the road all afternoon. He was ready to go home and take a hot shower, but just about then the phone rang. One of the night crew answered it and it was the auto club. Apparently some lady had locked her keys in her car at the community center and needed someone to come rescue her."

"So you, I mean this man, volunteered?"

"That he did, never dreaming she'd practically throw herself in his arms. And not because he'd unlocked her car, either, but because she was desperate for someone to take her to the Valentine's dinner."

"That part about her falling in your arms is a slight exaggeration," Dianne felt obliged to tell him.

"Maybe so, but it was the first time a woman had ever offered to pay him to take her out. Which was the most ironic part of this entire tale. For weeks he'd been trying to gain this woman's attention, practically killing himself to impress her with the amount of weight he was lifting. It seemed every woman in town was impressed except the one who mattered."

"Did you ever stop to think that was the very reason he found her so attractive? If she ignored him, then he must have considered her a challenge."

"Yes, he thought about that a lot. But after he met her and kissed her, he realized that his instincts had been right from the first. He was going to fall in love with this woman."

"He was?" Dianne's voice was little more than a hoarse whisper.

"That's the second part of the story."

"The second part?" Dianne was growing confused.

"The happily-ever-after part."

Dianne used her napkin to wipe away the tears, which had suddenly welled up in her eyes again. "He can't possibly know that."

Steve smiled then, that wonderful carefree, vagabond smile of his, the smile that never failed to lift her heart. "Wrong. He's known it for a long time. All he needs to do now is convince her."

Sniffing, Dianne said, "I have the strangest sensation that this woman has trouble recognizing a prince when she sees one. For a good part of her life, she was satisfied with keeping a frog happy."

"And now?"

"And now she's...now *I'm* ready to discover what happily-ever-after is all about."

* * * * *

She wasn't sure about that. "Yeah, but look at all the time
I'm taking from you. You're stuck babysitting me until
the Quinns get home."

He leaned back in the chair, and she couldn't help but
stare at his muscular chest and those massive shoulders.
Did the military do that for him, or the ranch work?

He caught her stare and she quickly glanced away.

"Hey, I'll take your kind of trouble any day. You
rescued me yesterday by helping me pack up all that
wedding stuff. You took charge yesterday like a drill
sergeant."

She felt a blush cover her cheeks. "What can I say? I
have a knack for getting things done."

Those dark eyes captured her attention for far too long.
She couldn't let this man get to her. Once he learned the
truth about her, he might not like that she'd kept it from
him.

He rested his elbows on the table. "Have you ever
ridden?"

She swallowed hard. "You mean on a horse?"

He gave her an odd look, but she could tell he was trying not to laugh. "Yes, as far as I'm concerned, it's the best way to see the countryside."

"You want to take me riding?"

"You seem surprised. I'm sure your sister will want to show you around, too."

"To be honest, I've never been on or around a horse until today."

Brooke's first instinct was to say no, but then she realized she'd never taken time just for herself. And why wouldn't she want to go riding with this rugged cowboy? "I'll go, but only if you put me on a gentle horse. You've got one named Poky or Snail?"

"Don't worry, I'll make sure you're safe."

She wanted to believe him, but something deep inside told her if she wasn't careful she could get hurt, and in more ways than one.

*Don't miss
COUNT ON A COWBOY by Patricia Thayer,
available March 2016 wherever
Harlequin® American Romance®
books and ebooks are sold.*

www.Harlequin.com

Turn your love of reading into rewards you'll love with

Harlequin My Rewards

**Join for FREE today at
www.HarlequinMyRewards.com**

Earn **FREE BOOKS** of your choice.

Experience **EXCLUSIVE OFFERS** and contests.

Enjoy **BOOK RECOMMENDATIONS**
selected just for you.

PLUS! Sign up now
and get **500** points
right away!

Earn
FREE
REWARDS
HarlequinMyRewards.com
Join
Today!

MYR16R

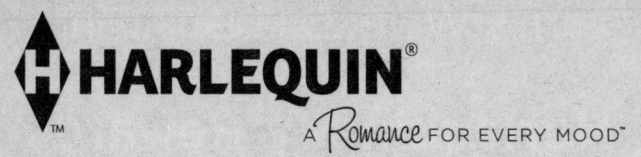

THE WORLD IS BETTER
WITH
Romance

Harlequin has everything from contemporary, passionate and heartwarming to suspenseful and inspirational stories.

Whatever your mood, we have a romance just for you!

Connect with us to find your next great read, special offers and more.

f /HarlequinBooks

🐦 @HarlequinBooks

www.HarlequinBlog.com

www.Harlequin.com/Newsletters

◆ HARLEQUIN®

A *Romance* FOR EVERY MOOD™

www.Harlequin.com